The Collected Issues
of
THE A.P.R.O BULLETIN
AERIAL PHENOMENA RESEARCH
ORGANIZATION
For The Years: 1962-63
Coral E. Lorenzen

SAUCERIAN PUBLISHER

ISBN:9798634303307

ISBN-13:9798634303307
GTIN- 14: 9798634303307

© 2020, Saucerian Publisher

Coral E. Lorenzen, co-founder of the Aerial Phenomena Research Organization in 1952, and co-author of several books with her late husband, Leslie James Lorenzen

The above is a candid photo of the staff taken during a coffee break after an evening's APRO chores. From left to right: A. E. Brown, Director of Research; Elinore Brown, Secretary; L. I. Lorenzen, Director of Public Relations (standing); Coral E. Lorenzen, Director, and Terry Clarke, Assistant Director of Public Relations. PHOTO BY A. E. BROWN. Taken from THE A.P.R.O. BULLETIN-July, 1958.

Prologue

It is generally a good idea to return to the classics in any genre. This also goes for UFO literature. Rereading a book after ten or twenty years is a rewarding experience. You will discover new data and ideas you didn´t notice before. The reason, of course, is that you are, in many ways, not the same person reading the book the second or third time. Hopefully you have advanced in knowledge, experience, intellectual and spiritual discernment. A good starting point is to reread the contactee classics of the 1950s,in order to understand the deeper mystery involved in what happened during that era.

THE A.P.R.O BULLETIN was published by Coral Lorenzen at Sturgeon Bay, Wisconsin under the banner of the AERIAL PHENOMENA RESEARCH ORGANIZATION. This publication was a forum for Fortean experience and saucer sightings. It was first published in 1952.

Aerial Phenomena Research Organization (APRO) APRO was founded in January 1952 by a Wisconsin couple, Jim (Leslie James) and Coral E. Lorenzen who later moved to Alamogordo, New Mexico, and finally to Tucson, Arizona, where the organization was based until it was dissolved in 1988, when Coral E. Lorenzen passed away on April 12, 1988. The organization was founded on the premise that the UFO phenomenon is important enough to warrant an objective, scientific investigation. Toward this end, APRO became a pacesetter in many ways. APRO was the first organization of its kind in the world in that it always maintained representatives in most foreign countries who kept headquarters in Tucson informed concerning UFO activity around the globe. About 10 percent of its membership were outside the United States.

Saucerian Publisher was founded with the mission of promoting books in Science Fiction. Our vision is to preserve the legacy of literary history by reprint editions of books which have already been exhausted or are difficult to obtain. Our goal is to help readers, educators and researchers by bringing back original publications that are difficult to find at reasonable price, while preserving the legacy of universal knowledge. This book is an authentic reproduction of the original printed text in shades of gray. Despite the fact that we have attempted to accurately maintain the integrity of the original work, <u>the present reproduction may have minor errors beyond our control like: missing and blurred pages, poor pictures and readers' pencil markings from the original scanned copy.</u> Because this book is culturally important, we have made available as part of our commitment to protect, preserve and promote knowledge in the world. Some of the issues could be missing. These issues are an authentic reproduction of the issues of *THE A.P.R.O BULLETIN* for the years: 1962-1963. Great, but unpretentious, these issues are extraordinarily rare symbols by themselves of what was going on in those early years of the modern UFO phenomena. This title has the following issues: **THE A.P.R.O. BULLETIN- MAY, 1962; THE A.P.R.O. BULLETIN- JULY, 1962; THE A.P.R.O. BULLETIN-**

SEPTEMBER, 1962; THE A.P.R.O. BULLETIN- NOVEMBER, 1962; THE A.P.R.O. BULLETIN- JANUARY, 1963; THE A.P.R.O. BULLETIN- MARCH, 1963; THE A.P.R.O. BULLETIN- MAY, 1963; THE A.P.R.O. BULLETIN- JULY, 1963; THE A.P.R.O. BULLETIN- SEPTEMBER, 1963; THE A.P.R.O. BULLETIN- NOVEMBER, 1963.

Editor
Saucerian Publisher, 2020

CONTENST:

Saucer Dunks in Reservoir
Submarine Saucers
Object Seen AgainNear Quarry
1837 Sighting Of 80-Minute Meteor
Another Wandering "Star"
Yellow Light At Amboy, California

THE A.P.R.O. BULLETIN- JULY, 1963

SAUCER PANICS CATTLE
"Meteor" Panics Baseball Crowe/Barometers React To "Meteor"
Another "Mother" Ship?
Antarctica Sightings Corroborated
Rancher Sees Hovering Object
Seattle-- Another Fire Ball
Monitor·ing and Scanning UFOs
Clues On Mysterious Cremation

THE A.P.R.O. BULLETIN- SEPTEMBER, 1963

THE CASE Of THE FRIGHTENED COWS
Solar Transit Made By UFO
Disc Buzzes House
Blue Light Seen In Ark.
Ice Fall In Russia
Menzel's Book-A Further Extension on An Old Theme
Do Scientists Stifle New Knowledge?
Division of Meteorological Physics
High Altitude Satellite Type Object Seen
Fiery Object Over Fijis

THE A.P.R.O. BULLETIN- NOVEMBER, 1963

FAMILY BESEIGED BY DISCS
What Did Cooper See?
News Photog Snaps UFO
House Heated Up Like Oven
Slow Moving Discs
Widely Seen UFO In Calif.
Pear-Shaped Object Over Balto
Sky Object Stri·kes Building, Causes Fire
Scout Leader Observes Strange Light

THE A.P.R.O. BULLETIN

The A. P. R. O. Bulletin is the official copyrighted publication of the Aerial Phenomena Research Organization (A.P.R.O.), 4145 E. Desert Place, Tucson, Arizona, and is issued every other month to members only. The Aerial Phenomena Research Organization is a non-profit group dedicated to the eventual solution of the mystery of the unidentified objects which have been present in the skies for hundreds of years. Inquiries regarding membership may be made to the above address.

TUCSON, ARIZONA — MAY, 1962

Extraterrestrial UAO Thesis Gains Support

Glow Seen, Numbness Follows:

A group of 5 teenagers, ranging in age from 15 to 18, observed a strange glow near Modesto, California, in the early hours of 13 April 1962.

The five teenagers were visibly shaken as they related their experience to Stanislaus (Calif.) County Deputy Sheriff Ron Hackett.

The youngsters were parked near a canal bank on Ustick Road when they noticed a strange glowing object or light in the west. It appeared to be two to five miles away, over the Riverdale tract area on Hatch Road near the Tuolomne River.

At first the light was about 500 feet high but it descended toward the ground and got brighter as it neared the horizon. It faded away, however, when it appeared to reach the ground. The observers started to get out of the car but when they did, their bodies began to feel numb. They said they could hardly move but later rushed to the home of one of the party where they called the sheriff.

Pilot Reports Speedy Globe

On 21 May an Irish International Airlines pilot, Capt. Gordon Pendleton, and his crew told reporters at Dublin, Ireland, that a globe-shaped object had been sighted while they were flying across Southern England.

Pendleton's plane was at 15,000 feet altitude when he spotted the brown-colored object which appeared to be smaller than his aircraft as it approached from the opposite direction. It had irregular antenna-like protuberances. Pendleton estimated its speed at 500 miles per hour. He said it definitely was not a balloon.

The object passed 3,000 feet below Pentleton's Viscount when he was 35 miles southeast of Bristol on the Cork-to-Brussels run. The co-pilot also observed the object but neither he nor Pendleton informed the two hostesses and 60 passengers.

NASA Is New Subscriber

We welcome the Washington Headquarters of NASA (National Aeronautics and Space Administration) to APRO's tiny list of subscribers. As most know, APRO exists solely to provide information to members only through their individual active cooperation. The only exceptions have been various libraries and research laboratories. We sincerely hope our work will be of value to NASA as it has to our other group subscribers.

In view of this new interest, (foreign and pre-1947 evidence aside) it is even more difficult to accept Dr. Leon Davidson's theory that UAOs are a propaganda weapon of the U. S. Central Intelligence Agency. It would seem unlikely that NASA would be interested in a propaganda tool, or be completely unaware of its existence.

In answer to the many vehement reactions to his original thesis, Dr. Leon Davidson recently mailed an open letter to UFO Researchers plainly marked "not for publication." In it he lists his qualifications as an expert—among them his degrees, work record at various secret labs and the confidence of the USAF UFO Project and the CIA. The latter two make Dr. Davidson open to question concerning unbiased research in the UFO field.

On Page 2 (Item 4, paragraph 3) of his open letter, Dr. Davidson quotes Allen Dulles' statement in Leonard Stringfield's book, "By use of injunction, if necessary," he could prevent anyone from testifying in court concerning Adamski's book "because maximum security exists concerning the subject of UFOs." Davidson infers that he believes that the statement Dulles made indicates Adamski's book was the CIA's promotion. But there are too many factors involved to enter into that argument here.

At the end of the open letter, Dr. Davidson invites people to write for detailed references but not for discussion. If we are not allowed to discuss the issues presented by Dr. Davidson via correspondence (although we realize it would

(See NASA, page 2)

In April U. S. news wires hummed with a brief condensation of Dr. Frank B. Salisbury's (Colorado State University) theory concerning the nature of the biology of the planet Mars. As usual, news stories were comprised of bits and pieces of the original theory, all of which added up to sensationalism.

Shortly after the first wire story was read at this office, Mrs. Lorenzen forwarded a copy of her book to Dr. Salisbury and requested a copy of his paper, of which several copies subsequently arrived.

Salisbury's complete dissertation on Martian Biology is far more interesting than the short UPI-AP version. The complete text appears in the April issue of "Science." In a telephone conversation with the Director, Dr. Salisbury stated his feeling that scientists interested in the exploration of other planets should read Mrs. Lorenzen's book and said he would recommend it. Subsequently the Doctor joined the ranks of APRO members, thus increasing the number of scientists on record who are interested in the subject of UFOs. It is this sort of recognition by sound-minded individuals which will accomplish much in UFO research.

In May, Dr. Carl E. Sagan of the University of California at Berkeley stated that Mars is the most likely abode of life in our solar system. He also theorized that although it is generally believed that the Moon cannot support life on its arid and airless surface, "conditions are appreciably milder some distance beneath the lunar surface, and the likelihood of living things beneath the moon's surface is probably small but it is not negligible." Dr. Sagan's ideas were expounded on a "Voice of America" science lecture broadcast.

At least one sighting which was forwarded to Dr. Salisbury as a result of his recent publicity will appear in this issue.

MEMBERS

Please check your cards and receipts and renew!!

The A. P. R. O. BULLETIN

Published by

THE AERIAL PHENOMENA RESEARCH
ORGANIZATION
4145 E. Desert Place
Tucson, Arizona

Copyright 1962, Coral E. Lorenzen

Editor and Director

Information appearing in this bulletin may be used
by other UAO research periodicals providing names
and address credit is properly given to this organization and periodical.

Coral E. Lorenzen ..... International Director and Editor
A. E. Brown, B.S.E.E. .... Director of Research
L. J. Lorenzen .... Director of Public Relations
John T. Hopf .... Photographic Consultant
Oliver Dean .... Photographic Consultant

SPECIAL REPRESENTATIVES

(The following listed individuals participate in planning and policy-making as
Staff Members, in addition to coordinating investigative efforts in the areas indicated following their names.)

Dr. Olavo T. Fontes, M.D. .... Brazil
K. Gosta Rehn .... Sweden
Graham Conway ...... Eastern Canada
Idame Burati .... France
Horacio Gonzales Gauteaume
                                Venezuela
Peter E. Norris, L.L.D. .... Australia
Jun' Ichi Takanashi .... Japan
Juan C. Remonda .... Argentina
Sergio Robba .... Italy
Arist. Mitropoulos .... Greece
Rev. N. C. G. Cruttwell, New Guinea
Eduardo Buelte .... Spain
Norman Alford .... New Zealand

SPECIAL CONSULTANT

Prof. Charles Maney,—Physics

ALAMOGORDO PRINTING COMPANY, INC.

NASA . . . .

(Continued from page 1)
be a gargantuan task for Dr. D. to under-
take such a correspondence) the letter
becomes a one-sided attempt at indoc-
trination, not an unbiased attempt to
get at the truth.

By 1957, when Dr. Davidson claims
he became aware of the "truth" concerning the CIA's role in the UFO mystery, UFO research had become effective and well-organized. By then the extremely important works of Aime Michel
and Dr. Olavo T. Fontes had contributed
to the weighty evidence. Was it THEN
that the CIA decided on a new maneuver
to disorganize the research which was
turning up some distburbing answers
to the UFO mystery? I have a couple
of questions for Mr. Davidson:

1. Was Michel fed phony information
by French peasants who were coached
by the CIA?

2. Was Olavo Fontes fed phony information via hundreds of private citizens
or was he also a CIA pipeline or plant?

There is another theory or two which
have not yet been thoroughly probed.

Inasmuch as there seems to be a question as to who is doing what to whom
and why, we will continue this discussion in a subsequent issue.

UAO Over North Philly

In a personal report to APRO member Michael J. Campione, Mr. Zigmund
Hill of Philadelphia, Pa., described his
experience of 23 May 1962. Mr. Campione informs us that some of the names
have been fictionalized to some extent
as the observers were hesitant about
publicity.

On the date mentioned above, Mr.
Hill, his wife, daughter Rosemarie and
niece Valentine London were relaxing
in front of their home at 4th and Ontario in the north area of Philadelphia.
Mr. Hill's son Michael suddenly tugged
at his arm, pointed to the sky and said,
"There's a flying saucer and it's all lit
up."

Hill jumped out of his lawn chair, and
looking in the direction indicated by his
son, saw several people at the street corner looking upwards into the sky. The
neighbors were John Site, John Saw,
Robert Kind, Leonard Leon and Rosalee
Haven. They beckoned to Hill.

When Hill arrived at the street corner,
Rosalee Haven thrust a pair of binoculars into his hands. Hill sighted the object almost immediately. It appeared to
be hovering about 2 blocks away at
about 2500 feet altitude. The object appeared as an inverted "saucer" with six
port-like holes surmounted by a dome-
like cabin with a large window which
was lit up by a greenish light.

Moonlight on the object made it appear light grey or silverfish in color
and the portholes were also of a greenish color. A hissing or humming sound
emanated from it and the bottom half
seemed to rotate in a counter-clock-wise
manner. A light belt of greenish color
came from the section where the dome
met the inverted saucer top portion, but
the belt was fuzzy and spinning slowly
like the bottom. Hill estimated the object's total diameter as about 20 feet.

Shortly after sighting the object, Hill
heard the familiar roar of jets as two
of them, with riding lights, came into
view at about 5,000 feet and circled the
area. Within several minutes two prop-
driven planes also appeared on the
scene and were apparently on a collision
course with the saucer-shaped object.
When the planes were approximately
half mile away, the lights on the UAO
went out completely after making a fast
maneuver which resembled a "6".

Hill timed the sighting as lasting a
full five minutes. The planes continued
to circle for several minutes and then

left the vicinity. The observers watched
the lights of the planes until they were
obscured by buildings and were about
to leave when someone shouted: "There
it is again."

During the course of the next 40 minutes, the saucer reappeared three times,
as did the jets and the prop-driven
planes. The maneuvers were the same
in each of the second and third instances
but in the fourth reappearance, when
the aircraft showed up, the UAO zoomed
straight up into the sky at very high
speed until it became a pinpoint of light
and sped away in a northwest direction.
The jets attempted (apparently) to pur-
sue but were swiftly outdistanced.

Mr. Hill further stated that although
he heard "scuttlebut" about UAO in
WW II, and other rumors since, he had
never put any stock in stories of flying
saucers.

Additional information pertaining to
the sighting: Object passed in front of
the moon at one time, bolstering the observers' feeling that it was a solid, material object. A bright moon and many
stars were evident in the sky. The object's light pulsated during the times
it was hovering and brightened notice-
ably during flight. Hissing or loud hum
was heard during hovering, but no data
is available concerning sound during
maneuvers and flight. Color of the object was light grey or silver, slightly
fuzzy appearing on edges. Object was
so close it's apparent size was the size
of a grapefruit held at arm's length.

Railroad Men Spot Bullet-Shaped UAO

At 3:30 a. m. on 16 May 1962, two
New York Central freight train crews,
working miles apart, spotted and subsequently reported their observation of a
fire-spewing object.

One crew was working near the O. H.
Hutchinson power station between
Franklin and Miamisburg in Warren
County, New York. George Enneking, a
trainman, said the object traveled from
northwest to southeast and looked like
a rocket with blue-white flame issuing
from the rear. Enneking also told newsmen that four other members of the
crew, working the length of a 95-car
train, also observed the UAO.

The other crew, working near the Earl
and Daniel plant at 525 Carr St., saw
a "fireball" streak across the sky over
Northern Kentucky. The flash lasted
about 7 or 8 seconds, and appeared to
be "shedding" or throwing off fiery
sparks.

UFO Seen By Prof. Maney, Others

A UFO was seen at Defiance, Ohio, between 8 and 9 p. m. on 20 May 1962 by Prof. Chas. A. Maney, of the Department of Physics, Defance College. The professor is also consultant in physics for APRO and a member of the board of governors of NICAP in Washington, D. C.

First spotted by Don Reimund, the object was a round, blue ball of light moving in a horizontal path from the northwest, about 10 degrees above the horizon. It changed to a bright orange, became dull and disappeared in the southwest at 8:22 p. m. Reimund called Maney at 8:20, by the time the professor arrived at Reimund's residence the object was out of sight.

Reimund began describing the object to Maney and the object reappeared in the southwest at 20 degrees elevation, moving horizontally toward the north. Maney then viewed the object with unaided vision and binoculars of 7 magnifications for 10 minutes as it travelled north about 40 degrees. Maney watched the object for 3 or 4 minutes with binoculars, turned them over to another observer, during which time he lost sight of it. A minute later he caught it again, and the object had turned a brilliant yellow in color. Presently the object stopped, hovered 5 or 6 seconds, then reversed direction, traveling south. At times it appeared to move rapidly, then hover, apparently motionless. It continued to travel south getting closer to the horizon, becoming fainter until it disappeared in the southwest at 9 p. m.

During the sighting both jets and prop-driven planes were observed from west to east, presenting a good opportunity for comparison observation. Professor Maney decided the object was closer to observer Reimund in the first sighting as it was clearly defined as a ball whereas in the second sighting it was just a brilliant light.

The sighting was published in the Defiance Crescent-News on May 21, where in Professor Maney asked for accounts from other possible observers. Subsequently he received the following information which he hailed as "very significant additional information:

The sighting from 8 to 8:22 was possibly observed by Quincy L. Dray, Jr., from St. Johns, Ohio, about 55 miles south of Defiance. He said: "I sighted the same object outside St. Johns moving west and south at "an altitude lower than a star." It was blue and became quite bright, remaining at the same level and I thought it might be Echo II but was quite skeptical. It was visible for about 20 minutes, 8:10 to 8:30 p. m. It would be impossible to identify this as it was not a meteor, not a shooting star nor a comet. It moved erratically, seemed to dip or back up, then start forward fast."

Miss Linda Baker of Hamilton, Ohio, with three members of her family and a neighbor, Jerry Conrad, observed an aerial object between 9:30 and 10 p. m. on the same night—one hour later than the sighting made by Prof. Maney. The object was viewed in a northwest direction over a hill, both with and without binoculars. They observed it as it shimmered as a star, constantly shifting colors from blue to orange. It moved with a "frenzied motion"—it stopped once. It was watched for 15 minutes before the group retired.

See article elsewhere in this Bulletin for a 1960 sighting by a scientist which was passed on to Prof. Maney as a result of publicity regarding sightings noted above.

Scientist Reports Sightings

Upon hearing of Prof. Maney's sighting of a UFO on May 20, a scientist at a University in Ohio informed the Professor of an incident witnessed by him in 1960. Following are the pertinent details:

At 10 a. m. on Thanksgiving Day, Nov. 24, 1960, "Dr. Blank" he requests anonymity) of the Science Department of "Blank University" was driving south on a highway not far from the campus. A member of his family was a passenger. Low in the sky ahead of him appeared a black spot which he at first assumed to be an approaching plane. But as the object got closer the professor could see that unlike a plane the object had no wings. His curiosity aroused, the professor stopped his car at the side of the road adjacent to a golf course where he and his companion got out to get a better look at the approaching object.

As viewed by the two observers when at an altitude (elevation) of approximately 70 degrees and two or three blocks to the west (estimated), and at a straight line distance of 1200 to 1500 feet, the object was clearly visible. It was egg-shaped or elliptical, perfectly smooth, no protuberances or markings, clear curbed edges and a bright chalk-white on top with just a narrow band of shadow across the bottom.

This appears to be a view of a disc-shaped object with the top tilted toward the observers. The apparent diameter of the horizontal major axis of the ellipse shape viewed at arm's length and 1300 feet for the straight line distance of the aerial object, evolves an approximate diameter of about 100 feet.

The object moved at moderate speed like that of a conventional propeller-driven airplane, but silently with no trace of noise whatever. The object traced a smooth arc of travel with no up or down travel. It was in sight some five minutes, moving toward the northwest until it disappeared from view.

In explaining why he did not want his name to be released in connection with the report of his sighting, the Ohio scientist wrote as follows: ". . . I have been thinking about permitting my name to be released, and have decided that I do not want my name released. I hope you will understand. I have grants here at the University for research which I do not want to jeopardize should someone that is prejudiced against analyzing UFOs truthfully and scientifically (and you know there are many) make an issue out of this sighting . . . I am sorry I must ask you to keep my name confidential but I hope you understand. Sincerely, I hope that I have helped in some way, nevertheless, by telling you of what I saw . . . Sincerely Yours, Dr. Blank of Blank University."

UFO Color Photo In Antarctica

An unidentified "very strange" object was seen over Cape Hallet, Antarctica, at 11:10 p. m. on the evening of 9 July. Harold T. Fulton, president of Civilian Saucer Investigation New Zealand (now in recess) forwarded several news clips as well as the text of a radio broadcast containing the information:

Mr. C. B. Taylor, scientific leader at Hallet station, reported by radio-telephone on the 10th. The object had three yellowish-white lights, the center light being midway between the other two and much brighter than the others. It travelled from southwest to northeast, with its highest point in the northwest about 35 degrees from the zenith. When the object was in the northern sky, it emitted a brilliant flash of white light. As it neared the horizon, the smaller lights disappeared in the auroral glow.

"It took about three to four minutes to cross the sky, from about 11:10 to 11:13 p. m." Mr. Taylor said. "We have no idea what it could have been. It was too slow for a meteorite but too fast for a satellite."

Seven of the station's crew of 18 saw the object, and it was photographed by the all-sky auroral camera, in color. Further information will appear as it is received.

An Engineer Looks At UFOS

By Glenn D. Bryant

(The writer is a graduate of Mississippi State University, holding a Master of Science degree in Aeronautical Engineering. He is a rated pilot, has spent 10 years in the Aerophysics Department of Mississippi State U. and served as Project Engineer for Modification, Design and Production of Research Aircraft. Mr. Bryant belongs to the Institute of Aerospace Science and is a member of Phi Kappa Phi and Tau Beta Pi. He is married and has three children).

Please don't read this article if you are absolutely sure Unidentified Flying Objects can all be explained as terrestial objects. I will make no attempt to prove they are the space ships of another planet, which I am convinced they are. Instead, those who admit there may be space craft lurking in the Earth's skies may find here an aeronautical engineer's analysis of what this all adds up to. This summary is entirely based on several years of observation and study of available unclassified material. The writer's background includes design studies on unconventional aircraft and their relation to certain military and civilian applications. This account, in a like manner, considers U. F. O 's as machines either designed for or adapted to a particular type of mission.

First, what do I assume is their mission? A study of reports gives convincing evidence of a mission of surveillance of the Earth by extraterrestial beings. Their lack of aggressive action suggests they are not in process of colonizing the Earth. Lack of formal contact casts doubt on a trade motive. Evidently, these gifted creatures are in a far more favorable environment on their native planet than on Earth, and their advanced technology would probably put them in a position of self-sufficiency. Lack of formal contact, however, also indicates something more than curiosity or scientific interest.

The remaining likely motive is concern over their own security. The increased surveillance to keep pace with our own technological explosion is evidence that they consider us to soon be in a position to threaten their native planet. The advent of the use of atomic energy and the beginnings of space flight by man are putting him in just this position. Our space visitors are obviously aware of the instability and frequent violence of Earthly society. This uncertainty of intent completes the menace imposed by our growing capability for harm to them. On the other hand, we must assume that theirs is a mature, self-restrained society with concern for the well-being of others. If this were not so, they would likely have waged preventive war against the Earth at the first sign of a threat. Some may argue that they are yet considering the preventive war alternative. Their weapons and means of delivery are still so far ahead of us that for some years to come they could defeat us without serious losses to themselves. The date would be set by a level of our development which is high enough to pose an inevitable threat to themselves, but low enough to assure an easy victory.

This gloomy alternative, preventive war, is by no means the only one available to them, however. It is most likely such an advanced race has long ago renounced war as a method of settling disputes between societies. They must therefore, have advanced know-how in getting along with other civilizations. It is most reasonable that these diplomatic methods would be tried before restorting to all-out violence.

The question now is why the delay? Why have formal contacts not been made with major Earth governments or the United Nations? An early start would be advantageous in bridging the gaps between our backgrounds. There would be more time to arrive at a mutual working understanding. There must be good reasons for delay which outweigh these considerations. Is there an actual communications barrier between us? Are formal relations impossible because they cannot decipher our spoken or written language? Are they unable to articulate a reply? Evidence from reports and even a superficial examination of the problem render these assumptions unlikely.

Reports indicate space creatures have been prowling around the Earth for many, many years. What would be more likely for a science-minded race than taking specimens of terrestial flora and fauna back to their planet for study under laboratory conditions? It would be surprising if they did not have a whole "Bureau of Earth" with hundreds or thousands of employees working in numerous laboratories and offices specializing in various features of our complex planet. It would be surprising, indeed, if they overlooked the most interesting and pertinent of terrestial fauna, man.

Without formal contact with Earth, a large number of humans would have to be collected, studied, and interrogated to keep up with the state of the Earth's civilization. Surely some of the crop of missing aviators and others must suddenly find themselves living in an artificial environment in a Martian or Venusian laboratory colony. No, I am sure there is not a serious communications barrier. If the Earth's monitors cannot hear our spoken words or voice replies, I am sure they could train human interpreters or even translate by machine. Our written language would be even less of a problem.

Note the above reference to Martian or Venusian. Why do I assume Mars or Venus or both as the home of our visitors? Some well-informed persons state these creatures come from planets around distant stars. If that is true, why is there such an impression of urgency in their surveillance? They monitor our advances in the space arts with exacting thoroughness. The cost of such an operation at a distance of four to ten light years would be staggering even for a highly advanced civilization. Would all this be for the absurdly remote security threat that we could pose for an unknown planet at such a distance? The home of our uninvited guests must surely be in our Solar system and, indeed, right next door.

The apparent primary reason for lack of formal contact goes back to the security threat. It is an engineering matter and gets to the real point of this essay. There is yet one major step for mankind to make technologically before he will be a serious potential menace to our space neighbors. This one momentous bit of know-how is paradoxically utilized by the very space craft which monitor our progress. If one of these craft fell into our hands, the odds are very great that the secret would soon be disclosed to us.

Our feeble attempts at space flight are now achieved by rockets which fire for a time to build up velocity and then coast along. Though much lauded at the present time, these space craft compare with those of our celestial neighbors like a glider with a jet air liner. The vital difference comes from the fact that we have only one tool with which to overcome gravity and inertia. That is inertia itself used in various forms. initially, a large part of the mass of our ships must be jettisoned at high velocity in order for a small part to coast along to its destination. Our neighbors' ships do not require any such means to oppose gravity. No deafening rocket with billowing smoke from enormous boosters is required for their ships to hover, maneuver, or race skyward to outer space. Instead, they accomplish these feats with

(See Engineer, Page 5)

Engineer . . . .

(Continued from Page 4)

the silent ease of riding a bicycle around a park.

The only reasonable explanation for the reported performance of the U. F. O.'s is that they are able to generate a field to directly counteract gravity. Also, since gravity and inertia are related, it is not surprising that some of these ships are reported doing fantastic maneuvers. Evidently this anti-gravity device enables our observers to also control inertia forces so that their ships can turn or accelerate at unbelievable rates. This may likewise explain why they fly through our atmosphere at supersonic speeds without the sonic boom of high speed terrestial aircraft. In other words, their field generator not only opposes gravity and controls inertia within the ship, but controls the inertia of the air flowing past, as well. Apparently, the field generator requires a large amount of power in one form or another, and a nuclear power plant is carried on board. Any power plant must reject heat and the most practical way to reject heat in space is by radiating electromagnetic waves, such as infra red or visible light. It, therefore, comes as no surprise that large quantities of both heat and light are reported emanating from U.F.O.'s. Further, the color is often reported to change with the intensity of the maneuver. When cruising steadily along, the color may be rather dull. Indeed, I and others have seen them switch off their radiators completely at intervals of about every ten seconds when cruising along in straight flight.

It is interesting that these ships make no attempt at concealment. They are conspicuous by their light and are easily picked up by radar without any apparent use of electronic counter measures. They evidently rely entirely on vastly superior performance and armament for safety among their potentially hostile hosts. As to their armament, impressions from bits and pieces of reports here and there indicate that at least one form is of the "ray" variety that can be turned on and off independently of the main propulsion system of the ship. Rays have been reported which cause heat, radiation burns, temporary failure of electrical equipment, and even mechanical force on their targets.

Can you imagine the military significance, of these missing technological links in human hands? Is it any wonder, then, that our space neighbors do not risk this vital security information by making a formal contact that could only be our advantage at this stage of the game. Such contact would expose their handiwork to close scrutiny, and the utmost of Earth's resources would be rushed into the quest for their secrets. Once given the clue that a secret is to be wrested from nature, and a general impression of what direction to go, man, with all of his weaknesses, will persevere to the solution. Anti-gravity is no exception. The ironic fact is that our visitors have already given us just this clue. A few years ago gravity research was very unfashionable among scientists mainly because no one thought it was possible to do anything about it. Now, the picture is rapidly changing, thanks partly to the example of the U.F.O.'s. The very security serveillance we are undergoing is helping to stimulate mankind into a feverish quest for the missing links which will threaten that security.

It is easy to see that this shocking knowledge is also raising very interesting terrestial security problems. What a hot potato this is for the world's major governments. What, for instance, would happen if the Russians get it first? All the free nation's defense strategy would become obsolete. Is it any wonder, then, that governments go to ludicrous lengths to soft-pedal it. The official denials of the problem's existence do not fit the impressions one gets of the attention it is getting under the wraps of security.

Of course, I do not have any concrete proof to offer that I and thousands of others have actually seen visiting space ships. Perhaps they are just what many are convinced: Mistaken identity of familiar objects, mirages, hoaxes, and the like. On the other hand, perhaps these thousands are not all fools or knaves and the Earth really does stand on the threshold of the greatest historical event of the millenium: The formal meeting of two worlds.

Robots Scare Woman

An official Argentine TV Station, with the assistance of the Argentine Air Force, released to the press an account of a woman rancher who saw a disc-shaped unconventional aerial object on the ground at close quarters. The woman had to be hospitalized for shock.

The woman's name was not revealed by the TV station or the Air Force but they did state that she was from the province of La Pampa. She reportedly saw two strange robot-like creatures near the unidentified object. The report also said that experts had confirmed that grass in the area where the object presumably landed, was singed in a six-yard-wide circle.

Some members will note the similarity of this report to the one reported in the November 1961 issue concerning burned grass roots at the site of a UAO landing in Venezuela, last fall. Also, this is not the first time the sight and proximity of such objects has thrown an observer into shock.

At this writing we have no further details but have requested same from Mr. Remonda and other South American representatives. No exact date was given but the incident is presumed to have occurred in early May.

1947 Pilot Sighting Revealed

The following report was submitted via letter to Dr. Frank Salisbury (see article elsewhere in this issue) by a friend pertaining to the sighting of a formation of UAO's in 1947:

"I did not make a report. Those making reports were looked on as some sort of nut and even the few friends I mentioned it to seemed to think I had joined the "club." Beulah, Ron and I were flying from Los Vegas, Nevada to Salt Lake and while over Utah Lake saw the six or eight objects coming towards us and slightly to our right. They were at the same altitude as we. I did not notice them until we were practically to them. As they passed I banked the plane sharply and flew after them for a few minutes during which time they left us as if we were standing still.

"Size is difficult to estimate in the air but I would guess they were not over six feet in diameter. They were silver-white, oval top and bottom much like two saucers face to face. They were closely spaced. They fluttered as a group for a second or two and then stabilized for a second or two, alternately between these two modes. The incident happened on July 12, 1947, at approximately 2:30 p.m. P.S.T., according to my flying log."

Bullet Speeds Over New Zealand

A mysterious, bright, bullet-shaped object flashed through New Plymouth, New Zealand skies on the night of 4 February 1962. Fishermen who watched the object for at least 10 seconds said it definitely was not a falling star or comet. Mr. H. Edwards, who was fishing off rocks near the New Plymouth Railway station said the object traveled from north to south, was white with a reddish tinge on the leading edge. It had a short tail which flickered as the object disappeared.

MEMBERS . . .

Please check your cards and receipts and renew!!

Mystery Object Over Whakatane, NZ

An unidentified object hurtled over the central Bay of Plenty coast at 9 o'clock on the night of 9 July, leaving a fiery trail hanging in the sky for several minutes.

The object, which witnesses described as appearing larger than the moon, traversed the sky in a couple of seconds and disappeared behind hills west of Wakatane. Eye witness Contable Douglass Gray of Whakatane said the object seemed to come from north of White Island, an active vovlcano 30 miles off the coast and lit the whole sky with a whitish glow. The center of the ball appeared multi-colored, and the rim was surrounded by lines resembling rocket trails.

Noises, Lights Over Cincinnati

Dave Wahler and Mike Benesch of Bridgetown reported seeing a light moving east to west across the sky and changing from red to white, on the evening of the 25th of May. A Mt. Washington man said he saw a moving light which was 3 to 4 times brighter than Venus, going north to southwest at low elevation.

A housewife in Ft. Thomas also reported seeing a large moving light during which time she heard a zooming, "swishing" noise.

The FAA tower at Greater Cincinnatti airport reported no strange objects and Dr. A Presnell of the Cincinnati Astronomical Society said he thought the object probably was Venus, which is large and bright at this time of the year. Presnell did not say he had personally seen the object, however.

Another Sighting In New Zealand

On the same evening (July 9) as the sighting of a UFO by Antarctica scientists, two residents of the Stokes Valley, Mr. and Mrs. J. W. Skeet, observed a similar phenomenon. The couple were in their back garden when "suddenly this blue-white shape appeared in the sky." Skeet said that both he and his wife thought that it was heading due north.

Mr. Skeet said the object appeared about as large as an orange, and that the overcast sky and dense clouds made the object look fuzzy at the edges. The object appeared to be throwing off pieces, "like sparks jumping from a hot fire." Skeet estimated that the craft was crossing the sky at about 40 degrees above the horizon, somewhere over the Wairarada.

"Platillos Valadores Sobre Venezuela"

The above is the name (in English—"Flying Saucers over Venezuela") of a new book in Spanish authored by APRO's Venezuelan Representative Horacio Gonzales G. and published by Tipografia Olimpis of Caracas. With heavy dependence on a Spanish-English dictionary, abetting some very sketchy Spanish, the Director managed, finally, to finish reading the book. Some of the strangest, most inexplicable sightings of UFOs including landings and "little men" are carefully documented and discussed. We can recommend without qualification t h i s great book for those able to read Spanish. Any suggestions concerning an English edition will be appreciated also.

The Disappearing TVMs

On Page 12 of the American Legion Magazine for April 1962, Allan W. Eckert documented the case of the disappearance of 5 Navy TBM Avengers off the Florida Coast. Radio contact indicated the planes were lost and their compass apparently of no help. When radio communication was broken off after many conversations indicated the men were frightened and helpless, a Martin flying boat with full rescue equipment and crew of 13 men took off in search of the planes. It gave several routine reports, then lapsed into silence. During the conversations the obviously frightened men said the sea and sky "looked strange".

Eckert goes on to document other strange aircraft disappearances in the same area—all at approximately the same time of the year. For a hair-raising explanation other than the UFO kidnap possibly, get this and read it! Extra copies could be obtained by inquiring at American Legion Magazine, P. O. Box 1055, Louisville, Kentucky. Price is 15c—suggest an extra 5c to handle mailing in the U. S., Canada and Mexico.

Same Old Stuff—USAF

On or about 8 February 1962, the USAF issued its usual debunking news (?) release pertaining to UFO. Inasmuch as there was no new innovations to the usual line, we only present announcement of this denial of the reality of the UFO for the record.

Shiny Ball Speeds Over Norway

Police investigated reports of a mysterious "shiny, ball-shaped object" which sped across the sky at Honningsvaag, Norway on the 4th of May. No further details at this time.

Gonzales Writes For Army Magazine

APRO's Venezuelan Represent a t i v e Horacio Gonzales G. authored an article entitled, "The Real Facts of the Flying Saucers" for the September-October 1958 issue of the official Venezuelan Army Magazine. The article gives a short history of the phenomena of the UFOs in the early years and outlines various explanations.

More On Mantell

After reading the Director's book, "The Great Flying Saucer Hoax", Mrs. Charles Brunes of Pequot Lakes, Minnesota writes to APRO to offer more information on the Mantell incident of January 1948 which still puzzles UFO researchers today, and has never been solved due to unavailability of military dossiers pertaining to the case.

Briefly, the Mantell case involved the chase of a UAO by 3 P51 fighters. Mantell, one of the pilots, closed in, described it, then no more was seen or heard of his plane til it was found later smashed to bits over a wide area of the terrain.

In one of his books, Donald E. Keyhoe of NICAP, said that Mantell's body was found, but that because of a "mysterious wound" a closed-casket funeral was held. At least two other members of the Air Force at Godman Field at the time have said that they were in a position to know and that Mantell's body was never found.

Mrs. Brunes and her son John were listening to short wave when they were startled to hear an excited voice say: "It has a metallic look and it's moving fast." Later, the voice said—"It's huge", and then, "I'm going to try to ram it."

After hearing this somewhat shocking monologue, Mrs. Brunes and John attempted to learn more about it via the radio. According to reports they heard later, the object was seen from at least two different points about a hundred miles apart. Those same radio reports indicated that Mantell's plane was found in bits and pieces "like kindling wood", scattered over a wide area. This may be the reason there were no reliable reports of its fall.

The Mantell case may be one of the first incidents in which instruments, particularly the radio, were knocked out prior to actual destruction of the plane itself. It is obvious that the Brunes just happened to hear what they did through a freak of radio waves.

MEMBERS . . .

Please check your cards and receipts and renew!!

HE A.P.R.O. BULLETIN

The A. P. R. O. Bulletin is the official copyrighted publication of the Aerial Phenomena Research Organization (A.P.R.O.), 4145 E. Desert Place, Tucson, Arizona, and is issued every other month to members only. The Aerial Phenomena Research Organization is a non-profit group dedicated to the eventual solution of the mystery of the unidentified objects which have been present in the skies for hundreds of years. Inquiries regarding membership may be made to the above address.

TUCSON, ARIZONA — JULY, 1962

Saucers Shoot Rockets over Tucson, Arizona

Support NICAP?

From time to time we receive letters from members and others urging us to "throw our support to NICAP" or "back NICAP policies" or "help NICAP press for congress hearings," etc. Until now we have remained tacit on this matter but we feel the time has come for a clarification of our stand.

The major difference between NICAP and APRO is that NICAP concentrates on lobbying while APRO is primarily concerned with research. We do not participate in lobbying efforts for two reasons: (1) We would lose our tax-exempt status (2) We feel that we are more effective in other areas; that, in fact, lobbying would lessen this effectiveness.

APRO's efforts, especially the Director's book, are gradually drawing the endorsements of the scientific community. This we feel, is real progress. Such endorsement would arise with more reluctance we feel, had we the reputation of using such for purposes of direct political pressure. A scientist, once aware of the true nature of the problem, becomes a firm supporter. Politicians, on the other hand, are notoriously fickle.

To illustrate a point, we quote from a letter from Dr. Frank Salisbury, Plant Physiologist with the Colorado State University. "Both Monday and Tuesday of this week I gave talks about life on Mars and of course inserted the up-to-date section on UFO's. The first talk was to a group of scientists (about a dozen), and sure enough, at the end of the talk one of them came up with an account of a personal sighting. This person was the organizer of the group and a rather well established chemist of many years standing. I was really quite amazed to hear her tell of two objects that came over the horizon and descended into a valley below her ranch and then headed straight upwards toward the zenith . . . On Tuesday I talked to an institute of humanities and again I put in a healthy pitch for the UFO subject. I even went so far as to say that in a group of that size (50 or

(See NICAP, page 2)

Cigars, Discs Over Argentina

A Reuters Dispatch from Buenos Aires, Argentina dated June 18, 1962, reads: "Unidentified Flying Objects — saucer or cigar-shaped—are becoming a common sight for Argentinians. The last of a recent series was reported in Olavarria—a town in the province of Buenos Aires.

Farmer Jose Muro telephoned the local newswpaper El Popular reporting the presence of an unusual object which he had spotted with a small telescope.

Reporters, neighbors and photographers went to Muro's home and 20 minutes later the object was still hovering overhead, barely moving. Witnesses claimed that shortly afterward it vanished upwards, only to reappear closer than ever several minutes later. The color of its light appeared to change from red to blue, from blue to green and again to red. Other residents in Olavarria claimed ot have seen similar objects.

Buenos Aires press dispatches say a confidential report to the authorities compiled by officers of the naval base of Puerto Belgrano, at the southern tip of the province of Buenos Aires, confirmed the presence of unidentified objects in the skies over Argentina. The officers cross-examined scores of witnesses, particularly those who reported unusual activity of flying objects during the night of May 14 in the neighborhood of the base.

Still Available

The first edition of the Director's book, "The Great Flying Saucer Hoax" is going fast but copies are still available from headquarters to those who have not obtained their copies, or who may wish to order for friends. Some members, among them John Hopf, our photo-analyst and Jeanne Gregory, recommend that those who can afford it should buy an extra copy for placement in the local library. Copies are still available at the $3.95 price—10% off for members.

By Coral E. Lorenzen

"Some doors opened in the bottom and something came out." An unconventional aerial object hovered for a period of time at Tucson, Arizona and a strange device had lowered to the ground. The boy relating the details was 14-year-old John Westmoreland. He and his brother James and next-door neighbor Ronnie Black had spent the night of June 25, 1962 in the tent in the Westmoreland back yard and during the course of four hours had witnessed a strange but revealing chain of events.

On the evening of the 26th of June I opened the Tucson Daily Citizen newspaper. When I came to the local news section, these words seemed to pop right out of the page: "Saucers, Rockets Inhabit Night Sky."

I scanned the article briefly and reached for the telephone book. Seconds later I was talking to Mrs. Logan Westmoreland, the mother of John and James Westmoreland. She graciously invited Mr. Lorenzen and me to come to her home and interview the boys. Three hours later we were seated in the comfortably furnished living room of the Westmoreland home in southeast Tucson.

The boys were eager to talk about their adventure, partly I suspect, because they were met with doubt at first. As soon as we got the gist of the story we started the slow process of cross-examination.

The three boys had been given permission to spend the night in the tent, so, armed with a deck of playing cards, pad and pencil, they settled down to a game of 500 Rummy by lantern light. Shortly before nine they were bored with cards and not sleepy, so they decided to go outside, watch for meteors and look at the stars and try to catch an errant, cooling breeze. The summer rains were in the offing and the air was warm and humid. The day had been hot; the night air was a welcome change.

At about 9 o'clock John noticed a star at 5 degrees south of due west, 30-40 degrees elevation, which didn't behave

(See Saucer Shoot page 3)

The A. P. R. O. BULLETIN

Published by

THE AERIAL PHENOMENA RESEARCH
ORGANIZATION

4145 E. Desert Place
Tucson, Arizona

Copyright 1962, Coral E. Lorenzen
Editor and Director

Information appearing in this bulletin may be used by other UAO research periodicals providing names and address credit is properly given to this organization and periodical.

Coral E. Lorenzen ..... International Director and Editor
A. E. Brown, B.S.E.E. .... Director of Research
L. J. Lorenzen .... Director of Public Relations
John T. Hopf .... Photographic Consultant
Oliver Dean .... Photographic Consultant

SPECIAL REPRESENTATIVES

(The following listed individuals participate in planning and policy-making as Staff Members, in addition to coordinating investigative efforts in the areas indicated following their names.)

Dr. Olavo T. Fontes, M.D. .... Brazil
K. Gosta Rehn .... Sweden
Graham Conway ..... Eastern Canada
Idame Burati .... France
Horacio Gonzales Gauteaume
                     Venezuela
Peter E. Norris, L.L.D. .... Australia
Jun' Ichi Takanashi .... Japan
Juan C. Remonda .... Argentina
Sergio Robba .... Italy
Arist. Mitropoulos .... Greece
Rev. N. C. G. Cruttwell, New Guinea
Eduardo Buelte .... Spain
Norman Alford .... New Zealand

SPECIAL CONSULTANT
Prof. Charles Maney,—Physics

ALAMOGORDO PRINTING CO., INC.

NICAP . . . .

(Continued from page 1)

60 people), that it was quite likely that one or two would have had a personal sighting. Sure enough, after the end of my hour talk and half hour discussion (most of the discussion about UFOs) two people came up and told me their stories. Unfortunately the accounts are rather cold by now, but I think it is extremely interesting that even with such a limited sample one can find 2 or 3% of an audience that has personal accounts to tell about. If this were really true on a national level, it would mean that literally hundreds of thousands of people in the United States have witnessed UFOs in the past 15 years. In none of the cases which I have passed on to you in recent weeks has the person ever reported his sighting to anyone else other than close friends." Unquote.

The point is that it only took a serious treatment of the UFO subject by an established scientist to bring the others out of "hiding." Professor Maney's experience seems to bear this out. We quote from the Defiance (Ohio) Crescent-News:

"Among reports of other sightings of unidentified aerial objects received by Professor Maney the last few days is one which Prof. Maney regards of special significance. The report was received in the person of a scientist from one of the universities in Ohio, who made a special trip to Defiance for the sole purpose of conferring with Prof Maney concerning his experience. The scientist whose identification is withheld for reasons given by himself below, had told no one previously about his experience. He had just learned through the account of the Defiance sighting in the press of Prof. Maney's serious scientific interest in the study of unidentified aerial phenomena and desired to contribute his personal first-hand observation, which he felt to be of value in the study of these phenomena." The account of this sighting appears in this issue, incidentally.

When scientists speak up, laymen are encouraged to do the same and when enough of this has taken place, congressional investigations will follow automatically if still needed. It is our feeling that the Air Force UFO program is a public relations program. It's an advertising scheme which explains UFOs as conventional objects because that's what it's designed to do. Why dispute them?

You might just as well claim that king-size Coca-Cola doesn't give you that refreshing new feeling.

Space Visitors—A Review and Comments

By Coral Lorenzen

From time to time in the past 20-odd years, I have exposed myself or have been exposed, to various and sundry writings concerning theories pertaining to the Origin of Things, Life, and Man. In the course of my pursuit of the Unknown, and attempts to find logical explanations for same, I have noted and duly studied data pertaining to unexplainable artifices and artifacts.

Recently, an article entitled, "Space Visitors" was featured in "Australian Flying Saucer Review," published in Melbourne, Australia and edited by APRO's able representative, Peter E. Norris, a Melbourne attorney-at-law. The article is a translation and condensation from the Soviet magazine "Smena," No. 10, 1961, and was authored by Alexander Kazantsev.

Mr. Kazantsev, after duly philosophizing concerning life beyond earth and the possibility of space travelers, proceeds to recite the details of various strange findings. Among them are:

A purported shoe print made on sandstone in the Gobi Desert "millions of years ago." Kazantsev says its size and pattern suggest that this is the print of a space traveler's sole who had landed on earth at a time when there were no human beings. We ask this question: What criteria determines that this print did not belong to a member of a race which inhabited this earth and was long since destroyed?

Another case listed by Kazantsev is a polished steel block 2½"x2¾"x2" weighing 785 grams, found by an Austrian physicist in the Alps in a coal stratum of Tertiary period.

Case number three which is also germane: The mountain lake of Titicaca in the Andes has still preserved a well-defined line of a seashore. Remains of sea weeds, shells . . . and ruins of a sea harbour can be seen there.

The Gate of the Sun in Tiahuanaco is covered with unique hieroglyphics which, deciphered by Epstein, turned out to be an astronimical calendar of great precision but which gives the year only 290 days. Kazantsev automatically concludes that the calendar was brought to earth by spacemen.

Also listed is the strange light-colored stones of the Nasca Plateau, in the Andes, which from the air form various animals and other symbols. Kazantsev assumes that these markings are signals or landing guides for space ships.

There are many, many more including the strange but famous iron pillor erected near the ancient tower of Kutb-Minar in Delhi, India "over 1500 years ago." The pole is eight meters high and weighs twelve tons. It can be circled by a pair of hands. It does not rust, indicating that it is made of highly pure iron.

Considering the obvious tentative conclusion of Mr. Kazantsev that these strange artifices and artifacts came from a race of space dwellers, I feel that he has fallen into a common and most tender trap. This trap consists of a compulsion to attempt to apply one theory to all of the erratics, no matter how one must bend the facts—or logic.

In a letter to the editor of the Alamogordo Daily News, Alamogordo, New Mexico, a resident of the Tularosa Basin recounted his discovery of a large, symmetrical metal ring and eye-bolt set into solid rock on the face of a high rock wall near one of the highest peaks of the Sacramento Mountains.

The ring was located about 2 to 3,000 feet above the floor of the Tularosa Basin which is 3500 feet above sea level. Fossils found in the Basin and the general alkaline nature of the soil indicate

(See Visitors page 5)

Saucers Shoot

(Continued from page 1)

like a star. It was very bright, white in color, and "moved around a little," in the boys' words. Soon it dimmed, moved a little toward the south, lost a few degrees in altitude and then became stationary.

The boys soon lost interest and went back into the tent to another game of Rummy. From time to time they peeked out and took a look at the strange "star" but it "just stayed there." Then at about 11:45 things began to happen.

The bright "star" became much brighter and seemed to move closer. Instead of looking like a star, it assumed a triangular shape as it grew larger. Then it became stationary again. How long this process took the boys did not know, but according the kitchen clock (they kept peeking in the window to check the time), a surprising thing happened at 12:15. Three green flares or rockets were fired horizontally from the main object.

At this time, John scrambled into the tent and emerged with the score pad and pencil. He decided to keep notes. On the pad he wrote: "At 9 o'clock at night we saw a flying saucer. At 12:15 it shot three green things that traveled faster than any plane." These rockets were too fast to track visually.

After the first "rocket" was fired, John noticed the second "saucer" which we will hereafter refer to as Number Two. It came in racing from west to east across the northern sky, "turned a flip" and came to rest at about 15 degrees east of north at a slightly greater elevation than No. 1. Shortly No. 2, which appeared closer and larger than No. 1, was approached by the "flare-like object," which came in from underneath and appeared to be absorbed through the bottom of No. 2.

Then the first "saucer" spat out another of the small objects. About three minutes later No. 2 was again approached by the tiny object and again the boys watched as it seemingly disappeared into the bottom of No. 2.

No. 1 was still in the same position, appearing to be triangular in shape, and No. 2 appeared much closer and round-shaped with two leg-like or stilt-like proturberances on the underside.

A third flare emerged from No. 1, and was shortly "received" by sauce No. 2. Things were getting interesting. No. 2 then shot out a rocket which quickly disappeared into the night sky. No. 2 began to dim and fade into the night sky and was not seen again. No. 1 retained its same position.

At this time, Saucer No. 3 was spotted

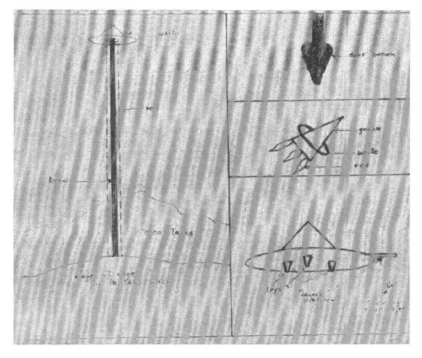

at about 100-110 degrees and about 45 degrees elevation. It appeared the largest and highest of the three, which suggests that it was closer. The detail reported by the boys bears this out.

But the best part of the show was yet to come.

Number three sported a cone-shaped superstructture above an apparently round airfoil. Its color was white and like the others it made absolutely no sound. At 1:16 a jet plane went over—we later decided it was probably in the flight pattern of Davis-Monthan AFB, a Strategic Air Command installation a scant 3 or 4 miles from the Westmoreland home.

The new visitor closed in and three of the stilt-like proturberances "popped out." Then the object gained altitude. An elongated dark "something" slid out from above the circular rim and three of the small rocket-like objects emerged in quick succession. In a few brief minutes they were back. Two doors swung open, down, and back up against the underside of the saucer. As the doors opened, the "legs" receded into the object. The little rockets, now clearly seen, swiftly entered the opening, one by one. The big object elevated slightly, and moved sideways, then became stationary again.

The newspaper had printed only the boys' notes which were not detailed ex-

cept for general movement of the objects. In describing saucer No. 3, John had written: "Something lowered from the bottom. Something came out."

I asked John what he meant by that. He said that something which looked like a rope or cable came out and lowered to the ground. I asked him what color it was, and two voices—his and James', piped up and said "brown." I wondered how they could tell colors at that time of the night and asked them. "From the light," they said.

"What light was that?" I asked. Then then told me that when the doors opened a red light shone down from the inside in a perpendicular narrow beam, that extended to the ground. When the long, ropelike object began to come out, it was clearly visible and appeared to be brown in color.

The boys estimated that the "rope" was extended for from three to five minutes, after which it began to come up into the saucer again. After it had cleared the top of the ridge bordering the wash, they realized that something was on the bottom of it. It was slowly pulled up into the large object, the doors closed and the object moved up and into the east until it was out of sight.

The youngsters stayed up a little longer, watching for more activity in the sky but before long the excitement of

(See Saucers Shoot, page 4)

Saucers Shoot . . . .

(Continued from page 3)

the night and their lack of sleep overcame their curiosity and they retired into the tent. As soon as they had awakened in the morning they rushed in to tell Mrs. Westmoreland what they had seen.

Pat Westmoreland, about 40, is an understanding mother but a firm one. The thought at first that perhaps the boys had had a touch of imagination and set about using all the "trapping tricks" she knew to trip them up in their story, but to no avail. She began to realize that they had had a real experience. She decided the newspapers should know what had happened the preceding night and called them. Thus the article which had drawn my attention came about. It should be noted here that the newspaper printed the notes, pointing out that it could be imaginary or real—they printed it because it was a sensational story.

The matter of the boys' honesty comes to mind as a matter of course in these investigations. After three long visits with the boys, during which time Mr. Lorenzen walked with them to the wash over which they thought the UAO had hovered, and I had sketched the objects from their instructions, we found no indication that the boys were not telling the truth. Mr. Lorenzen said that he had not caught any signs of strain, rehearsed conversation or trickery during his talks with them while walking to and from the wash. Nor did I ever detect any evidence that the boys were attempting to perpetrate a hoax. Some of the things which impressed me concerning the sighting as well as the honesty of the boys were these:

When attempting to describe the object which was brought up by the rope or cable, John Westmoreland said he got the impression that the object was about as long as his father—in other words, its length equalled approximately the height of his father who is about 6 feet tall. If saucer No. 3 was above Pantano wash as the boys felt it was, we have an idea of its size as well as the size of the rockets or flares and the size of the object which was pulled up into the large object.

The rim of the saucer appeared to have the same angular displacement as a five foot cross-arm on a utility pole at the corner of the Westmoreland lot. If it was over Pantano wash (quarter mile distant) it was approximately 80 feet in diameter. The small objects then would be about 6 feet long, and the object which was taken up into the saucer

would be about the same size as the "rockets," and certainly the same general configuration. (See sketches).

It is interesting and tempting to speculate that one of the rockets, at some time or other, had become disabled, a search initiated, and eventually, a recovery effected. The latter phase of the sighting, in which a device was lowered to the ground and returned to saucer No. 3 with a triangular-shaped object at the end of it, could have been that "recovery." This may further be supported by the fact that after the object was taken into the saucer, the saucer left. The recovery of that object may have been the sole purpose of the presence of the saucers that night.

It is interesting to note that after the case was fully investigated, the local newspapers were not interested in further information or a follow-up story.

On the 29th, a group of local college students sent up some balloons filled with ordinary kitchen gas and lighted by candles encased in fireproof crepe paper. Although this was not accomplished until three days after the Westmoreland sighting, the idea of saucers had been firmly implanted in the public mind. A local professor of atmospheric physics who is interested in UFO, was told of the strange lighted object in the sky, and went to the U. of A. meteorological lab to track the thing. The story of his sighting was in the Arizona Star morning paper for Friday 29 June 1962. Upon reading the details, plus his theory that the thing was an "extended source of light," I wondered if some hoaxers might have been at work. I called the Tucson Citizen asking that they mention APRO and ask for further sightings of the Thursday evening object and suggested that the object seen that night might have been the result of a prank. Later, I talked to the physicist who had been viewing the object and found that he had also decided that the object was a hoax.

Later news stores stated that the college boys involved in the "prank" were "carrying out experiments dealing with wind velocity and other weather conditions." Considering the type of homemade balloon, and the fact that it contained dangerous highly inflammable gas which was tied to a device with an open flame, it is not likely that any such experiment was being carried out. It appears more likely that a childish prank was being played and the "young men" involved did not want to admit their part in it, attempting to write it off as an experiment.

It is lamentable that the newspapers were satisfied with the experiment ex-

planation and stated that these "experiments" may have been the cause of the saucer sightings in Southern Arizona in the past few months. Certainly, the easiest way to dispose of the perplexing UFO problem is to ignore the evidence which prolongs its mysterious nature. A large percentage of the press is inclined to do precisely that.

In the case of this latter sighting, the only two observers of the lighted plastic bags who called me felt the object was a balloon. The local press gave the impression that those who viewed the hoax objects were completely fooled, but that certainly was not the case.

The events of the week of June 24-30 very aptly demonstrated the contention that I have had for years concerning the psychology of the disbeliever. The skeptic is often so intent upon disproving that which he does not care to believe, by attempting to label it a hoax or a misconception of a conventional object, that he sets about to perpetrate a hoax to support his own convictions and allay his subconscious fears.

A thorough perusal of newspaper stories concerning the Westmoreland sighting as well as ensuing reports of unidentified sky objects emphasizes the foolhardiness of accepting en toto the information pertaining to UFO sightings as presented by the news media and points up the need for thorough investigation. Had I accepted the Westmoreland story as presented by the Tucson Citizen, I would have had a short dissertation completely lacking in detail. A few hours spent in investigation yielded some very important facts, and enabled APRO to log one of the most detailed sightings of an unconventional aerial object which has ever been observed.

Ice Cutter Encounters "Lake Lights"

On March 17, 1962, strange lights off the shore of Erie, Pennsylvania, got the ice cutter Ojibwa out of dock to investigate. Chief Warrant officer Kenneth N. Black (Coast Guard) said the lights were seen by several individuals including the ship's crew. The ship got underway, cutting through heavy ice all the way to the Canadian shore and Black said "The closer we moved toward them, the farther away they seemed to be." Black also said he believed the lights were the result of unusual atmospheric conditions causing lights to be refracted on the lake. It is interesting to note that the obvious explanation — that they were chasing moving lights — was apparently not mentioned or considered by Black.

Visitors . . . .

(Continued from page 2)

that the Basin was once an inland sea— a body of salt water.

The ring and eye-bolt, apparently made of brass or bronze, appeared to have been set by first drilling a hole and inserting the hardware, then pouring in molten sulphur which later hardened.

This finding indicates that fairly advanced people lived on the land called the Sacramento mountains and also suggests the ring was a device for tying or mooring a vessel. Obviously, because of the metal and workmanship, this ring was not a product of the Apache Indians who were a barbaric tribe which predated white men of that area. The known history of the Apaches does not record the presence of a sea or any body of water in that locale. It does not mean, however, that space men came to the Tularosa Basin and moored ships at that mooring place.

The foregoing is only a few of many examples of evidence suggesting past civilizations. This evidence is found throughout the world—some of which was mentioned in Mr. Kazantsev's article.

In the interest of objectivity, students of the unexplained should avoid accepting theories which could be based on possible emotional preference. Facts which have for the most part been ignored by orthodox science and religion are now being seriously considered. These facts include the evidence of past civilizations as well as the evidence of visiting space travelers.

Some of us show a strong inclination to link these two groups of facts, and sometimes even attempt to tie in other completely disassociated fields such as ESP and parapsychology.

In my book, "The Great Flying Saucer Hoax," I mentioned, however briefly, the tendency of the Russian scientist toward feelings of inferiority. This is evident quite often by demonstrations of boasting and further especially in regard to speculation concerning space travel by extraterrestrials. When theorizing about the artificiality of the Martian moons, one Russian scientist (Schklovsky) assumed they were the product of a recently evolved technology rather than a very advanced race with hundreds or thousands of years of space travel experience behind them. The recognition of a race of nearly the same scientific accomplishment as ours would be far more preferable to a person or people with feelings of inferiority than the idea of a race thousands of years ahead.

Mr. Kazantsev, who is probably a member of a political party known for its atheistic convictions, seems to reach out for security of a kind — we might say "technical-type" angels" in his speculations concerning space travelers who have visited earth in past milleniums, teaching new scientific concepts, etc.

Several years ago, I became engaged in a lengthy conversation concerning the origin of man with a world famous astronomer. The scientist, who undertook a study of geology in order to better equip himself for planetary studies, said that Earth was a favorable abode for man at least millions of years before man apparently (according to present-day science) made his appearance here.

If we view Mr. Kazantsev's data with an emotional inclination against the idea of extra-terrestrial visitors because of the apparent evidence, we come up with the conclusion that man has existed on earth before, and due to causes and effects about which we know nothing, was, along with what civilization he had attained, utterly destroyed. And perhaps these cataclysms have happened many times. This theory of devastating cosmic cataclysms is dealt with in detail by E. Velikovsky in his books, Ages in Chaos, Earth in Upheaval, etc., and seems well substantiated. Such occurrences could account for a carefully wrought steel block being buried in a coal strata—an indication that a very advanced civilization had been utterly destroyed eons ago. It could also account for a 290-day calendar which survived an orbital disturbance which gave us, depending on which cataclysm is involved, the 365-day calendar of the present. The IGY studies of 1956 concluded that the north pole was once located somewhere in the Pacific Ocean.

Why could not the stone arrangements of the Nasca Plateau be remnants of the ancient Indian cultures which worshipped the sun? Some, of these arrangements, at least, could be exhortations to the god of the Sun and it would be a simple matter to transfer the concept of the various animal-shapes, etc., from small to large proportions encompassing acres and miles.

There is a budding theory prevalent among some researchers which postulates the escape from destruction by space travel of advanced earthmen a millenia ago. These same theorists feel the space beings visiting earth today are descendants of those same migrating races, and related to man. Why is it so important to associate these beings with man?

Is it because the idea of a race evolv-

ing elsewhere makes God a less personal entity and man a more puny, insignificant cog in a machine which is so huge as to be impossible to comprehend? Do some of us prefer to juggle and warp the facts to suit our own emotional needs? Sadly enough, this seems to be the case, for all of us cannot be entirely correct. Perhaps the answer to the origin of the erratics lies in a combination of these speculations. But — UFO researchers are concerned with the unconventional flying machines which obviously do not have an earthly origin.

If one can prove something has happened once, it is reasonable to assume that it could happen again. Such is the case with the UFOs. If we could prove that space ships have traversed space and landed on earth in the distant past, we could reasonably speculate that it could happen at this time.

However, there is no proof of space travelers in ancient times — merely speculation based on arbitrary association of erratics.

Conversely, we do have massive evidence supporting fact of space travelers today! Let us proceed from there. To wean the orthodox masses from their dearly held convictions of the exclusiveness of man is a task of tremendous proportions—this is not a time to meddle with John Q.'s ideas of history which are deeply rooted in his religious inclinations. Easy does it.

Back Issues

The office has many back issues of the Bulletin for sale at 50c each. In some instances, however, the stock is so large that it is taking up needed space. We urge members (especially fairly new ones) to order back issues. Three or more issues will be sold for the price of 3 for $1.00, 4 for $1.50, postpaid.

Also in stock is a small supply of Special Report No. 1, the Barra da Tijuca Saucer, illustrated with photos and diagrams. This is the first and only complete account of the famous four detailed photos taken near Dio de Janeiro, Brazil in May 1952 by photographer Ed Keffel. The report is by Dr. Olavo T. Fontes of Brazil.

UFO Over Argentina

Miguel Thome, news photographer of "La Nueva Provincia" took four exposures of a UFO over Bahia Blanca, Argentina in May, obtaining one picture out of four attempts. The photo shows only an illuminated ovoid object against a black sky. When further details are available they will be presented in this Bulletin in the future.

Fireball Lights
Pacific Northwest

On the evening of 28 May, a giant fireball was observed by thousands over the Pacific Northwest. At 10:45 p. m., the large, multi-colored ball of fire trailing smoke and flame raced across the sky in a southeast direction, as observed by Canadians. Most observers in the U. S. as well as Canada observed the spectacular object for a period of at least 15 seconds.

One observer near Royal Oak, British Columbia, Canada, spotted it while driving, had time to stop the car to look. Research scientist Frank Hughes of North Gurrey, B. C., says he's seen 200 meteors, that this was the biggest. "It was on a 20 degree angle from the earth, 10 degrees in width and traversed about 30 degrees in 5 seconds. It was glowing with a white brightness like a magnesium flare—the different portions of it glowed with varying intensity," Mr. Hughes said.

Upon reading the initial descriptions of the fireball in news clippings, we were struck by the extraordinary length of time the object was observed. Mr. Arthur H. Randell of Victoria, B. C., was one of the eye-witnesses, and furnished this first-hand report:

"We had been into the city and were driving home at about 10:45 p. m. We were within a quarter mile of home, on the coast road, at Cordova Bay, where our home is situated. The Patricia Bay Airport is eight miles north of us, near Sidney and we are on the route used by TCA (Trans-Canadian Airlines) and other commercial airplanes to Seattle and other USA points, and are quite used to all types of planes and helicopters passing overhead.

"The night was dark with some stars, but few clouds, the sky being quite clear. When we first saw this object or rather lights, we thought it must be a Seattle plane. However, we immediately saw it was not, as the lights were of a different intensity and color. They were of a luminous quality, white with also some blue, almost like lighted cabin windows. It was travelling southeast towards Seattle, and was over the sea, the Haro Straights. It was not travelling very fast, but about usual plane speed, or a little faster. We could not discern the shape due to the lights and luminous glow from it. It was definitely not like any meteor we have ever seen, did not travel like one, and resembled an object intelligently controlled and going somewhere. It did not appear to be up at any great height, about usual plane height. After about 2 or 3 minutes it disappeared into the southeast in the general direction of Seattle. As it was seen in Alberta, Vancouver, here and Idaho, it must have been on some course, made several turns, and was not falling to earth in a straight line like a meteor."

Paul Quam, APRO member at Spokane, also observed the spectacle and adds further mystery to this so-called sighting of a large "meteor."

"A very large mass of material traveled in a southwest direction, coming from the north-northwest at a very high speed and not too high an altitude; at least in Spokane it wasn't close enough to be above us. It traveled parallel to the horizon. Most so-called shooting stars usually fall or streak from above to the earth. This display was quite different. It was very large, its color was beautiful, but the distance it travelled and the perfectly straight line it held was something to wonder about. Even when it began to fade away, (the "head" of it) it just traveled straight on. Almost like a jet plane shooting along.

"It is difficult to determine the altitude and speed of something like this but reports show it was seen over the larger part of the Pacific northwest. I would say it was visible to us for about 12 to 15 seconds, perhaps longer, but there were trees in the way at the north entrance and it was possible it could have been in the atmosphere longer than when we first saw it."

Flashing Lights
Seen In Colorado

APRO member Martha T. Nichols of Wheat Ridge, Colorado, has forwarded the following information concerning a sighting made by herself, her husband Charles R. Nichols, and their sons, Philip and Ross:

First sighted by Philip Nichols, the object was seen in the East-southeast about 25 degrees above the horizon at 1 a. m. MST on 26 June 1962 from the 7000 block of W. 48th Ave. Philip called his brother Ross, who arrived in time to see the object, after arriving at an overhead position, turn in a tight curve and fly toward the south. When it turned it did not tilt or bank, and proceeded to disappear at about 30 degrees from the horizon.

To the naked eye the object appeared to be a white light about the size and brightness of Jupiter. Through 8 power binoculars it appeared the size of a penny held at arm's length. Through the binoculars three white lights, spaced like the points of an equilateral triangle could be seen. In the center of the triangular formation of lights was a smaller, flashing red light. The bottom of the triangle was faintly illuminated. It flew with one light leading, point first.

Duration of the sighting was about 8 minutes, there was no sound and observers said it was impossible to judge the size of the object or its speed.

Both Philip and Ross observed the object through the binoculars while it was close enough for them to study it. They both decided that it could not be any plane that flies, as there were no wingtip lights and no sound, and the object did not bank at the turn. Mr. and Mrs. Nichols, their parents, can attest to the white light visible to the naked eye, and to a flashing red light but by the time they saw the object, it was too far away to be seen clearly.

Ross Nichols was employed (outdoors) at Stapleton Airfield at Denver for six months. Both Ross and Philip Nichols worked as helicopter mechanics on the flight line at Fort Ord, California, during basic training. Both have watched planes, both military and civilian through binoculars for years. Most of the planes in this area come and go from the west in full view of their home. Mr. and Mrs. Nichols are members of the Denver Astronomical Society and are familiar with astronomical phenomena.

It might be added that the Martin Missile plant at Littleton, Colorado, is south of Wheat Ridge, as are Colorado Springs and NORAD.

It is also interesting to note that approximately 8 minutes after the object mentioned above left that area, a round object with three legs showed up at Tucson, Arizona. See front page story.

What Were The
Green Fireballs?

The great, glowing green fireballs of 1948, 1949 and 1950 still remain pretty much of a mystery to UFO investigators and theorists. APRO member Steve Erdmann of St. Louis, Missouri, forwarded pages 93-98 and 240 of Popular Science for July 1953 which contains an article entitled: "Man-Made Meteors to Spy on Space" by Edward Hutchings Jr. and Olin J. Eggen.

Erdmann says: "Just as we planned to shoot man-made meteors to the moon and analyze the flash of impact (spectographically) in order to learn its chemical constituents, could it be possible that outer-space beings have the same ideas and have been bombarding our planet and spectroscopically charting our chemical constituents? (Example: the green fireballs of 1948, 1949 and 1950)."

Mr. Erdmann's reasoning is fresh and clean and may well be a beginning of the solution of the green fireball systery.

THE A.P.R.O. BULLETIN

The A. P. R. O. Bulletin is the official copyrighted publication of the Aerial Phenomena Research Organization (A.P.R.O.), 4145 E. Desert Place, Tucson, Arizona, and is issued every other month to members only. The Aerial Phenomena Research Orgazination is a non-profit group dedicated to the eventual solution of the mystery of the unidentified objects which have been present in the skies for hundreds of years. Inquiries regarding membership may be made to the above address.

TUCSON, ARIZONA — SEPTEMBER, 1962

MAN KIDNAPPED BY GLOBES

UFO Over Titan Site

On or about the 7th of August, 1962, a brilliantly glowing object descended over a Titan missile site near Tucson, Arizona, in the vicinity of Oracle. Because of fear of reprisal, the witness first contacted was not willing to give his name for publication and because of this APRO was in doubt as to the authenticity of the sighting. However, within five weeks after the initial report, two other reports reached us which indicated that indeed something strange had happened at the site on or about the 7th. The first report was that at about midnight on the 7th, one of the night crew while outside the complex spotted the brilliant light overhead which began to appear larger and larger. He realized the object was ascending directly over the site, went inside and notified another man who came out and watched with him. Shortly, the object appeared to be coming so close that the men were somewhat frightened and they took refuge. Davis-Monthan AFB had been notified, and two jets streaked in from the direction of Tucson. As the jets approached, the objects took off fast and was out of sight in seconds. The jets circled the area, then headed for Tucson. Minutes later the "visitor" was back again. Witnesses said the bottom of the object was similar to the color of the moon in the night sky. Shortly after the second ascension over the Silo, the object ascended vertically and moved off at high speed, disappearing in seconds.

Another witness' testimony indicated that the object or a similar one was seen either the night before or the night after the above-described sighting, with similar maneuvers taking place.

Boy Snabs Photo Of UAO Covey

Alex Birch, a 14-year-old schoolboy of Moor Crescent, Mossborough, Sheffield, England, snapped a box-camera photo of a group of NAOs on or about 25 February 1962, in the presence of two other boys, Steward Dixon and David Brownlow. He and his friends were in the old nursery garden in the back of his home when they spotted the five dark objects over the currant hedges and trees. The picture was taken with a simple Brownie camera, shows five dark fan-shaped objects, slightly out of focus above the trees.

Air Ministry experts examined the photos but would not comment on them. Theye questioned the boy for nearly two hours. Alex's father said he was told he would get an answer if he came to London with the photo and negative, but after the meeting, officials said they would have to make more inquiries.

The Yorkshire Post said the Ministry officials smiled when they saw the boy and his box camera but did not smile when they saw the photograph. They later referred to the objects as UFOs and Aerial Phenomena, and say the photo is not a hoax.

On the glossy pictures and the negative, there are several clusters of white or clear spots. One cluster is immediately above one of the objects.

Landings In Italy

In addition to the Zuccula sighting (or experience), there was several other close-up sightings of UFOs—especially in the vicinity of Florence. On the evening of the 11th of April, Iller Benazzi, 28, accompanied by three friends, was driving along the Saronno-Legnano road. He stopped the car so that he and his company could watch a strange looking flying machine. He said it made no noise, dived on their car, then landed on the road some distance from their car. The Edinburgh Evening News for 14 April did not give a detailed description, but quoted Benazzi as saying the objects had "three smaller tail lights with a violet gleam." The four drove on. He told police that he and his friends decided not to talk about the object, as they feared no one would believe them. He changed his mind after reading of the Zuccala sighting which described a similar type of craft seen on the same night. No further details; see Zuccala sighting.

Report by Olavo T. Fontes, M.D.

The tragic case I am going to relate here was investigated to the limits that any investigation can reach when every piece of evidence is analysed and evaluated, when every clue is exhaustively followed, and when every conventional explanation is explored and dismissed for lack of proof. In a case of this kind, however, we could only establish a definite conclusion if that conclusion could be negative. We could be sure, in other words, if the body of the victim was found; if facts or motivations in the past life and personality of the victim or witness were demonstrated, showing that they couldn't be trusted, were psychotic, or had reasons to simulate the whole thing; or if additional evidence was not uncovered connecting the facts in the case with the sighting of unconventional aerial objects. As the body was not found, facts or motivations of such a kind were lacking and there was definite evidence concerning the sighting of UAOs—the case must be accepted as possible despite the lack of absolute proof. On the other hand, we must recognize the witness obviously cannot present more than was presented: his report about the mysterious disappearance of his father. You can believe it or not. The absolute truth, that only the witness himself can be sure about it.

The readers may not like this report. For one reason—it will show them that such things as UAOs from other planets could be interested in kidnapping humans, in order to become better acquainted with them. In fact, personal experiences such as the one related here will cause you to wonder about missing people—about how many of the individuals who are yearly reported as missing might have chanced to come upon a UAO in some lonely spot and were captured as specimens.

A noise of running steps, a shadow seeming to float into the dark room, two ball-shaped objects emitting light and discharging a strange yellow smoke, a human being disappearing into that yellow mist before the eyes of his terror-stricken son—such is the fantastic story

(See Kidnapped, page 3)

The A. P. R. O. BULLETIN

Published by
THE AERIAL PHENOMENA RESEARCH
ORGANIZATION
4145 E. Desert Place
Tucson, Arizona
Copyright 1963, Coral E. Lorenzen
Editor and Director

Information appearing in this bulletin may be used by other UAO research periodicals providing names and address credit is properly given to this organization and periodical.

Coral E. Lorenzen .... International Director and Editor
A. E. Brown, B.S.E.E. .... Director of Research
L. J. Lorenzen .... Director of Public Relations
John T. Hopf .... Photographic Consultant
Oliver Dean .... Photographic Consultant

SPECIAL REPRESENTATIVES

(The following listed individuals participate in planning and policy-making as Staff Members, in addition to coordinating investigative efforts in the areas indicated following their names.)

Dr. Olavo T. Fontes, M.D.........Brazil
K.Gosta Rehn .... Sweden
Graham Conway ...... Eastern Canada
Aime Michel .... France
Horacio Gonzales Gauteaume
　　　　　　　　　　　　　Venezuela
Peter E. Norris, L.L.D. ....Australia
Jun' Ichi Takanashi .... Japan
Juan C. Remonda .... Argentina
Sergio Robba .... Italy
Arist. Mitropoulos .... Greece
Rev. N. C. G. Cruttwell, New Guinea
Eduardo Buelte .... Spain
Norman Alford .... New Zealand
Austin Byrne .... Ireland

SPECIAL CONSULTANT
Prof. Charles Maney,—Physics

ALAMOGORDO PRINTING CO., INC.

Salisbury On "Life On Mars"

In "Popular Science" magazine for September 1962, APRO member Dr. Frank B. Salisbury tells "Why I believe in Life on Mars."

The reasons: 1. The color change fits nicely into a spring-summer vegetation cycle, and 2. When the yellow clouds do cover the planet they don't permanently tinge it. Whatever is there appears to grow through it or shakes it off. This rules out lichens which also require a lot of water, algae and fungi for existence.

He points also to the riddle of the Martian satellites—and the canals — in support of possible "higher forms of life."

Moving Lights Over Philly

On the nights of April 25 and 26, 1962, objects were reported over Philadelphia which moved, stopped short, changed direction and faded from sight. Authorities suggested airplane landing lights or fireballs. What'll you have?

PALO ALTO, Calif., Monday, Sept. 10, 1962—Research scientist Alvin E. Brown, of Lockheed Missile & Space Co., finds his way through a wooded area with a "bat radar" device which uses the principal of the bat hearing system in detecting objects in its path.

Brown Plays "Batman"

With pardonable pride we wish to call attention to some recent accomplsihments of Al Brown, our Research Director.

No. 1 is a portable electrocardiograph so small that the heart patient can wear it under his clothes while pursuing his normal daily activity. Heart activity is recorded on a tape capsule which is removed and interpreted later. Al designed and patented the device in the course of his work at Lockheed Missiles and Space Co. It is already on the market.

No. 2 is described briefly in the following excerpts from a Lockheed Missiles and Space Co. news release:

"FOR RELEASE: Monday, Sept. 10, 1962. BAT RADAR DEVICE ENABLES MAN TO 'HEAR' OBJECTS IN HIS PATH. PALO ALTO, CALIF.—A "bat radar" device which, when fully developed, may allow a blind man to throw away his cane, has been produced by Lockheed Missiles & Space Co. scientists.

"In its present preliminary form, the instrument enables a blindfolded person to detect and make his way around such objects as filing cabinets, cars, trees, and other people.

"If scientists can learn more about the mental mechanism of bats—as well as other animals—they may convert this knowledge to great value for man. This is the real object of bionics research and

development at Lockheed and elsewheree.

"But Lockheed's "bat radar," built to enable a man to navigate sightless like a bat, is expected by its inventors to have broad applications. Studies connected with the instrument, or with devcies based on the same principle, may teach scientists much about radar and sonar that is not now known.

"Experiments with bats are continuing, but research scientists in the Lockheed Laboratories at Palo Alto decided to attempt to reproduce, at least in crude form, the bat's navigation system. The specific task was given to electronics research scientist Alvin E. Brown, 36-year-old graduate of the University of Washington." (See photo of Brown testing the device above).

Red Ball Speeds Over Phoenix

Earl Vaughan, his wife and guests, Mr. and Mrs. Allen Beckman from Colorado Springs, Colorado, observed a huge glowing reddish-orange ball (about the size of tennis ball held at arm's length) on 11 August 1962 at 8:20 p.m. The object's course was from north to south, and was seen in the eastern sector of the sky. It proceeded swiftly south in a flat, horizontal trajectory, and was in sight about 5 seconds.

Kidnapped . . .

(Continued from page 1)

told by a 12-year-old boy, Raimundo de Aleluia Mafra. His father, Rivalino Mafra da Silva, is missing. Raimundo states that he was kidnapped by two strange objects, on the morning of August 20, 1962, just in front of his house, in a place called Duas Pontes, district of Diamantina, State of Minas Gerais.

The sixteen thousand citizens of Diamantina are divided in their opinions about the happening: some believe there was merely a murder with a missing body; others thing that Rivalino ran away for some unknown reason and his son is telling a tale to cover him; still others think the whole think was 'the work of the Devil"; many others are certain that the child is telling the truth On the other hand, the situation is quite different in Biribiri, Mendanha and Rio Vermelho, small villages in the vicinity of the area where the strange events took place. The residents at those places—those who still remain there—are living with panic in their hearts. They do not dare to go outside at night. They do not risk walking alone through the fields. Their doors and windows are closed after 8 p.m. Their streets are empty and silent at night. Many families are leaving toward Diamantina.

You cannot laugh at them — they are too frightened, haunted by the pitiful cries of a child: "They've got my father! I want my father back! Help me!..." They are under the terror of the almost unreal, of something alien and unexplainable, something so different from common sense that your mind is repelled by it. This may sound to you like the science fiction stories you customarily read in Science Fiction magazines.

Perhaps this is best for your sanity—if you don't believe in UAOs from other planets.

Raimundo Aleluia Mafra's Report

Rivalino disappeared on August 20. That same day the police was called and the investigation started. Rumors began to spread and reporters were alerted on August 24. The case hit the headlines on August 26. On the evening of August 25, the boy Raimundo was interviewed by the press about the circumstances related with the disappearance of his father.

In spite of his undernourished aspect and obvious anxiety, the youngster was able to give a clear and detailed account of the tragic event. He falters only when forced by direct questions about his father; then he begins to cry. He is only a small boy, who has never attended school and doesn't even know the alphabet. He lives in a small house in a lonely spot, about 28 kilometers from Diamantina. He helps (or helped) his father as the oldest son, taking care of the two small brothers and doing all the house work. His mother died about one year ago. In his ignorance, living in a deserted place outside the civilized world, he has never heard about flying saucers, "space beings" from other planets, comics, or even radio and television. His report was given in the presence of Lieutenant Wilson Lisboa, Police chief at Diamantina. For the twentieth time — according to the information of that authority—he tells about the incredible drama lived by his father before his startled eyes. He says that things started in the night of August 19. The whole family was in bed—himself, his father and his two brothers (Fatimo, 6-year-old, and Dirceu, 2-year-old). He cannot tell the time, because there is no clock in the house, but he was awakened by the sound of steps and got the impression that people were walking hurriedly through the room. He called his father who lit a small candle. Then, under the flickering light, they saw a strange silhouette more like a shadow, floating in the room without touching the floor.

"It was a weird shadow, not looking like ours because it was half the size of a man and not shaped like a human being. We remained in the bed, quiet, and the shadow looked at us—then it moved to the place where my brothers were sleeping and looked at them for a long time, without touching their bodies. Afterwards, it left our room, crossed the other room and disappeared near the outer door. Again we heard steps of someone running and a voice said: 'This one looks like Rivalino.' My father then yelled: 'Who goes there?' There was no answer. Father left the bed and went to the other room, when the voice asked again if he really was Rivalino. My father answered it was right, that Rivalino was his name, and there was no answer. We came back to bed and heard clearly their talk outside, saying they were going to kill father. My father started to pray aloud and the voices outside said there was no help for him. They talked no more.

"We passed the night awake. In the morning, still afraid, I had the courage to go outside to get my father's horse in the field. But then I sighted two balls floating in mid-air side by side, about two meters from the ground, one meter from each other and a few meters away from our door. They were big. One of them was all black, had a kind of irregular antenna-like protuberance and a small tail. The other was black and white, with the same outlines, with the antenna and everything. They both emitted a humming sound and appeared to give off fire through an opening that flickered like a fire fly, switching the light on and off rapidly. I was frozen by fear. I called father to see those strange flying objects. He came out of the house, still praying and asking about what those things could be, his eyes locked on them. He warned me to stay away and walked toward the objects. He stopped at a distance of two meters. At that moment the two big balls merged into each other. There was only one now, bigger in size, raising dust from the ground and discharging a yellow smoke which darkened the sky. With strange noises, that big ball crept slowly toward my father. I saw him enveloped by the yellow smoke and he disappeared inside it. I ran after him into the yellow cloud, which had an acrid smell. I saw nothing, only that yellow mist around me. I yelled for my father but there was no answer. Everything was silent again.

"Then the yellow smoke dissolved. The balls were gone. My father was gone. The ground below was clean as if the dust had been removed by a big broom. I was confused and desperate. I walked in circles around the house looking for father, but I found no tracks, footprints or marks. Was this the work of the Devil? My father had disappeared in mid-air. I have searched the plains, fields and thickets with no results. I have watched the flight of vultures, looking for clues to locate his body, but I saw nothing. Five days have passed and nothing was found. Is my father dead, taken by the globes? I want my father back . . . " (Unquote—Belo Horizonte DIARIO DE MINAS, August 26. Rio de Janeiro CORREIO DA MANHA, September 4. Lieutenant Lisboa's report, transcribed verbatim).

The Police Investigation

Lieutenant Wilson Lisboa, Police chief at Diamantina, was called the same day of the strange disappearance. He put the Raimundo boy under cross-examination but failed to make him change his incredible story. He then decided to make a complete investigation. Policemen were ordered to look for Rivalino's body, to find him at any cost. The search was started inside Rivalino's house. No clue was found. The surrounding country was covered by trained men. At the spot Rivalino had been kidnapped by the ob-

(See Kidnapped, page 4)

Kidnapped . . .

(Continued from page 3)

jects—according to the boy's report — the ground was clean of dust in an area about five meters in diameter, but no tracks or marks were visible. About fifty meters away, a few drops of blood were found. Lieutenant Lisboa collected samples and the analysis identified them as human blood. The search for the missing body spread through the whole district of Diamantina. It took ten days. Police dogs were sent from Belo Horizonte, bloodhounds trained by the military police to follow tracks and find missing people. They found nothing. A complete investigation of Rivalino's past life, possible love affairs, enemies, friends, relatives, etc., was undertaken. No clues were found.

Another investigation was made concerning the possible sighting of UAOs over the region by other witnesses. The following reports are of interest:

(1) The vicar at Diamantina's cathedral, priest Jose Avila Garcia, contacted Lieutenant Lisboa to inform him that, by a strange coincidence, a friend of his had reported an unusual fact the night before Rivalino's disappearance. That friend, Antonio Rocha, was fishing at the Manso river, close to Duas Pontes, when he sighted two ball-shaped objects hovering over Rivalino's house. Priest Garcia believed that the boy had dreamed and his father had been murdered, but it was his duty to report all facts to the police — even those opposed to his own opinion.

Mr. Antonio Rocha, who worked at the Mail Department in Diamantina, was called and confirmed his story. On the evening of August 19, he was fishing at a place near Rivalino's house. "At 4:00 p.m.," he said to Lieutenant Lisboa, "I sighted two strange ball-shaped objects in the sky. They were flying in circles over Rivalino's house. They came very low and were gone a few minutes later. I don't know anything about Rivalino's disappearance, but—from the report given by his son Raimundo—I have the impression he saw the same objects I sighted."

(2)—Rivalino Mafra da Silva was a diamond prospector. Lieutenant Lisboa interviewed other prospectors in the district who did their mining work with Rivalino. They told him a startling story. Rivalino had informed them that, on August 17, when going back home, he had seen two strange persons digging a hole in the earth at a spot near his house. When approached, the creatures ran away into the bushes. They were

approximately three feet tall. A few moments later, he sighted a strange object which took off from behind the bushes and disappeared into the sky at high speed. According to Rivalino, this object was shaped like a hat and surrounded by a red glow. They didn't believe him, of course.

(3)—Doctor Giovani Pereira, a physician living at Diamantina, went to the police to report the sighting of a disc-shaped object over his own house two months before. He had had a night call from a patient and was driving back in his car. When closing the car's door to go inside his home, he suddenly sighted a brilliant object, shaped like a disc, hovering low over his house. He stopped and watched it for several minutes. Then it moved away at high speed after crossing over the sleeping town. He said he had kept the sighting secret because he knew nobody would believe him.

(4)—On the morning of August 24, a UAO crossed over the town of Gouveia, about 42 kilometers to the south of Diamantina. The sighting was witnessed by more than fifty people, including the local Police chief, Lieutenant Walter Costa Coelho. According to the observers, the object was white colored, shaped like a soccer ball and encircled by a kind of fluorescent glow—remaining in sight for about two minutes. It was traveling to the north (toward Montes Claros), then changed course to the northwest.

A few minutes later, the same (or similar) object was spotted in the sky by more than one hundred citizens at Brasilia de Minas, a small town about 120 kilometers to the northwest of Montes Claros. Again it looked like a soccer ball and was surrounded by a white glow. According to the local priest, this UAO hovered for a long time over the town's church before disappearing to the west at high speed.

This sighting was printed in the papers on August 28. The news had a deleterious effect on the residents of small towns and villages in the same area of Duas Pontes. The coincidence was too much for them: a ball-shaped object, sighted over the same region, just four days after Rivalino's disappearance. The consequence was panic and hysteria.

The last step in Lieutenant Lisboa's investigation was to check and recheck the sanity of Raimundo and the reliability of his report. Raimundo was intensively questioned by the police and, at police request, a psychiatric examination was made by Dr. Joan Antunes de Oliveira. He was found to be sane. Dr. Oliveira then decided to make a last

experiment. It was a cruel test, but justified due to the circumstances in the case. In the presence of witnesses, the boy Raimundo Mafra was taken to a room where there was a human body covered by a cloth. "Raimundo," said Dr. Oliveira, "this is the body of your father. He is dead. You lied when you told us that he had been kidnapped. Tell now the whole truth(what really happened on the morning of August 20." The boy began to cry, in a state of great emotion, but continued to affirm that his story was not a lie, that his father could be dead but had been taken by the two objects. "Perhaps they brought him back, dead," was his conclusion. This ended the experiment. Dr. Oliveira was interviewed by the press. He said: "I don't wish to discuss the facts in the case. They are beyond my competence. But I can tell you that the boy is normal and he is telling what he thinks to be the truth."

An attempt was also made to cross-examine the kid applying the technique known as hypo-analysis. The attempt failed because Raimundo was not receptive to hypnosis.

So Lieutenant Lisboa came to the end of his investigation and found himself in a very peculiar and difficult position. He was certain that Rivalino had been murdered, but the corpse had vanished. He had thought that the boy was lying or out of his mind, but failed to get proof showing he couldn't be trusted, was psychotic, or had reasons for simulation. He didn't belief in flying discs or balls—yet the evidence he had collected pointed in that direction. At this point, he decided to do two things: (1) to continue the search for Rivalino's body; (2) to make a written report to the Secretary of Public Security of the State and send Raimundo Fafra to Belo Horizonte, the State capital.

Raimundo Mafra Goes To Belo Horizonite

On August 30(the boy arrived at Belo Horizonte. He had a companion, Mr. Antonio de Carvalho Cruz, the Commissioner of the State Child's Department at Diamantina, who had the mission of taking the boy to the proper authorities in the capital. At that moment, general curiosity had been aroused about the kid, and he was interviewed by the whole press and even appeared on a television program. Then Colonel Mauro Gouveia, Secretary of Public Security in the State of Minas Gerais, took charge of the case. Raimundo was questioned, cross-examined, photographed and again

(See Kidnapped, next page)

Kidnapped . . .

(Continued from page 4)

submitted to medical and psychiatric examination. Three days later he was taken into custody by military authorities. An Air Force plane took him to Rio de Janeiro, where he disappeared behind the protection of a tight security ring. No one knows where he is now.

Epilogue

A month after the mysterious disappearance of Rivalino Fafra da Silva, the police at Diamantina decided to stop their investigation and to close the case. The body is still missing and every effort to find new clues has met with complete failure. Lieutenant Lisboa and his policemen are depressed. One of them, policeman Clemente, said to the press: "Nobody expects to find a satisfactory explanation with respect to Mr. Rivalino's disappearance." (Belo Horizonte ULTIMA HORA, September 22, 1962).

At this point, it would be preferable merely to present the evidence and to allow the reader to draw his own conclusion; but I find it necessary to call attention to a very important thing: Reports indicate space creatures have been investigating the Earth closely for more than fifteen years. They appear to follow a very methodical plan, step by step. Available evidence indicates they have already taken specimens of terrestrial flora, water, rocks and soil. An investigation of the fauna was apparently lacking, as far as the collection of specimens is concerned. However, would it not be logical that they eventually turn their attention to collecting specimens of fauna? It would be surprising, indeed, if they overlooked the most interesting example of terrestrial fauna—man himself.

The case of Rivalino Mafra da Silva appears to be the first one—in the whole UAO history—where vanishing people and UAOs are definitely connected by direct evidence. Therefore, in spite of some incredible details we cannot explain (i.e., the happenings at night inside and outside Rivalino's house), I am forced to conclude he was kidnapped by two ball-shaped UAOs—in the presence of his own son. There is no other alternative. And—as they always repeat their moves—it is reasonable to expect that other similar cases will happen soon.

PLEASE!...
REMIT DUES
PROMPTLY
$3.50 PER YEAR

Low Flying Disc In Washington

The "Whisky Ridge" area east of Marysville, Washington, played host to a disc-like object which was reported by many residents in the summere of 1962, and a reporter recently suggested that Whisky Ridge be re-named "Disc-Slope" if any more are seen. The most recent object was shaped like a whale, dipped down toward a field as though it were going to land, then headed off into the northwest. It made no noise, and travelled at about the speed of a small aircraft. The latter sighting was made by Mr. and Mrs. Floyd Brooks on 17 September 1962.

AF "Bugged" By UFOS At Truax

APRO member Herb Thrune of Milwaukee, Wisconsin, reported the following information which he heard on the radio on June 30 and about which he inquired and recorded: "For the past week reports of UFO have been reported to Madison, Wisconsin police. The objects were first thought to be "Echo" balloon. There have been three UFOs which fly erratically, mostly in the vicinity of Truax AFB, and they cannot be tracked on radar. Reports also came from Green county, to the west of Madison." Nothing was found in the Milwaukee Journal, and the Sentinel was inactive because of a union strike at the time, so no further confirmation was received.

UFO Over Milwaukee, Wis.

At 1:45 a.m., CST, on August 3, 1962, Mr. and Mrs. Herb Thrune of Milwaukee, Wis., observed the passage of a huge light from south to north above their home. The couple said it appeared to revolve to the right, going faster than any airplane with which they were familiar. As it approached overhead position, a "huge sunflower-shaped light" blinked on and off. Mr. Thrune went out on the lawn between his house and the one next to him and watched as it sped due north over the Miller Brewnig Co. He said the incident happened so fast that it was difficult to determine the altitude. He felt the object was cigar-shaped, and it did not arc, but adhered to a flat, straight course at a very high rate of speed. The color was golden or orange, and there was no sound or contrail of any kind. Thrune is conversant with the types of planes usually in the area, and cannot identify the strange luminous body as anything conventional. Mitchell AFB is 8 to 10 miles south of the Thrune home.

Light On Moon Observed

At 9:50 p.m., on August 12, 1962, Donald R. Westlake of Yorktown Heights, New York, observed a small star-like object on the dark portion of the moon. According to the report he submitted to a Valhalla, N. Y. APRO member, the moon was in its gibbous phase and the light was quite obvious. He was using a 16 power, 3-inch Bausch and Lomb Naval "Spy Glass." He at first thought it was a defect on the glass itself, and after checking this on a starfield, he turned his attention to the moon again. The object was as bright as the Ray system in Tycho but was well into the dark of the moon. He thought then it was a mountain top or peak just catching the rays of the sun. Westlake then got out his 2.5" refractor telescope and with 50X lens the object seemed to take on an oblong narrow shape. He used 90X and although it looked clear, the shape of the object remaineed the same. The object at no time seemed to move as would be th ecase if it was a star or planet occulted by the moon. Westlake then called his wife Mary and neighbor Alex Zajac. As they watched the object Mr. Westlake attempted to call a friend who lived down county and was also interested in this type of occurence. As he talked to his friend, Mr. Zajac reported the object was beginning to fade. Westlake went back to the scopes and looked but the object was gone from sight. His friend with whom he talked on the telephone had told him that he also had been watching the moon prior to being called, but he had noticed no object. They all watched the moon until clouds covered it at about 11 p.m. EST and the object did not return. Westlake checked his Sky and Telescope magazine and could find no occultation scheduled for stars on that date. "Anyone who has ever witnesseed an occultation knows tht the star disappears instantly and does not fade out as this object did. The object in question appeared to be as bright as the lighted side of the moon. Any explanations sent to APRO will be forwarded to Mr. Westlake, who, incidentally, is a UFO skeptic.

Teacher, Friends, See UFO

Arthur Sketchley, a school teacher, and five companions, observed two unidentified objects while driving near Winfield, 140 miles northwest of Calgary, Alberta, Canada at 7 p.m. on Thursday, May 17, 1962. The objects were described by the observers as cigar-shaped,

(See Teacher, page 6)

Teacher . . .

(Continued from page 5)

long and slender and golden in color. The objects were observed in the western skies, and when in silhouette, appeared long and slender, but when viewed from another angle, looked fluffy at the sides. One eventually disappeared behind a cloud, the other was in view for some time. There is not sufficient detail in this sighting to thoroughly evaluate, but the description could fit a high altitude aircraft contrail reflecting the setting sun, thus appearing to be golden. This is also indicated by the "fluffy" description. However, the testimony that the objects were viewed from two different angles suggests that they changed position and this might lead to doubt as to their identity as contrails. As for the one object disappearing behind a cloud, if the contrail were from high altitude aircraft as, say, 50,000 feet, cloud cover at 10,000 could easily obscure them.

Liberal, Kansas Sightings

On August 2, 1962, personnel at the Liberal, Kansas airport were shaken considerably when various colored brilliant objects "lit up the runways." Whether or not this indicates the objects were low enough and bright enough to actually shed light on the ground is not known. However, similar reports came from Albuquerque, N. M., Pueblo, Colorado, Garden City, Kansas, and Guymon, Oklahoma. Central Airline Agent Fred Jones said about a dozen individuals at the Liberal airport saw the phenomena at about 8 p.m.

According to Jones, Capt. Jack Metzker, CA pilot enroute from Wichita, Texas, to Amarillo, told airport officials he saw the objects which he said were moving higher and faster than any plane he had ever seen. Metzker's aircraft was at between 5500 to 7000 feet at the time he sighted the objects.

Witnesses described the lights as about the size of car headlights, and they varied in color from white, green, blue to brilliant orange. There were four of the objects, Jones said, which moved singly across the sky. One became stationary over the airport and seemed to produce a landing-type light directly under it.

All sighting took place at approximately 8:45 p.m. The reports came to Liberal over the airport's telephone communications system. The FAA said no planes which could produce such lights were scheduled in the area at the time.

At Amarillo, Metzker made this statement: "People I talked to after landing here seemed to think it was a meteorite, but it wasn't like any meteorite I've ever seen."

Witnesses at Pueblo described a blue ball of light traveling north.

Rotating Ball—Wisconsin

APRO member Mrs. Forence Cummins reports a sighting by a friend who lives about 12 miles north of Thorpe, Wisconsin. Said friend was visiting daughter the week of 19 August, cannot place exact date, but incident took place during that week. The observer was outside with 1-year-old granddaughter when she saw a balloon-like object which was speeding across the sky—"sort of whirling." She illustrated with her finger, and Mrs. Cummins said the observer indicated a horizonal flgiht, although the object was rotating—somewhat like a circular "penmanship exercise." The woman called her daughter to see it, but the object had disappeared from sight by the time the daughter arrived outside.

UAO Formation North Of Toronto

On July 2, 1962, an observer in Toronto, Canada, witnessed the flight of a formation of three white, round objects which passed overhead, directly north to the horizon. The observer said each was about the size of his thumb at arm's length. No noise was heard, but he said he heard a jet airliner go over shortly before or after the objects' flight. Time: 5:25 p.m., EDS. Nothing appeared in local papers about other observations, but a neighbor told the observer he and several others had seen a huge object hovering over the new Highway 401. No newspaper reports on this sighting, either. Observer in first named sighting is friend of APRO member and remains anonymous.

Boys Sight Maneuvering UFO In 1961

On August 7, 1961 Danny Okrasinski, 12, Route 1, Gresham, Oregon, and James Towell, 12 also of Route 1, camped out in a field near their homes and while looking at the starts sighted a strange light which circled, hovered and started at intervals. They claimed it made several passes over Gresham and appeared to be very large as it came down close to the ground. They had seen it two weeks previously and the August 7 sighting made the second time they observed it.

Books

It is with considerable pleasure that we say a few words about "Mars, The new Frontier—Lowell's Hypothesis" by Wells Alan Webb. In addition to reading the book, the Lorenzens had the pleasure of meeting the author in August while visiting APRO's Research Director, Mr. Brown, in California.

Some of the more humble of the saucer buffs will feel somewhat embarrassed to learn that this scientific contribution to our knowledge of Mars was published way back in 1956 (Fearon Publishers, 2450 Fillmore St., San Francisco 15, Calif.). Others, of course, may have already read it.

Although a clear and concise analysis of Lowell's Hypothessi constitutes a maor part of the book, some pearls of wisdom inevitably take the reader's attention. Two chapters of considerable interest are Numbers 1 and 2: "Science and Controversy" and "Science and the Personal Factor," respectively. A close perusal of these two chapters will give the reader a larger insight into the necessary objectivity of a scientist, however frustrating the caution may seem to the layman.

To be brief, we would like to quote a few words from Capter 10, Page 130, entitled "Strange Sightings": "The end that I hope to have accomplished by all of this is to induce scientific men at last to take that quantum jump, that revision in basic philosophy essential to tentative acceptance of Lowell's Hypothesis, an explanation that I believe correctly orients the phenomena of Mars. But I urge such acceptance as a trial, to stimulate inquiry; for I do not maintain that proof-positive has been established for intelligence on Mars, but that my correlation is corroboratory evidence, the best present answers for the facts of the network. I think that future research will establish for certain that Mars' canals are either the beaten footpaths of lower migratory animals or they are engineered conduits devised by intelligent beings for their survival on an oxygenless planet. Every effort should be made by scientists to resolve this question promptly."

Mr. Webb, a chemist with Hexcel Products, Inc., Berkeley, Calif., has also forwarded a copy of his paper entitled "Mars as an Object of Exploration and Settlement" and which was presented to the International Astronautical Federation, XIIth Congress, in October 1961, at Washington, D. C. The paper is a carefully outlined plan by which humans may be able to establish self-sustaining colonies on Mars. Mr. Webb's conclusions are interesting, to say the least.

THE A.P.R.O. BULLETIN

The A. P. R. O. Bulletin is the official copyrighted publication of the Aerial Phenomena Research Organization (A.P.R.O.), 4145 E. Desert Place, Tucson, Arizona, and is issued every other month to members only. The Aerial Phenomena Research Organization is a non-profit group dedicated to the eventual solution of the mystery of the unidentified objects which have been present in the skies for hundreds of years. Inquiries regarding membership may be made to the above address.

GLOWING LIGHTS INVADE HOME

Monitoring And Scanning Discs

The 'Ears' and 'Eyes' of the UFO's

By C. W. Fitch

Numerous and varied reports of small flying objects, diminutive saucers and night-flying balls of light, leave little doubt as to their reality.

Their true nature and activating motives remain a mystery which has given rise to considerable speculation. However, the most logical deduction would seem to be that these small objects are scanning discs or   devices or a combination of both—remote controll-

The following cases, among other things, are illustrative of the objects' maneuverability, with the resulting conclusion that they must, therefore, be under intelligent and precisely accurate control.

While certain of these occurrences have not involved the visual observation of small UFOs they have been included since it is quite possible that the phenomena observed in these cases was under the remote control of a spaceship.

—o—

The opening chapter of these recorded sightings takes us back to the war years of 1943-'44.

In his book "Black Thursday" Martin Caiden on pages 211-212 relates the following provocative account of a close-up sighting of diminutive saucers which took place on October 14, 1943.

"During the bomb run of several groups, starting at about the time the Fortresses approached the Initial Point, there occurred one of the most baffling incidents of World War II, and an enig-

(See "Monitoring", page 3)

Miehel Tells of New Findins

The following is a translation of an article by Aime Michel, entitled: "At What Point Have We Arrived in 1962, in Our Studies of Flying Saucers?"

"The following is a definite exclusive document announced within recent months. We have Aime Michel, the author, to thank most sincerely for the results of this long research, who has been so gracious as to give the first fruits of his labors to the readers of "Lumieres dans la Muit."

"This document includes not one but five discoveries of the greatest importance: (1) The certainty of the origin of the instruments (perhaps not of their real origin, but in any case of a base or of a relay serving their exploration); (2) orthotenic lines are planetary, and do not stop as one might have supposed after a few hundred kilometers.

On the subject of orthoteny, let us refresh people's memory as to what it is, especially those who are not informed and can no longer get the authoritative work, now out of print of Aime Michel: "Mysterious Celestial Objects"; "It is the rectilinear disposition, causing networks, of the immense majority of observations relative to flying saucers in 1954 — as the author (Michel) wrote in "Science and Life," in February, 1958. This disposition is authentic for the observations noticed during the same day and seems all the more powerful as it was possible to determine the trajectory of the object precisely (for example its landings). Some scientists have calculated that the probability that such a rectilinear disposition was an effect of chance   does not exist, especially if one reflects that   of the o servations are   on straight lines, and that this phenomenon was repeated over western Europe for week uring all of September and October, 1954,   which is fantasti .

"Reading nothing further in the newspapers on the subject of flying saucers, the public may be led to think that no observation is being registered any more

(See "Michel", page 5)

On the 10th of October, residents on Spring Park Road, Jacksonville, Florida, observed strange small fireballs which had fuzzy outlines and stole silently around and among houses on that street. House lights dimmed and some went out entirely as the phenomena occurred. Mrs. J. P. Baker said she was in her upstairs kitchen at twilight when her husband told her he had seen a ball of fire moving through a field behind the house. Mrs. Baker looked out her kitchen window and saw a "round ball, big as a No. 2 wash tub" which was pinkish in color and so brilliant it almost blinded her. She said it hovered outside her kitchen window apparently less than 6 feet away. then floated around the corner of the house and cross Spring Park Road. Harold Whitehead of Browning Fuel Oil Co. on Spring Park Road said he and two others saw a fireball gliding along a utility wire a block south of the oil company. "It was the size of a washtub, a blinding, whitish ball of fire. I watched it about five seconds. It moved about 10 or 20 feet during that time, then went out with a big "pop." Our lights were dim for about a half hour after," Whitehead reported.

On Pampas Drive, which connects with Spring Park Road, an unidentified woman (by request) said a formless "glow" moved through her house, out through the front door and along Pampas Drive. She said it was about a half a block long, and brilliantly illuminated a car and other objects in the vicinity. She said that as the glow moved through the house, it enveloped her, her hand tingled "as if it had gone to sleep" and her children screamed through fear.

Mrs. Gladys Faucette of Cascade Road, the street from which Mrs. Rakers' fireball seemed to come, said she saw a glow descend to within 3 feet of the ground between her home and the adjacent house. She said the form was too vague to be described as ball-shaped, but she called it a "terribly big brilliance." She said the circuit which carries electricity to her bathroom and bedroom was knocked out about this time, and was still out the next morning.

The A. P. R. O. BULLETIN

Published by
THE AERIAL PHENOMENA RESEARCH
ORGANIZATION
4145 E. Desert Place
Tucson, Arizona
Copyright 1963, Coral E. Lorenzen
Editor and Director

Information appearing in this bulletin may be used by other UAO research periodicals providing names and address credit is properly given to this organization and periodical.

Coral E. Lorenzen ___ International Director and Editor
A. E. Brown, B.S.E.E. ___ Director of Research
L. J. Lorenzen ___ Director of Public Relations
John T. Hopf ___ Photographic Consultant
Oliver Dean ___ Photographic Consultant

SPECIAL REPRESENTATIVES

(The following listed individuals participate in planning and policy-making as Staff Members, in addition to coordinating investigative efforts in the areas indicated following their names.)

Dr. Olavo T. Fontes, M.D. ___ Brazil
K. Gosta Rehn ___ Sweden
Graham Conway ___ Eastern Canada
Aime Michel ___ France
Horacio Gonzales Gauteaume ___ Venezuela
Peter E. Norris, L.L.D. ___ Australia
Jun' Ichi Takanashi ___ Japan
Juan C. Remonda ___ Argentina
Sergio Robba ___ Italy
Arist. Mitropoulos ___ Greece
Rev. N. C. G. Cruttwell, New Guinea
Eduardo Buelte ___ Spain
Norman Alford ___ New Zealand
Austin Byrne ___ Ireland

SPECIAL CONSULTANT
Prof. Charles Maney,—Physics

ALAMOGORDO PRINTING CO., INC.

1960 Sighting Of UAO Carrier

The following was forwarded to us by a member, but the name of the contributor is not on the original report, nor the names of observers. Will the contributor please inform us of his identity just for the record?

On the last Sunday of December 1960 a man and his family were visiting relatives at Cottonwood, Minnesota. At about 11:45 p.m. the husband went outside for a breath of fresh air, then noticed an unusual light traveling in the north. Not knowing of any satellite which would be in that sky sector, the observer watched the object, which obligingly came closer. In about 30 seconds it was close enough so that he could observe the following details: It was shaped like a "half-ball" with a dome on top, which was about half the size of the bottom portion. On the extreme left was what he took to be a porthole, as light was shining from it. At the base of the object was an opening which revealed a small part of the interior. All that was observed of the inside was what looked like a white string. The UFO itself was a tan color and had a silvery glow outlining it, and was quite large.

The object seemed to flutter down, rocking gently from side to side, somewhat like a "falling leaf." It came down at an angle, stopped, hovering a bit, then it ejected a whitish object the size of a pea held at arm's length. It appeared to come from the back side of the large object.

The small UAO floated in a westerly direction until it appeared "about the size of a star." After this, the first UAO, the large one, went straight down and let out two reddish objects, Nos. 3 and 4, which came out together, rather than one at a time. They were the same size as the first small one. After clearing the mother-ship, they flew southeast at the same distance from each other, appearing to flash green light beams at each other. As the observer put it, "For example, No. 3 would shoot out the beam, and hit No. 4, and in turn, No. 4 would return a similar beam. After three or four such exchanges they separated and went different directions.

The mother ship (object No. 1) went a short distance in the direction of No. 4, then stopped briefly and began moving up and down in the opposite direction; finally it went twice as high as its original apparent altitude, where it hovered. Suddenly the observer noticed two reddish objects, apparently No. 3 and 4, near the opening of the big ship. They entered the opening or port, and while they were doing so, No. 2 (the small white UAO) was spotted coming back to the big object. When No. 2 had entered the opening, the "port" closed, and the large object left in the same direction it had come.

The duration of the sighting was from ten to fifteen minutes, and there was only one witness. We note the similarity between this sighting and that of the Westmoreland boys of Tucson in June 1962.

Boys Watch "Shooting Star"

Robert Santillo and Thomas David of Garrett Mountain, N. J., watched a strange, blinking star in the sky on September 21. The star grew brighter and brighter, shooting off beams of light, which brightened up the area. It then gave off a variety of colors, they said. Then the star shot off red blasts and disappeared. The whole display lasted about four minutes. As usual, few details were given by the newspaper and the boys did not respond to inquiries.

Where Is Private Irwin?

The above is the title of an article concerning the sighting of an unusual aerial object and the unexplained amnesia and subsequent disappearance of the young soldier who observed it, in 1959. The article was written by Mr. L. J. Lorenzen, our Public Relations Director, for the November 1962 issue of "Flying Saucers" (Ray Palmer, Amherst, Wis.). Members who recall the incident from the pages of the APRO Bulletin will want to read this complete documentation of the incident. Gerry Irwin's case is not closed in our files, but we have come to a standstill. Because it was too detailed and ponderous for the Bulletin, and we hoped to establish contact with Irwin, the article was submitted to the magazine. For one of the most puzzling incidents in the annals of UAO history, don't miss this one.

Man And Dolphin— A Book Review

The above is the title of a new book by John C. Lilly, M.D. (Doubleday and Co., Inc.) Garden City, New York. Just a few words from the preface should suffice as an introduction: "Within the next decade or two the human species will establish communication with another species: nonhuman, alien, possibly extraterrestrial . . . "

Carrier UAO Launching

We would like further information on the following incident which took place near Tri-City, Washington, possibly in July or August. Taken from the Pasco, Washington, Tri-City Herald, it was reprinted in "SPACE" — 267 Alhambra Circle, Coral Gables, Florida. No date was given and we need a date plus additional details.

Ed Olson, 20, of Kennewick, and neighbor Don Sprinkles, 17, watched a large, brilliant object (larger than Venus) at 45 degrees elevation in the east at 10:45 p.m. It appeared to move south, then up for some distance—then it stood still. "The thing that puzzled us most was the small objects that seemed to come out of the top of the big one and then float away," Olson declared. According to Olson, the large UFO lingered in the sky for a moment after the small ones disappeared, then "it went out like a light." He said the big object emitted a white light and appeared larger than either Venus or America's satellite.

Monitoring .

(Continued from page 1)

ma that to this day defies all explanation.

As the bombers of the 384th group swung into the final bomb run after passing the Initial Point, the fighter attacks fell off. This point is vital, and other pilots were queried extensively, as were crew members, as to the position at that time of the German fighter planes. Every man interrogated was firm in his statement that "at the time there were no enemy aircraft above."

At this moment the pilots and top turret gunners, as well as several crewmen in the plexiglass noses of the bombers, reported a cluster of discs in the path of the 384th's formation and closing with the bombers. The startled exclamations forcused attention on the phenomenon, and the crews talked back and forth, discussing and confirming the astonishing sight before them.

The discs in the cluster were agreed upon as being silver colored, about one inch thick and three inches in diameter. They were easily seen by the B-17 crewmen, gliding down slowly in a very uniform cluster.

And then the "impossible" happened. B-17 Number 026 closed rapidly with a cluster of discs; the pilot attempted to evade an imminent collision with the object, but was unsuccessful in his maneuver. He reported at the intelligence debriefing that his "right wing went directly through a cluster with absolutely no effect on engines or plane surface."

The intelligence officers pressed their questioning, and the pilot stated further that one of the discs was heard to strike the tail assembly of his B-17, but that neither he nor any member of the crew heard or witnessed an explosion.

He further explaineed that about twenty feet from the discs the pilots sighted a mass of black debris of varying sizes in clusters of three by four feet.

The SECRET report added: "Also observed two other A/C flying through silver discs with no apparent damage. Observed discs and debris two other times but could not determine where it came from."

No further information on this baffling incident has been uncovered, with the exception that such discs were observed by pilots and crew members on missions prior to, and after, Mission 115 of October 14, 1943." Unquote.

The New York Herald-Tribune of January 2, 1945, carried an article relating to similar phenomenon under the heading "Nazi Balls of Fire Race Along with U.S. Night Raiding Planes — Weird New Weapon Keeps Pace With Planes for Miles, Following Every Turn; Does Not Attack or Explode and Purpose May Be Psychological." — By the Associated Press.

"A UNITED STATES NIGHT-FIGHTER BASE, France, Jan. 1, 1945. The Nazi have thrown something new into the night skies over Germany—the weird, mysterious "foo-fighter," balls of fire, which race alongside the wings of American Beaufighters flying intruder missions over Germany.

Pilots have been encountering the eerie weapon for more than a month in their night flights. No one apparently knows exactly what this sky weapon is.

The balls of fire appear suddenly and accompany the planes for miles. They appear to be radio-controlled from the ground and manage to keep up with planes flying 300 miles an hour, official intelligence reports reveal.

"There are three kinds of these lights we call 'foo-fighters'," said Lt. Donald Meiers, of Chicago. "One is red balls of fire which appear off our wing tips and fly along with us, the second is a vertical row of three balls of fire which fly in front of us, and the third is a group of about fifteen lights which appear off in the distance—like a Christmas tree up in the air—and flicker on and off."

The pilots of this night fighter squadron—in operation since September, 1943 —find these fiery balls the weirdest thing they have yet encountered. They are convinced that the "foo-fighter" is designed to be a psychological weapon as well as military, although it is not the nature of the fireballs to attack planes.

"A 'foo-fighter' picked me up recently at 700 feet and chased me twenty miles down the Rhine Valley," Meiers said. "I turned to starboard and two balls of fire turned with me. We were going 260 miles an hour and the balls were keeping right up with us.

"On another occasion when a 'foo-fighter' picked us up I dove at 360 miles an hour. It kept right off our wing tips for a while and then zoomed up into the sky.

"When I first saw the things off my wing tips, I had the horrible thought that a German on the ground was ready to press a button and explode them. But they don't explode or attack us. They just seem to follow us like will-o-the-wisps."

(An Associated Press report from Paris, Dec. 13, said the Germans had thrown silvery balls into the air against the raiders. Pilots then reported they had seen these objects, both individually and in clusters, during forays over the Reich.)

But apparently the mysterious "foo-fighters" which our pilots thought at the time were psychological weapons of the Germans were something else for seven years later, in late 1952 and early in 1953 U.S. Airmen flying missions over Japan reported seeing "Mysterious flying objects—rotating clusters of red, white and green lights." Unquote.

The WASHINGTON POST of Jan. 21, 1953 carried an article entitled: "U.S. Airmen See 'Saucers' Hurtling Over North Japan."—AP.

"A U.S. AIR BASE, NORTHERN JAPAN, Jan. 21, 1953.

Mysterious flying objects—"rotating clusters of red, white and green lights" —have been sighted over northern Japan by American airmen, the Air Force disclosed tonight.

Intelligence reports placed the sightings close to Russian territory in the Kurile islands and Sakhalin. They added:

"There are too many indications of the presence of something to be considered an observation of nothing." And they discounted the possibility the lighted objects were mere "reflections of light."

Col. Curtis R. Low, in command of the northern division of the Japan Air Defense force, said the flying clusters were seen by fighter pilots and ground personnel and were tracked on radar. He released official intelligence reports on the sighting to the Associated Press.

The reports were similar to those describing "flying saucers" in the United States. One said the lights appeared to hang motionless at times, and at other times disappeared with blinding speed.

Col. Donald J. M. Blakeslee, World War II ace and commander of an escort fighter wing, took detailed observations on one rotating cluster and tried in vain to intercept it in a jet.

The report was signed by Lt. Col. Russell Powell, intelligence officer, U.S. Air Force.

The intelligence report said Blakeslee, of Fairport Harbor, Ohio, sighted a mysterious object twice on a night flight Dec. 29th.

The report said Blakeslee closed on the object after extinguishing all the lights on his aircraft "to make certain he was not getting some reflection from his canopy surface. When all lights were out he noticed no change in the appearance or brilliance of the object and its color scheme."

Col. Blakeslee chased the object in

(See "Monitoring", page 4)

Monitoring

(Continued from page 3)

his F-84 Thunder-jet for seven minutes at 600 miles an hour but couldn't get near it before it "disappeared into the night." Unquote.

The year 1948 witnessed a fantastic occurrence which took place the night of October 1st. In his book "A Report On Unidentified Flying Objects" former Air Force Capt. Edward J. Ruppelt refers to this case as "One of 'The Classics'," in UFO history.

On that evening Lt. George F. Gorman, a P-51 fighter pilot of the178th Fighter Squadron, North Dakota Air National Guard, had a 30-minute encounter with a mysterious round, brightly-lighted object in the night sky over Fargo, North Dakota.

The following is Lt. Gorman's experience as related to THE FARGO FORUM of October 3, 1948 and a subsequent article on the 4th:

"FARGO PILOT TELLS OF CHASING 'FLYING DISK,' Others Confirm Weird 'Dogfight.'

"A National Guard Air Squadron P-51 pilot Saturday told The Fargo Forum he had staged a dogfight with a "flying disk" object over Fargo Friday night. The object—which the pilot said was round with well defined edges, and brilliantly lighted — outdistanced him, then made a 180-degree turn and came at him head-on.

The pilot attempted to crash the object several times but it dodged out of his way.

That is the story of Lt. George Gorman—and it is corroborated by three other persons who declared that they also saw the object.

Maj. D. C. Jones, commanding the 178th fighter squadron at Hector airport, has Gorman's signed statement and is referring the incident to U.S. Air Force intelligence.

Gorman, Jones said, was so shaken by his experience that he had difficulty in landing. He had been in communication constantly with the airport control tower during the chase, giving a description of the object and its antics for the tower controllers.

—o—

This is what Gorman told his commanding officer:

About 9 p.m. he sighted the object, dimly lighted, slowly circling over the city. He decided to investigate, but as he approached the object suddenly became brillaintly lighted and put on a burst of speed.

At first, Gorman told Jones, the object apparently was traveling about 250 miles per hour. But after Gorman began the chase it speeded up to what Gorman thought was about 600 miles per hour. At that time Gorman's plane was doing about 400 miles per hour, near its maximum speed.

When the object had outdistanced him considerably it made a 180-degree turn and came straight at him, Gorman said. He attempted to crash into it, he said, but as it neared him it veered suddenly upward and passed him overhead.

Another time, Gorman told Jones, the object began an almost vertical climb. Gorman said he gave chase and climbed to about 14,000 feet, where he nearly stalled out. He gave up the climb and started down. When he reached about 12,000 feet, Gorman declared, the object again "made another head-on overhead pass" at him.

Lloyd D. Johnson and H. E. Johnson, both CAA controllers at the Fargo control tower, and Dr. A. E. Cannon, 1330 Eleventh Ave., S, an optician, also asserted they saw the object.

Jensen declared that through binoculars "the object appeared to be only a round light, perfectly formed, with no fuzzy edges or rays leaving its body. The edges were clear cut. No other shape was observed. The main identifying characteristic was the high rate of speed at which it was apparently traveling."

Gorman Saturday confirmed the story to The Fargo Forum.

"Once," he said, "when the object was coming head-on, I held my plane pointed right at it. The object came so close that I involuntarily ducked my head because I thought a crash was inevitable but the object zoomed over my head. It was the weirdest experience I've had in my life."

Gorman said it was impossible to determine the outline of the object—"it just looked like a big light"—but he saw a Piper Cub below and could make out its silhouette.

Gorman during World War II was a pilot with the U.S. Army eastern flying training command, flying a B-25 overseas. Unquote.

—o—

The Fargo Forum of October 4th, carried another follow-up item relating to Gorman's experience: "WRIGHT FIELD OFFICERS PROBE 'DISK' REPORT.

"A group of Air Force officers from Wright-Patterson Field, Dayton, Ohio, flew to Fargo Sunday to investigate reports that a pilot here had staged a dogfight with a "flying disk" object Friday night.

They conferred with Maj. Donald C. Jones, commanding officer of the 178th fighter squadron, North Dakota Air National Guard. They left today in an Air Force B-25.

The visiting officers, termed by Dayton field headquarters as "one of its investigating teams" assigned to probe "aerial phenomena" left instructions here that no information was to be released." Unquote.

Considerable enlightenment as to how the military operate to prevent too much information from reaching the public in an authentic UFO sighting such as this case represents, is contained in a letter written by Lt. George F. Gorman to Mr. Kenneth Arnold of Boise, Idaho, under date of December 18, 1948, reprinted in Arnold's interesting booklet "The Flying Saucer as I Saw It." The following is a pertinent exttract from it:

"I am sorry that I have been unable to answer your letters. However, I think that you can understand my position better when you know the facts.

First of all I am under the military control of the Tenth Air Force and they have issued direct orders concerning the disc or object.

Second the Air Material Command has issued orders classifying the information as Secret. And this makes it a General Court Martial to release any more information. The Command has asked that my commanding officer and myself be court martialed for releasing what information we did. I have General Edwards or some high officer to thank for refusing to carry it out.

Third the Counter Intelligence Corp. have asked that I turn over all information to them. And I have no doubt that the F.B.I. will get around to sending a few letters too.

The public relations officer released more than he should have and now we are being given a rough time; and they can do it too.

I have a normal amount of curiosity and I have a lot of questions to ask. But then I had a lot of them answered that night. The rest that I have will have to wait until they get ready to answer them." Unquote.

—o—

The writer made attempts to contact Lt. (now Capt.) Gorman who, in Feb. 1962, was stationed with the 818th Air Division at Lincoln Air Force Base, Lincoln, Nebraska, but his Certified letters went unanswered. No doubt Gorman, who would be subjeect to AFR 200-2 and JANAP 146, finds it necessary to refrain from any further discussion of his experience.

(Continued next issue)

Michel . . .

(Continued from page 1)

and that the study commissions for the explanation of the mystery have ceased their efforts.

"There is nothing to this, of course. The observations continue to be as numerous, and as far as research goes, I can vouch for the fact that never, since it began nearly 15 years ago now, has it been as active and efficacious. In reply to our friend Raymond Veillith's request, I am going to two aspects of the situation, observations and studies, up to date.

"A. Observations. It is sufficient to follow regularly the specialized reviews (Flying Saucer Review, London, and APRO Bulletin in the U.S.A.) to realize that the activity of non-identified flying objects is actually very intense considering the cyclical aspect of the enon, to which I'll return shortly. Without speaking of the photos taken by the American jet plane Scot the time the last A erican trip into space, photos w ich lead to discussion, I shall cite but one episode: that of the numerous cases studied since mid-May 1962 by the Navy and military aviation in the Republic. Between the 12th and 25th of May, numerous observations were registered at Cordova, Chumbicha, Bahia Blanca, Salta, etc. Witnesses were innumerable. At Bahia Blanca, photographer Miguel Thome, was even able to take several pictures. Brilliant objects passing quickly at night, stopping, changing direction, putting forth colors, came close to earth and even landed; one finds the whole gamut described in my book, "Mysterious Celestial Objects" in 1958. The best observed landing took place on the 12th of May at 4:10 a.m. at Kilometer 72 of Road No. 35, in the province of Pampa, three truck drivers were able to see at 70 meters distance, for a minute, an object as big as a railway coach, brilliantly illuminated, with approximately 20 "portholes" showing intermittent lights. Captain Luis Sanchez Moreno, of the Marine Information Service, gave hmiself at once to a serious protracted investigation. A conference of the press held at the Ministry revealed that 4 other persons had noticed the object. Rear-admiral Eladio E. Vasquez and the 2nd in command of the Naval Zone, Captain Aldo Golivari, added that they themselves had observed a similar object the day (evening) before. In the succeeding days, many other observations were made. A few days later, G. Ariel Ciro Resti, president of the Commission of Inquiry, CODOVNI,

was pointing out the predominance of the apparitions on the ort o joinin Bahia B confirming once again the discovery made the first time in France from the study of the wave of 1954.

As I write these lines, the observations continue.

B: Studies of the Saucer Phenomena since 1958:

These have been carried forward by my collaborators and myself, essentially, in France, Dr. Olavo Fontes in Brazil and by the engineer, Buelta, in Spain.

(1) In France: We have carried our investigation in two directions: generalizations of orthoteny, and study of the periodicity of the waves.

As far as orthoteny is concerned, the question which was posed in 1958 was to know if the orthotenic lines discovered in Europe were planetary lines. the work of my collaborator . . working with a powerful electron alculator, we know the answer: it is yes. We ave thus discovered that the line of 24 September 1954 (Bayonne-Vichey) is in reality a great earthly circle, crossing not only Europe, but Brazil, the Argentine Chile, New Zealand, New Guinea. In all these countries, observations have been found on this line, with the fantastic of 40 meters of error for a great circle of 40 million meters. Other lines have identified, and we are presently working to recognize their location on the terrestial globe.

Insofar as the periodicity of the waves is concerned, J. V. has been able to show while studying separately two distinct catalogues (mine and Mr. Guy Quincy's of Constantine) that there exists a period of 26 months separating the waves of recurrences. That means that the frequency of the observations in the world varies, and passes through maximums every 26 months.

2. In Spain:

Buelta has separately found this same periodicity working with a third catalogue, different from Mr. Quincy's and from mine. While comparing the successive periods, Buelta has found that the form of the curve of frequencies could be an exponential function. Now these in define the amortized movements. That means that everything takes place as if the energy utilized by these instruments were delivered to them 26 something like the polar ex editions w ic receive their fuel once a year.

3. Finally, and quite separately, Dr. lavo Fontes, eminent Brazil researcher has als fo.... t i eriodicity studying his own catalogue. But Fontes

has made another observation, a very curious one: according to him, this 26-month periodicity is covered by another, the latter of 5½ years. That would result in a definitive periodicity rather more complex and would explain well the slight variations observed by experience, for it permitted him to announce a recrudescence for June-July 1962, and indeed that is what the wave presently being observed in Argentina is showing.

But, some will say, what does the periodicity of 26 months found separately in North Africa, in France, in Spain and in Brazil, mean? All who have some knowledge of astronomy have already guessed it: There exists in astronomy only one cycle of 26 months, the one of the approach of the planet Mar

C. Conclusions:

We French researchers have in the last few weeks met our South American colleagues, Dr. Olavo Fontes and Mr. Christian Vogt, of CODOVNI. We have discussed at length all these new facts. And here are our conclusions, published here for the first time:

1. Flying objects not identified are advanced astronautic objects.

2. They are of extraterrestrial origin.

3. They are piloted by intelligent beings who are not men.

4. They come from Mars. not necessarily their real origin. This planet plays the part, perhaps of a between ear and a more distant world.

6. The question of the intention of the beings which pilot these instruments remain unknown. These intentions may be inconsequential to our terrestrial destiny; it is, until further absolute proof, my personal opinion; they may be well-though nothing leads us to believe it; They may be aggressives or malevolent; and I must say this is Dr. Olavo T. Fontes' opinion which is based on a very troubling tistic: the number of aviation accidents seems to augment with the number of observations of flying saucers; that is, every 26 months. In order to be certain of this, it would be necessary to establish statistics, something which is difficult to do.

Such is the actual shape of the research. As one may see, it has not remained inactive since 1958. But one must recognize that if certainties are required, the depth of the mystery remains. We do not know whence, exactly, these flying saucers come, or what they do in our heaven." Unquote.

The following may be added to what is currently known about UFO: Through

(See "Michel", page 6

Michel

(Continued from page 5)

the preliminary study of data gathered in the calendar months of 1962 ,Mrs. Lorenzen verified her prediction made in her book, "The Great Flying Saucer Hoax," to the effect that 1962 would be the next "5-year" big flap, the last having been 1957. The sightings, however, are expected to lap over into 1963 with a diminishing, yet substantial number of sightings being reported. Several other curious correlations should be noted: The high incidence of   or hovering UAOs in the vicinity of reservoirs, lakes, etc., brilliant exploding fireballs accompanied or followed by blinding flashes of
flying   lights
launched satellites except for their orbits and time of transit.

Several people, after reading Mrs. Lorenzen's book, wrote and indicated great curiosity pertaining to the small bipeds which have been observed on occasion in the vicinity of landed UFOs. Mrs. Lorenzen deliberately refrained from theorizing to any great extent in this respect inasmuch as even experienced UFO researchers have a tendency to discount the occupant accounts, and also she hoped to create an atmosphere of intellectual freedom, urging the reader to fill in the gaps for himself, rather than imposing her ideas. However, the demand, even from researchers, for her impressions concerning the non-human occupants helped her to decide to elucidate the following:

The appearance of non-human occupants, sometimes in the company of the humanoid types, in the vicinity of the UFO was a great puzzle, except for a possibility of an "interplanetary alliance" of a sort, until the U. S. launched their pre-manned satellite, sending first th echimpanzee, "Ham," then "Enos" into controlled orbits around the earth before sending a human space pilot. These anthropoids, although of a lower species were trained to   certain functions while in orbit.

Would it not be possible, then, for the human-type higher species connected with the   to recruit and train lower   for certain functions? Perhaps these creatures are indigent to our own solar system and have been recruited our   who actually originate in another star system. Perhaps they (the hairy dwarves, etc.) were imported along with other materiel, by the UFO occupants, to supplement work crews, etc. However—there is a strange coincidence which may indicate that lower species from within our solar system

have been recruited and trained: In 1956 or 1957 (the clipping is not immediately at hand) an anthropologist's theories concerning life on other planets in our solar system came to our attention via a small wire service bulletin. In it, the anthropologist described the probable inhabitants of Jupiter thusly: They would be short, about 3 feet tall, in   but extremely strong, with an external skeleton and hairy bodies. The height and weight would be a result of   factors from the strong gravitational pull of Jupiter. The external skeleton and great strength would be results of the same. The profuse hairy   would be protection   the bitter cold thought to prevail on the surface of Jupiter.

If we compare this physical description with that of the small hairy bipeds seen frequently in South America, and Venezuela in particular in 1954, and recall their great strength, and invulnerability to weapons, we find an astounding similarity.

If, as we suspect, the UFO inhabitants did indeed come from another star system, the   is not to difficult to explain. The two (or 26 month) cycle coincides with the close   of Mars. A colony of Mars would have to be supplied and reinforced periodically with new personnel —thus the   of in earth's atmosphere might indicate an orientation procedure for new personnel arriving from the home planet. If we again apply the reverse position procedure, theorizing what would be logical for earth colonists on a planet in another solar system, certain things about the UFO cycles become more clear. We would not land an   force on a strange planet in another system and desert them. We would periodically check on them, furnish them with ne-   supplies and reinforcing personnel. At the same time, if the colonists observed, through exploration or scientific observations (telescopes, etc.) any event on other planets which would have some bearing on their existence and/or future it would be duly reported to the next   and supply force and a check would undoubtedly made by the new arrivals. Thus we have an accounting for both the 26-month and   sighting cycles. rue, it is only speculation, but even if we had all the facts about all sightings of UFOs for a period of, say, the last 75 years, it would be necessary to speculate concerning those facts in order to discover their meaning.

A complete cross-indexing of all sightings gathered by APRO for 1962 will

be carried out during 1963 and there should be a report on our findings before the end of this year. Ideas and suggestions will be welcomed, but please do not ask for answers or comments as time is at a premium here and the 1962 study is an added task.

Flash, Boom Over Utah Fireball Lights Skies In Ten States

The huge "ball of fire" which flashed across the Western U. S. between 8:15 and 8:19 p.m. on 18 April 1962 was so brilliant that it triggered the photoelectric street lighting system in Eureka, Utah. The object was traveling from east to west. All street lights turned off in Eureka as the object passed over. Authorities thought the fireball crashed about 10 miles south of the small town. Residents saw a "blue flash" and heard a "rumbling" off in the distance immediately after the sighting.

Salt Lake City observers said the light of the "meteor" was as "bright as day." It was seen in Idaho, Montana, Oregon, New Mexico, Wyoming, Arizona, Nevada, Kansas and Utah. An FAA spokesman at Salt Lake City said the object vanished over southwestern Utah about 35 miles northeast of Delta. He also said aircraft and ground observers in the area confirmed the report.

Although not definitely established, a green glow seen by a tower spokesman at Peterson Field (Colorado Springs, Colo.) west of Pike's Peak, may have been connected with the sighting. The light was obstructed by the mountain.

Air Force officers from Hill AFB at Ogden, Utah, questioned sheepherders in the hills south of Eureka, Utah, who   observed the object. Bob Robinson of Eureka said it first looked like a "polliwog" with its tail on fire, going east to west in "sort of jerks." He said it suddenly exploded into a "sodium blue-white light brighter than day" and then continued on, looking like a vapor trail from a jet. He estimated it was 8 to 10 seconds before the sound became audible, sounding like cannons firing in the distance.

Most observers in Nevada declared the object was traveling west to east.

The thought occurs that this object was a perfect high-altitude flare—illuminating most of a two-state area to a point of daylight brightness. It so happens that the two states receiving most of the light were Utah and Nevada, both locations of U. S. Missile and nuclear test sites.

THE A.P.R.O. BULLETIN

fhe A. P. R. O. Bulletin is the official copyrighted publication of the Aerial Phenomena Research Organization (A.P.R.O.), 4145 E. Desert Place, Tucson, Arizona, and is issued every other month to members only. The Aerial Phenomena Research Orgazination is a non-profit group dedicated to the eventual solution of the mystery of the unidentified objects which have been present in the skies for hundreds of years. Inquiries regarding membership may be made to the above address.

TUCSON, ARIZONA — JANUARY, 1963

UAOs CAPTURE NEW SPECIMENS

Variety Of Objects In Colorado

"Flat, glowing objects" described as being quite close together and moving very slowly, were seen at 6:15 a.m. on 26 October 1962, in the southern part of the San Luis Valley in Colorado. Mrs. Alvie Frank, residing 11 miles south of Monte Vista reported the objects which were seen just as the sun was rising.

On the same morning, at 7:16 a.m., Mrs. Bessie Rogers of Fort Collins spotted a large black parachute-shaped object weaving back and forth over the mountains somewhere between the south end of Horsetooth Reservoir and Masonville. She said it flew around for about 10 minutes, disappeared and then returned. At 7:44 a.m., she called the police to report it again. Police and Sheriff's officers search the area but found nothing.

On the 29th, Mrs. Vera Rogers reported sighting a round, shiny object which was flying low over Fort Collins. The object, heading south, made a soft, whirring sound followed by a "popping" noise.

Further reports indicated a glowing low-flying object was seen in the sky late on the nights of the 26th and 27th, over or near Fort Collins, but no details given in newspaper articles.

Following are some of the sightings which included scanty details:

At 12:20 p.m. on 24 October, two "parachutes" were seen descending on the north side of Grand Mesa, in the vicinity of Cedaredge, Western Colorado. Mrs. Rex Allen of Cedaredge said she saw the two objects coming down on the northwestern edge of the mesa. A Fish and Game Department plane searched the area but found nothing. The FAA said it had no reports of missing aircraft.

Three hours later, at 3:20, an object was seen descending in the same general area by Mrs. Sydney Shoup and Mr. and Mrs. Gib Williams of Eckert, Colorado. None of the witnesses were

(See "Colorado", page 4)

Ball of Fire Demolishes Entire Block

Spokane, Washington, 17 March, 1962. The Sarnia Observer for Monday, 19 March 1962, had no explanation for the mystery blast which leveled an entire block of the   of North
        Some of

The blast was heard for 20 miles. Houses trembled, windows were broken and plaster cracked for blocks around. Display windows miles away were shattered. At least 31 people required hospital treatment. The explosion leveled a cafe, a used furniture store, a pizza parlor and an empty building.

Fire Chief W. A. Dunham said on the 19th that investigation hadn't been able to pinpoint the center of the blast.

an   firemen rushed
      debris   from
Mrs. Mary Keating, a waitress in the pizza parlor in the center of the block said she heard no explosion—just a
                    noise and then the windows popped out."

Fire Captain ack Wallter   reported seeing a huge ball of fire, then a deep, dull "wha-boom."

Compare these last two descriptions to those in back issues of the APRO Bulletin which reported strange balls of fire and blasts in Australia and New Zealand.

Missile, Contrail or UFO?

From Weatherville, and Eureka, California, from Burns, Oregon and Reno, Nevada came reports on 6 December 1961, of the observation of a westerly moving craft with a "tail" twice as long as itself. The object was officially explained as (1) a Thor missile launched from Vandenburg and (2) a vapor trail from a high altitude, high performance craft known to be flying in the area. Take your pick.

By Olavo T. Fontes, M.D.

In my studies of UAO sightings over a fifteen-year period, I have found a pattern indicating very careful and detailed plans being followed methodically, step by step, year after year. First, geographical surveys, then general military reconnaissance, then landings with surface sampling of botanical and geological specimens, then a very detailed examination of our terrestrial and aerial defenses with testing of at least two kinds of weapons against airplanes, automobiles, power stations and military installations, and with close watch over our satellite experiments and rocket developments. I have also found (together with many other fact) that the general curve of sightings follows a
of about 26 months; but also that a periodicity appears to be covered by another one of about five years. This last cycle makes the definitive periodicity of UAO sightings more complex than first believeed, but would explain well the small variations observed by experience. My first suspicion of this five-year cycle was born with the unexpected 1957 "flap", which started in June-July and didn't fit into the pattern of 26-month periods. The preceding cycle, according to this hypothesis, would be started with the 1952 "flap", which could have passed unsuspected because it fitted into the 26-month cycle. However, the next one would be started in June-July, 1962, in a time that also didn't fall into the 26-month periodicity. Therefore, the prediction of a new wave of UAO sightings for 1962, if confirmed, would be a good way to test the possible reality of such a five-year cycle. Such a prediction was discussed last May, in Paris, with
        the prominent French UAO re-
        and we agreed it was a fascinating possibility—at least from a theoretical point of view. In my opinion, however, this five-year periodicity is far more interesting than the 26-month periods—because there appears to exist a
        in   behavior of UAOs
with each neew cycle, or at   the
        of a new kind of procedure or operation not present in the preceding

(See UAO's Capture", page 3)

The A. P. R. O. BULLETIN
Published by
THE AERIAL PHENOMENA RESEARCH
ORGANIZATION
4145 E. Desert Place
Tucson, Arizona
Copyright 1963, Coral E. Lorenzen
Editor and Director

Information appearing in this bulletin may be used by other UAO research periodicals providing names and address credit is properly given to this organization and periodical.

Coral E. Lorenzen ____ International Director and Editor
A. E. Brown, B.S.E.E. _____ Director of Research
L. J. Lorenzen _____ Director of Public Relations
John T. Hopf _____ Photographic Consultant
Oliver Dean _____ Photographic Consultant

SPECIAL REPRESENTATIVES
(The following listed individuals participate in planning and policy-making as Staff Members, in addition to coordinating investigative efforts in the areas indicated following their names.)

Dr. Olavo T. Fontes, M.D. _____ Brazil
K.Gosta Rehn _____ Sweden
Graham Conway _____ Eastern Canada
Aime Michel _____ France
Horacio Gonzales Gauteaume
                                     Venezuela
Peter E. Norris, L.L.D. _____Australia
Jun' Ichi Takanashi _____ Japan
Juan C. Remonda _____ Argentina
Sergio Robba _____ Italy
Arist. Mitropoulos _____ Greece
Rev. N. C. G. Cruttwell, New Guinea
Eduardo Buelte _____ Spain
Norman Alford _____ New Zealand
Austin Byrne _____ Ireland

SPECIAL CONSULTANT
Prof. Charles Maney,—Physics

ALAMOGORDO PRINTING CO., INC.

Detailed Sighting Of Objects Over Dublin

Mr. Austin Byrne of Dublin reports the following sighting which he personally investigated: "The man, Mr. Patrick St ford, a C.I.E. bus driver of Dublin sai , ' was just getting up into the cab of my bus when I noticed this bright object coming from the Northeast.' He went on to say, 'It approached at about 300 mph—about the speed of a Viscount (commercial airplane usede by Irish air-lines), and 'it was at approximately 500 feet altitude.' The object was immediately unusual to him since it   off no sound. He said, 'it was like an aeroplane with   engines stopped.' He thought it was going to crash but what struck him was that it was not dropping, but in horizontal flight.

"On describing the object itself, Mr. Stafford said, "It was like the big spinning tops you sometimes see children playing with and it had portholes around the outside of it.' It was not spinning, he said, 'because if it was, you would see only a blur of light around the thing,

not just light coming out through each individual porthole.'

"Now, about this light he said was coming from inside of the thing through the portholes, he described it as being 'a   could have been somewhat   light. He said it gave him the impression that the light was centered inside the thing and 'you could see it coming from the center through the portholes.' but he emphasized it was a 'fierce' light. He said the object was as   as a bus. I asked him later, to elaborate on this by giving me some measurement and then he was somewhat unsure as he first said it was about 15 feet in breadth, and when I asked him the approximate height of the object by quickly guessing how many times the height would go into the breadth, he said, 'about three times.' I then said that would probably make the height about five feet, and he quickly said, 'Oh no, it was much bigger than that,' he said, stretching out his hands 'about 10 feet—and the width about twice that (about 20 feet)'. He emphasized the size and detail he could see by pointing out to me the size a Viscount airplane would be at a height of 500 feet.

"He then went on to describe a curious sort of light as he said, 'misty light' he saw come from the thing for about a hundred yards it was 'slightly tapered,' he said. It then went back into the thing and the flying saucer suddenly vanished. 'It just wasn't there anymore,' he said.

"All this took place in about ten seconds at about 6:28 a.m. as he had checked his watch to the 'Voice of America' time check on the radio that morning before going out.

"Stafford said 'it was a wonderful thing to see,' and he would 'love to see 1 again.' One of the bus cleaners at the bus depot observed the object also, as well as a conductor, Mr. Kevin Lynch. Lynch was near the same spot where Mr. Stafford made his observation, and could only add that the object's flight path was from northeast to southwest."

"Mystery Satellite" Sighted

Hong Kong, 9 July 1962. Local resident R. I. Hobson reported that he had seen an object which gave off a brightt white light, twice in two hours on the evening of 8 July. The "Bangkok World' from which this information is taken, reported that Hobson said the object traveled from south to north over the colony and took about 15 minutes to cross the sky. (Russian and American satellites take roughly 20 plus minutes for transit).

A member of a university scientific society (neither the person nor the society was named in the Bangkok World) reported having observed a satellite over Hong Kong on the night of July 4. He described it as being visible only for seven minutes and distinguishable from the stars by its relative motion and brightness. At the time the report was printed, the Royal Observatory had not been able to identify the object, according to government spokesmen. (This is only one of many reports of south-to-north satellite-like objects, which cannot be explained in a conventional manner. —The Editor).

Flying Egg In Massachusetts

Charles F. Kirk, 20, of Woburn, Mass., reported to the Woburn Times, Woburn, Mass., that on the 1st of November, 1962 he had sighted a "streamlined egg-shaped" object that hovered over Woburn for several minutes between 2 and 2:10 p.m. He said it looked like a streamlined (elongated) egg cut through the middle, and estimated its altitude at less than 2,00 feet. Kirk, who is a machinist and carpenter for the Wells Machine Company, was working on tope of the company's new building on Salem Street when he sighted the strange object. He said he thought the object was about 40 feet long, 30 feet wide and about 15 feet in height, but could have been much larger. He was obviously upset by his encounter and he described his "eerie   of   watched. (See   about Barney Hill sighting). He said he didn't want to see one of the things again.

The object was golden orange in color, flat on the bottom, with a black band near the   a   or   about ten feet the bottom. This strange device (th periscope) kept clicking at about 15 second   xcept or t e c icking sound, the object was silent, and it "produced a band of light around the building on which he was working." According to the Woburn Times, L. C. Anstey of the Woburn Civilian Defense found a slight increase in background radiation at the site of the incident.

Cone Shape Oxer Hamilton, New Zealand

Mrs. W. J. Crompton of Fow Street, Hamilton, reported to the Waikato Times that she had seen a "cone-shaped" object which looked like a rocket in the southwestern sky, apparently over the Waikato Hospital at 5 p.m. After a few moments the object disappeared over the southern horizon.

UAO's Capture

(Continued from page 1)

ones. For instance, in the first cycle (June 47 to June 52) the pattern only indicates geographical surveys and general reconnaissance by remote-controlled objects never close to the ground; in the second cycle (June 52 to June 57), that pattern changed into a very close and detailed examination of aerial and terrestrial defenses, plus landings and collection of botanical and geological specimens by humanoid creatures; in the third cycle (June 7 to June 62) the pattern changed again, with testing of weapons against airplanes, ground vehicles and military installations — and few landings, no collection of specimens.

The fourth cycle appears to have started two weeks before the expected time. The new wave of UAO sightings was first located over Argentina, then spread to Brazil, and now is going to Peru and other countries. But the amazing thing is the new change in the general behavior of UAOs: many landings since the beginning, everywhere, and attempts to collect specimens of terrestrial fauna —including man himself.

Flying Discs Over Barcelos, Amazonas

CHICKENS, PIGS AND COWS DISAPPEAR

On September 18, 1962, the Rio de Janeiro daily, A NOITE, carried a weird sequel to the events of the preceding month (i.e., the kidnapping of a diamond prospector, Raimundo Mafra da Silva, by two ball-shaped UAOs). This time it was the population of Barcelos which was worried by rumors related with the sighting of a flying disc over the area. According to the reports of three workers from a rubbeer tree plantation, a strong light was sighted over the river. They approached the place and saw, clearly outlineed against the dark sky, a huge, silvery disc-shaped object giving   s o   ire. It hovered over the river for a long time, then suddenly took off   a tremendous noise.

The town's Mayor was alerted by the witnesses. He decided to put them in   were ors to prejudice his administration." However, the corporal of the police squadron in the town was not convinced and decided to make his own investigation. He came to the conclusion that a flying object shaped like a disc was being really sighted around the town. He also concluded that its crew was low in supplies, or needing food, be-

cause 17 chicken, 6   and 2 cows disappeared from Barcelos — since the   the craft was first sighted. The Mayor, however, declared the three   will stay in jail just to learn   because "men   their   (grown   cannot fer hallucinations."

The reader might take this report as a humorous story, as an amusing tale produced by a good joker. But he may, perhaps, change his opinion after reading the next report, about an incident that took place in the same region a few days after the preceding one.

At Vila Conceicao: Soccer Referee Kidnapped By Flying Discs

On September 18, 1962, an unusual story hit the headlines in the newspapers of Manaus, capital of the State of Amazonas. Here is a summary of the news as reported in Rio's newspapers:

"MANAUS, 18   the news lated with the appearance of a flying disc over the town of Barcelos, in the interior of the State, a radio message was received at this capital, from Vila Conceicao, reporting the appearance of a flying disc also at that small village in the vicinity of the Padauri river. It seems to be the same one involved with the disappearance of chickens, pigs and cows from that first town. This flying disc came to Vila Conceicao last Sunday, September 16, after sunset.

"There was a soccer game at the village that afternoon, in a field behind the small town's church. It was a match between the team of Vila Conceicao and another one from a nearby village. The referee, Mr. Telemaco   had come with the visiting delegation. His decisions during the match showed he was not a good judge. He made several mistakes against the local team. He had the courage to invalidate two goals and to ignore four penalties against the visiting team. Such errors created an atmosphere of revolt and, at the end of the match, the angry local fans were decided to take their vengeance on the unjust referee. An incident was avoided   energic intervention of the   priest, who calmed down the more excited and convinced them to behave like good sportsmen.

"During the night, however — when everything appeared to be forgotten and both teams, together with the local population and the over visitors, fraternized with each other —   the absence of Mr. Telemaco   was noticed. A   to was found. After a whole night and a

day of frantic search, it was concluded that the referee had mysteriously disappeared. The only thing found was his whist   used during the match, which   as drop ed c   to a clearin in the middle of the forest that surrounds Vila Conceicao.

"It was only on the following day that the report from a rubber tree worker was   by the searchers. That man had seen, in the night of Sunday, a glowing, round-shaped obje   i -   off   of fire rapidly   That object   three men jumped out from it   a person who was walk-   i   e, a that momen   etween the   at   of the   Pro-tected behind the bushes, the witness watched the fight between the crew from the flying object and that person, who was finally grasped and   the attackers to the inside of their craft. The object then took off vertically at high speed and was gone. Investigation by the authorities revealed signs of the   where the worker said the fight had taken place. It seems evident, beyond any doubt, that Mr. Telemaco Xavier was kidnapped by a flying disc." Unquote.

I have the feeling that no more news will be heard about this incident. First, because of the location of the place where it took place — Vila Conceicao is a small village lost in the Amazon jungle, far to the northwest of Manaus, almost at the frontier of Venezuela. Second, because its communication lines with the civilized world are represented by a small radio transmitter only — and   messages are under government control. Censorship is very easy to effect   this case,   by the explosive implications of the incident. If explored by the press, this case might cause widespread panic and hysteria all over the country. Because here we have an incident where the kidnapping of a human being by the humanoid crew of a UAO was not only suggested—but witnessed; The second case, within an interval of 26 days, where vanishing people and UAOs are definitely connected by direct evidence.

A soccer game can be watched from space. To the observers, if they don't know anything about the game and its rules,   referee would seem to be a very important erson in the commun-   In act, he has the power to stop the game, to make the decisions, to force the players to follow the rules, etc. etc. If such was the reason for his kidnapping—then we can take his case as a very good interplanetary joke. Poor referee.

Colorado

(Continued from page 1)

sure of what they saw—but Mrs. Shoup said the parachute-like object came from an airplane. No one was able to identify the aircraft as to type, etc. Mrs. Shoup said the object appeared to be disc-shaped.

Lester Sandler an employee of the nd Southern Railroad at Fort Collins, reported on the 24th that he had seen a round, gray-white object at about noon. He said it appeared to fall to the ground west of the city. Sheriff Ray Scheerer sent deputies to investigate and shortly another report came in to the office pertaining to an object which   land at the base Dixon   Dam on Horsetooth Reservoir. However, the caller said the object was orange and huge in size, conflicting with the description given by Sandler. Airplanes sent up to search found nothing.

For two hours and 17 minutes on the night of Thursday, 25 October, the Colorado State Patrol dispatcher at Delta, a state patrolman, the Cedaredge city marshall and a number of other persons, watched two objects cavorting in the sky. The dispatcher, Mrs. Helen Mitchell said she spotted the object at 7:15 p.m. and watched them for about a half an hour. She said they were glowing like a fluorescent   then turning a deep red, dimming and turning white again. They appeared to be stationary in the sky between Delta and Cedaredge for a time before they began to ascend. Cedaredge Marshal Ed Marsh and State Patrolman Richard Kuta observed the same objects through binoculars for some time, and reported that the objects were, at various times, blue-white nd orange in color and shaped like inverted umbrellas with a number of bright, tail-like appendages. They disappeared from view at Delta about 7:50 p.m. and appeared over Glenwood Springs about 8:05 p.m. At 8:15 they were back over the Grand Mesa area.

Joe McDonald, civil defense coordinator at Delta, Colorado, said he had received several calls from area residents pertaining to unidentified or strange sky objects. Mrs. Mitchell estimated altitude of objects at 1,500 feet, but others felt they were probably at around 5,000 feet altitude. She said the objects were at least twice the size of the brightest astronomical objects—stars. They disappeared from view at about 9:32 p.m., traveling in a southeasterly direction.

Thus ends the summation of information pertaining ot the 1962 "flap" for Colorado. We hope to feature an article

dealing with the high incidence of sightings of UAO in the vicinity of water bodies in the near future,   above   sightings strengthens our theory that water is of more than a passing interest to the UAO.

Silver Ball Seen In Ontario

At 10 a.m., on Monday, October 1, 1962, a silver ball-shaped object was spotted by various residents of Thamesville, Ontario, Canada. It was still there at midnight and no explanations were forthcoming from responsibel authorities although a flippant newspaperman at the London Free Press informed one inquirer that "it would probably go away after the observer had some sleep." During the evening, jet contrails in the vicinity of the object were seen by observers. The reporter for the Thamesville Herald concluded his rather humorous article: "So, after analyzing all the answers, we swear never to look at another object in the sky. Even if we see it. We'll ignore it." This seems to be good advice, inasmuch as so few people take UFO seriously.

Minister Observes Yellow Object

The Reverend W. S. Mowery of Tipp City, Ohio, reports the following: On August 17 at 9:30 p.m., he was traveling north on County Road 61 just north and east of the Dayton (Ohio) Municipal Airport when a large and bright yellow light crossed the highway directly ahead of his car. It was at about 45 degrees elevation and appeared in about same flight altitude as a plane coming in for a landing at the field, but the speed and direction of flight made the Reverend question whether or not the craft could land. The light was a bright yellow and no other light was visible; it seemed to be about six inches in diameter and as it crossed the highway the Reverend could see the light reflecting upward on the bottom of the object but could not see its shape or size. It appeared to be just a flat, dark object just above and to the rear of the light.

The light was traveling in a northwest direction on a perfectly flat course. It was traveling so fast that Rev. Mowery; could easily observe the light growing smaller as it proceeded away from him and within a matter of 10 seconds it disappeared in the distance. The car window was down so he checked for sound and there was none. Rev. Mowery asserts that he is familiar with jets and other planes, but could find no explanation for this object.

"Low Glow" In California

Various residents in and around Corcoran, Calif., reported a strange glow which manifesteed itself in the early morning hous of 3 July, just before down. First reported to the Corcoran Journal by F. M. Montijo, the object was seen and reported by others later. Ray Thompson, a member of the Corcoran Forestry Division fire station, said that he was driving northwest of Corcoran when he first noticed the fiery luminous light near the horizon. He first thought it might be part of a missile experiment at Vandenburg AFB, but when it slowed down and hovered in the sky he stopped his pickup and listened for sounds, hearing none. The object remained on or near the ground for five minutes or more, then rose vertically and zoomed into the sky, leaving a blue and orange trail similar to that of a "shooting star."

Mrs. Jean Miller, driving a tractor in the ranch hayfield, also saw the brilliant orange glow which appeared to be almost on the ground at a neighboring farm. She stopped her tractor and watched and listened but heard nothing. Shortly, she said, the object rose from the ground and suddenly streaked off like a rocket, leaving a blue and orange trail in the sky.

Disc Illuminates Area

William Stock of Lodi, N. J., was making a routine check of the grounds at Sam Braen's Quarry, 662 Goffle Road, on Thursday, 20 September, when he sighted a round, disc-shaped object suspended in the air, which lighted up the entire area. When he   the of his   at the   it   side   then turned around. "As it turned around, I could see w at appeared to be headlights. It then disappeared very fast," Stock said. No further details, but this is one more of many sightings of objects water

Twin Fire Balls In Michigan

At 9:15 p.m. on April 27, 1962, Mrs. Fred Harris of Burt, Michigan, observed a brilliant green and speedy fireball with a tail which appeared half as large as the full moon. It was followed by another green ball of fire, slightly smaller, also with a tail. Both objects appeared to skim just above the tops of the trees which separated two lots. The witness said they were traveling "much faster than a plane."

Monitoring And Scanning Discs

(Continued)

By C. W. Fitch

Another incident, similar in many ways to the Gorman case, took place nearly five years later on the night of August 12, 1953, over Rapid City, South Dakota. Two F-84 jet pilots and a bright, fast-moving evasive light were involved in it with the F-84 pilots coming out second best after both had been badly scared by the tactics of the UFO. Ruppelt in his excellent work "The Report on Unidentified Flying Objects," pages 302-306 gives a detailed account of this case and closes it with the comment "This was an unknown—the best." Yet even so, somewhere strings were pulled which prevented it from reaching the press and the general public.

THE AMARILLO (TEXAS) SUNDAY NEWS-GLOBE of April 9, 1950 carried a headline: "SO YOU SAW A FLYING DISC?—This Boy TOUCHED One!" By Gordon Tompkins, Jr.

"Two young boys from River Road went fishing late yesterday morning, but instead of a string of perch, they came home with a flying saucer story.

This flying saucer landed. One of the boys touched it.

The pair are David Lightfoot, 12 years old, son of Mr. and Mrs. J. A. Lightfoot of Bluebonnet Drive and Charles Lightfoot, 9, son of Mr. and Mrs. O. W. Lightfoot of River Drive. The boys attend River Road School. David in the sixth grade, and Charles in thethird. They are cousins.

The two excitedly babbled out their eye-witness of the saucer to newsmen and radiomen yesterday afternoon. The accounts, except for minor differences in measurement estimates, were alike.

In substance, this is a composite of what David and Charles said happened to them yesterday morning: The boys went fishing shortly before 11 o'clock yesterday morning on a creek near the southern boundary of the Convalescent Home northeast of the city.

Before they had pulled in even a little one, they sighted what they thought at first was a balloon. It was about 20 degrees above the horizon, they indicated by arm motions. The object was traveling from the south.

As it came nearer, the object decreased in speed, and it became apparent that it wasn't a balloon.

The disk passed by only a few feet over the boys, and David shouted to Charles, "I'll bet that's one of those flying saucers, Charles, I'm going after it."

Charles did not follow. David said the disk circled slowly and disappeared over a small hill to the north.

Before David could top the rise, the saucer had landed.

"It was about as big　　　as a lar automobile　　　the youth remarked and about as high as my knee — maybe a foot and a half. I could see it good."

According to David's account, the object was rounded on the bottom and had a top part which resembled a flat plate. The top, he said, was separate from the bottom by a space perhaps one-half inch in depth, and was held to the bottom section by "some sort of screw or something in the middle."

"When I first saw it good," David explained, "the bottom was　　　but the top was　　　around real fast, and on　　e top of the part that was spinning around there was a little　　　k that had a ki　of spindle sticking out of it. The spindle was still, too. It must have been connected to the bottom part."

The object was blue-gray in color, and had no openings of any sort other than the space between the top　　and　　to the boys'

"When I came over that hill, the thing was only a little ways from me, and I ran a ways and dived at it." David related.

"My fingers just barely touched it and it felt slick, sorta like I guess a snake would. It was hot, too."

The youngster went on to relate that before he could "get ahold of the thing the top began revolving faster, and it made a sort of whistling noise and took off without warming up or anything." t disappeared in a straight line into the northeast in a matter of 5 to 10 seconds, he estimated.

In the process of taking off, though, the object emitted some sort of gas or s ray that turned the youngster's arms a　rig t red and cause　small his arms and face. That part of the story　the lad's father.

ing, his arms were just as white as could me," the father expained. "There wasn't hardly any sunshine this morning, and when the boys came running home talking about this flying saucer one of the first things I noticed was that his arms and face were red, and there were welts on them."

David explained that after his father had applied a type of skin balm to his arms and face the welts gradually disappeared, but the red remained.

The object was on the ground not more than a minute, according to Charles, who said he got no closer than 100 yards to it before it took off. "Boy, it took off just like it was on a string or something. It didn't wobble or anything."

David estimated the object to have been on the ground for about half a minute.

Both before it landed and after it took off, David explained, he could notice that the small area between the top and bottom sections of　　　red, like it was on fire in　　　or something."

　　　and　　　were sincere in telling the story.

And just for the record, neither of the boys believe the alleged flying saucers are from some other planet.

"I think it's something the United States is doing, don't you?" he asked.

Do you?" Unquote.

—o—

In July and August, 1952, there occurred the most important episode in the series of events involving small UFOs. These sightings took place over and around Washington, D. C. In the space of 33 days commencing on the night of July 14 and ending the night of August 15 scores of UFOs were observed over the Washington area. On three of these occasions the UFOs performed gyrations for hours at a time. Prof. Charles A. Maney comments that "Nothing like this series of occurrences has happened before or since in the skies over the United States of America." On page 209 of his book, "The Report on Unidentified Flying Objects." (Ruppelt) has this to say: "Although the Air Force said that the incident had been fully investigated, the Civil Aeronautics Authority wrote a formal report on the sightings, and numerous magazine writers studied them, the has　　　been told. The pros have been left out of the　　　accounts, and 　　　cons were neatly overlooked by the pro writers."

On several of these occasions when the unidentified targets were picked up by radar at the Washington ARTC Center and the Washington National Airport Traffic Control Tower, jets from neighboring fields were dispatched to investigate and, if possible, intercept the unknown objects. They were unsuccessful in their quest, save in one instance!

While the newspapers carried such captions as: INTERCEPTORS CHASE FLYING SAUCERS OVER WASHINGTON, D. C. — JETS ALERTED FOR SAUCERS — INTERCEPTORS CHASE

(See "Monitoring", page 6)

Monitoring

(Continued from page 5)

LIGHTS IN D. C. SKIES — FIERY OB-
JECTS OUTRUN JETS OVER CAPITAL
— INVESTIGATION VEILED IN SE-
CRECY FOLLOWING VAIN CHASE —
AIR FORCE DEBUNKS SAUCERS AS
JUST NATURAL PHENOMENA —
(temperature inversions), — MORE OB-
JECTS SEEN OVER CAPITAL, POKING
ALONG AT 90 MPH — AIR FORCE
DISCOUNTS SAUCERS, CALLS 'EM
COLD AIR LAYERS — The Miami Her-
ald," Wed., July 30, 1952, from news
released to them by Air Force spokes-
men said, no explanation was given of
the reported moving lights which the
jets had pursued. Presumably they were
the reflections of searchlights on the
cold air layers."

           the   of the
      had succeeded in   one
      the moving   and that th   t
ad got a lock-on and opened fire on
e o ject.

          knocked a small
      the rim of
ture inversion"   a 2'-3' diameter
disc-shaped object) which was seen to
fall earthward, glowing as it fell. It
dropped into a farmer's field and was
recovered by a ground search crew. This
segment, which weighed less than a
pound, was later cut into three pieces
and distributed for analysis.

According to M Wilbur B. Smith of
          Canada, who was affor ed an
opportunity to examine one of the pieces
a qualitative analysis disclosed its one
identifiable component to be magnesium
orthosi icate an having thousands of
    micron- iameter spheres scattered
t rough its matrix. The   had a
4.5 mc resonance. (See APRO Bulletin
March 1960, "Physical Evidence").

Later in a talk given to the Illuminating Engineering Society, Canadian Re-
gional Conference, at a luncheon on
January 11, 1959, in Ottawa; Mr. Wilbur
B. Smith, B.A. Sc., M.A. Sc., P. Eng.,
Supt., Radio Regulations Engineering,
Department of Transport, Ottawa, said
in part: "Various items of 'hardware'
are known to exist, but are usually
promptly clapped into security and are
not available to the general public."

Without doubt, the above mentioned
fragment was one such piece of 'hardware' to which he referred.

Major Donald E. Keyhoe on Page 272
of his book THE FLYING SAUCER
CONSPIRACY refers to a report given
to him by Lt. Commander Frank Thomas of a peculiar object which fell near
Washington during the mass saucer
sightings in 1952. Major Keyhoe states

that the object was retrieved by a naval
officer and later analyzed by the Bureau of Standards.

The comment is made that one side
of it was flat with odd markings, as if
if had been milled, also that an analysis
had failed to determine whether it was
an artificially constructed object or a
fragment of some unknown type of meteorite and that it was later sent to W.
B. Smith of Ottawa for further analysis
by Project Magnet engineers.

(Continued next issue)

Children Frightened By "Sky Ghost"

A strange elliptical-shaped object
which hovers stationary in the air above
the Fleetwood Elementary School at
Lethbridge, Alberta, Canada, has caused
a stir. APRO's W. K. Allan of Calgary,
interview Mike Williams and Miles
White of Lethbridge and forwarded the
following information to headquarters:

The object, which appeared about 6
feet in diameter, first appeared in 1959
and was seen "six nights in a row," by
school children and at least one adult.
It was seen again on November 23, 1962
at 10:30 p.m. After hearing about it,
White's mother and her son and the
Williams boy went to the school on Friday, November 30, 1962. The object was
sighted again. It was shining with a bluish light and appeared to be over the
school's bell tower.

On Saturday, December 1, the boy and
his mother returned at 9 p.m., and saw
it hovering over the school yard about
0 feet off the ground. It appeared to be
almost transparent. They threw stones
at it and after about twice the time expected for the stones to fall to the
ground they were heard falling on the
roof of the one-stor school anne   e-
hind their acks in the opposite direction to which they were thrown.

After the Saturday sighting, Miles
White and Mike Williams went to a
movie, during which Miles' speech became blurred, didn't make sense and he
fell asleep. He complained first of a
"buzzing in the head."

The story was published in the papers,
and the boys as well as Mrs. White were
reluctant to talk of their experiences,
fearing ridicule.

Tailor Talks To Saucer Man

A young Toscan, Italy tailor has claimed that he not only saw a "flying saucer," but talked to the occupants who
told him that "humanity will soon receive a message." The gist of it is this:
After spending the evening with a friend

Mario Zuccula, 27, from Cerbaia, near
Florence, went to his home, skirting the
cemetery. Suddenly he felt a current of
air behind him and looked around. He
was nearly pararlyzed with fear when
he saw an object, about 30 feet in diameter, appearing to be of whitish metal
suspended in the air a few feet from
the ground. Zuccula said a sort of me-
talic sylinder detached itself from the
object and came to the ground. From
a door through which an intense light
radiated, came two small men "about
4½ feet tall." The date: 11 April 1962.
The small "men" approached Zuccula,
and he noted their heads were covered
with a sort of hood. They lifted the man
bodily off the ground and took him into
the saucer where, with a serious tone,
which seemed to come from an amplifier, one of them told him that "at the
end of the fourth moon, about one hour
from morning, we will return to give a
message to humanity."

Without recalling the rest of the adventure, Mr. Zuccula found himself before his house. His wife opened the door
for him, reproaching him for being so
fightened, then stated that she hadn't
opened the door. Because of the strange
nature of his tale and his obvious emotional upset, Mrs. Zuccula and her father
advised Mario to go to the authorities
and tell the story in confidence. This
is the end of the information contained
in the newspaper. It should be noted
here that the "amplifier" is a new touch
in a contact story, as is the "cylinder"
gadget which apparently brought the
little men to the ground. In evaluating
this, it is necessary to recognize the
existence of two factors: The cemetery
and the "cold gust of air," both of which
are frequently connected with paranorm-
al happenings. We do not attempt to
disqualify the story as to authenticity
but feel that all possibilities should be
considered.

UFO In Gravel Pit

A mystery object landed in 40 feet of
water and mud near the Midway gravel
pit just off the Seattle-Tacoma Freeway
on 19 December 1962. Welder John Lied-
tke, who reported the incident to the
State Highway Patrol, said he saw a lot
of sparks flying, thought it was a car in
trouble. Then the object exploded into a
big ball of fire and smoke filled the rea.
State Patrol Headquarters said there was
a perfectly round hole, 15 feet across in
the mud where the object landed. The
Seattle Post-Intelligencer, which carried
the story, did not elucidate on physical
description of the object before it exploded, nor whether or not there was a
search for debris in the pit.

THE A.P.R.O. BULLETIN

The A. P. R. O. Bulletin is the official copyrighted publication of the Aerial Phenomena Research Organization (A.P.R.O.), 4145 E. Desert Place, Tucson, Arizona, and is issued every other month to members only. The Aerial Phenomena Research Orgazination is a non-profit group dedicated to the eventual solution of the mystery of the unidentified objects which have been present in the skies for hundreds of years. Inquiries regarding membership may be made to the above address.

TUCSON, ARIZONA — MARCH, 1963

UFO PHOTOGRAPHED IN ARGENTINA

UFOS Precede Echo

On the night of 30 July 1962, many reports from Oregon and Northern California indicated that two unidentified satellite-like objects preceded Echo's path at 9:18 p. m. Observers also stated that the objects were in the same orbit but moving faster. NASA was queried, but no satellites then in orbit could be seen visually except Echo. According to our information, NASA suggested that they were probably private aircraft. The NASA spokesman said that planes with steady white lights would give the effect of speedy star or satellite if Echo was being observed at the same time and if the craft were at high altitude or far away. Commercial planes were ruled out for they have blinking lights.

When queried as to how come these objects were seen from Salem to Tacoma, a distance of 170 miles, the NASA spokesman merely answered that NASA had no further information about the sightings.

We agree with NASA — the objects were probably private aircraft of some kind. But whose?

Astronomer: Visitors Likely

One of the few astronomers willing to extend himself into a discussion of the likelihood of space visitors is Dr. Carl Sagan of Hardvard University. In Marvin Miles' column in the Los Angeles Times for 16 November 1962, Sagan is quoted as saying that "earth may have been visited many times by various 'galactic civilizations' during geological times and it is not out of the question that artifacts of these visits still exist." He also said that some kind of a base may be maintained for such visits, the back of the moon being a likely place. "My conclusions are purely provisional," he explained, "and I advance them to stimulate further thought and study." Sagan was further quoted regarding the probable number of stars orbitted by inhabitable planets, a theory which has frequently been advanced in support of the possibility of extraterrestrial life.

Michel, Byrne To Represent APRO

Aime Michel, engineer, mathematician, author and UFO researcher, has consented to represent APRO in France. We hope, within the near future, to present some of the cases he has investigated which date back to the late twenties.

Another new representative is Austin Byrne of Dublin, Ireland, who will cover the Emerald Isle for APRO. A recent sighting investigated by Mr. Byrne appears in this issue.

That Wisconsin "UFO"

In the early morning hours of 5 September 1962, residents in Minnesota and Wisconsin witnessed a spectacular and awesome sight: Brilliant, glowing red objects appearing to be in formation, streamed down through the atmosphere. Several small and one large piece of residue landed in Manitowoc, Wisconsin. The cry of "UFO" and "censorship" went out among many UFO researchers and enthusiasts, but as the information streamed in to APRO headquarters it became quite apparent that the above-mentioned witnesses had observed the dying throees of a Russian satellite as it burned and broke up coming into earth's atmosphere.

Patrolmen Report Sky Lights

At 5:30 a. m. on 18 September 1962, Officers James Dugan of Neptune City, New Jersey, saw two strange "gigantic" lights in the sky. He spotted the lights while driving in his patrol car, then raced to headquarters where Officer Lawrence Leming was on desk duty. Leming went outside the building with Dugan and also saw the lights. Dugan estimated they were "about a mile apart," and hovered over the borough for a while. When Leming saw them they were traveling fast and heading out over the ocean, where they eventually disappeared.

Cesar Domingo La Padula, Ariel Kaplan, and Ernesto Jose Ind, students of the Institute of Mathematics, Astronomy and Physics of the National Observatory of Cordoba, sighted a UFO while on the terrace of Mr. Padula's home, attempting to adjust an antenna. They said the object was completely "irregular" and that once during the sighting the shadow of the object fell on buildings. Padula does not maintain that the object is a "flying saucer" and adds nothing to the report except the above. The newspaper, "Cordoba" published the photos (see cut) on their front page, remarking: "Are they or are they not from another world, flying special missions over our planet?"

The newspaper, "La Voz del Interior," besides publishing on that occasion two of the photos and comments about them, confirm the sighting of the object with the added comment that corroborating witnesses watched the object from the Airport of Cordoba.

The time of day of the sighting and subsequent photographs, was 5:30 p.m. Doubt concerning the incident was expressed in the newspaper "Los Principios" in an interview with the photographer of the National Observatory of Cordoba, Mr. Julio Albarracin who said he gave no credence to the report, and that he felt it was the product of a "youthful mentality" (juvenile hoax}. He also stated that the photos show an object that reflects a "strange light" from the lowerside and has a shadow on the upper side, the angles of the photo are contradictory and there are other details that make the whole incident suspicious.

However, the newspaper "Cordoba" said that members of the Institute decided to have the photographs analyzed by professional photographers who informed them the pictures were not fakes.

We are making inquiries to get prints from the original negative and additional testimony and details—if we are successful, more will be featured in coming issues.

(See Photos on page 3)

The A. P. R. O. BULLETIN

Published by
THE AERIAL PHENOMENA RESEARCH
ORGANIZATION
4145 E. Desert Place
Tucson, Arizona
Copyright 1963, Coral E. Lorenzen
Editor and Director

Information appearing in this bulletin may be used by other UAO research periodicals providing names and address credit is properly given to this organization and periodical.

Coral E. Lorenzen .... International Director and Editor
A. E. Brown, B.S.E.E. .... Director of Research
L. J. Lorenzen .... Director of Public Relations
John T. Hopf .... Photographic Consultant
Oliver Dean .... Photographic Consultant

SPECIAL REPRESENTATIVES

(The following listed individuals participate in planning and policy-making as Staff Members, in addition to coordinating investigative efforts in the areas indicated following their names.)

Dr. Olavo T. Fontes, M.D....... Brazil
K.Gosta Rehn .... Sweden
Graham Conway .... Eastern Canada
Aime Michel .... France
Horacio Gonzales Gauteaume
.... Venezuela
Peter E. Norris, L.L.D. ....Australia
Jun' Ichi Takanashi ....Japan
Juan C. Remonda .... Argentina
Sergio Robba .... Italy
Arist. Mitropoulos .... Greece
Rev. N. C. G. Cruttwell, New Guinea
Eduardo Buelte .... Spain
Norman Alford .... New Zealand
Austin Byrne .... Ireland

SPECIAL CONSULTANT
Prof. Charles Maney,—Physics

ALAMOGORDO PRINTING CO., INC.

Why Reservoirs?

The large number of sightings of hovering and landed UFOs during 1962 took place in the vicinity of various types of water bodies—lakes, reservoirs, etc. In Mrs. Lorenzen's book, "The Great Flying Saucer Hoax," she predicted that inasmuch as a military reconnaisance has been carried out, the next logical subjects for study by the UFO occupants would be power plants and water supplies. Some researchers have found this to be true in 1962, but there was considerable evidence to indicate interest in power plants and water supplies prior to 1962. Although there have been a considerable number of sightings of UFO in the vicinity of oceans, the main interest seems to be fresh water.

If the theory put forth in her book proves to be more than just theory, (and the bulk of evidence seems to support it) interest in water would be natural for a race of people which have colonized an arid planet such as Mars. Prior to 1962 many sightings were made in areas which are irrigated. The Ohio River Valley has been a prime target of the UFOs, and is replete with reservoirs, dams, and the accompanying power plants.

What the next 5-year-flap will bring, we do not know. We hope that a complete study of 1962 sightings will be of help in making an intelligent prediction. Perhaps, also, the 24-26 month interval flaps which coincide with the proximity of Mars, will be somewhat illuminating in this respect.

Scientist Theorizes On "Third Space Entry"

Frank Macomber's column in the San Francisco Chronicle for August 23, 1962, started out like this: "Did Martians beat Earthmen into space? 'Nonsense', say eminent American astronomers. 'It's possible,' say prominent space research scientists."

Macomber then goes on to quote Dr. Melvin L. Stehsel of Aerojet General Corporation Advanced Research Division at Azusa, Calif., who cites data about the Martian moons which seem to be artificial, etc. In fact, the whole quote, which also appeared in The National Metalworking Weekly, "The Iron Age," seems to have been a result of a thorough reading of the "Great Flying Saucer Hoax" by APRO's Director. Stehsel mentions the sudden discovery of the Martian moons, and the possible meaning of the so-called Martian canals.

Stehsel's opinions, as opposed to those generally put forth by astronomers, bolsters our contention that astronomers are prejudiced against the idea of space travelers and habitation on other planets in our solar system, while scientists in other fields are more objective.

Light Over Baltimore

On the first of August, 1962, Mr. and Mrs. Finck of North Point Road, Dundalk-Essex section of Baltimore county, also Mrs. Harper and son of Old North Point Road observed an amber light which appeared larger than the disc of Venus, in the eastern sky. Flashes were emitted at intervals of every two minutes, lasting for a few seconds, and proceeded by a soft, crumbling sound. Object visible from 9:15 p.m. until 9:55 EDT, when it disappeared below eastern horizon. Seen again at 10:20 p.m., a bit ESE of its original position by the Harpers and Fincks and one other anonymous couple who also noticed two small planes in the vicinity.

A short time later, a report from the towson area stated that a large, bright object was seen to move from the north to south, then reversed direction, going north, and eventually proceeding west until out of sight.

Scientists With Half-Closed Minds

The above is the title of an article which appeared in the November 1958 Harper's magazine and contains some nuggets of observation. Dr. Ian Stevenson, chairman of the Department of Neurology and Psychiatry School of Medicine, University of Virginia, makes some astute observations about the tendency of science to close its collective mind to new concepts. He cites some classic examples: the non-acceptance of the existence of meteorites, and the field of medicine's prejudice against the study of hypnotism. This latter is something which has been chuckled about with increasing frequency by those laymen who had been interested in the art of hypnosis and its possibilities in scientific application.

History is full of examples of truth being hidden by the veil of prejudice and ignorance. Dr. Stevenson's whole point is that scientists too frequently forget that they are human and therefore subject to human emotional frailties. Economic factors, such as the research grants which go to various scientific research projects and fields, are also discussed.

The reason we mention this article, incidentally, is because some of the thoughts expressed by Dr. Stevenson, help to explain the reason that science, and therefore the public and the government do not face the facts about UFO, and more important, the portent of those facts.

There are some half-closed minds in UFO research, as a matter of fact. For over 15 years, the main theme among researchers has been: the U.S. Air Force has been lying, and we must force them to tell the truth. Black and white. Too many people think black or white—the greys, the in-betweens are forgotten. There was little or no effort to analyze the psychological factors involved in the UFO prroblem until Dr. Jung wrote his book about UFOs, which, like much of his work, has been either maligned or completely disregarded by the very people who claim to be seeking truth. That book is extremely important to those of us who seek to better understand the self-deluded "contactees" (not including the confidence men who fabricate tales to benefit themselves monetarily), the "UFO" sightings which are hallucinatory in nature, rather than objective experiences, the various theories offered by various researchers, the various interpretations of evidence, sightings, etc., etc. The foregoing are as important to UFO research as the sightings themselves.

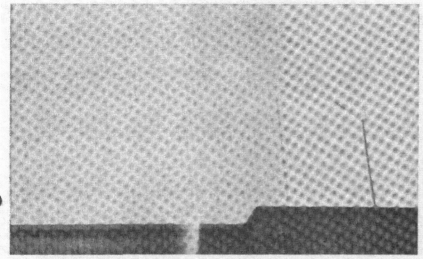

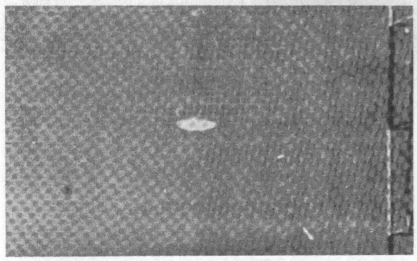

Above are shown 3 of 4 UFO photographed in Argentina. See page 1 for story, page four for photo No. 4.

Flaming Objects Fall

Reports of flaming objects falling into the Angeles National Forest west of Mount Wilson were made to sheriff's department and U.S. Forest Service officials shortly after midnight on November 7, 1962. The "objects" remained a mystery, however, and a search turned up nothing. Several Altadena citizens spotted the objects, which they said resembled the wing of an aircraft. Sheriff's office searchers scoured the area into which the objects reportedly fell but the hunt revealed nothing. The Civil Air Patrol said there were no missing planes. This report resembles that of the "flaming objects" which were identified as meteors, (flight time over Frisco about 25-30 seconds) and were seen to fall into the Isabel Valley near Lick Observatory in 1954. The objects in that case were seen "burning brightly" after they struck earth (or landed) in an area so wet that it was not likely that anything could have burned. The morning after the objects were seen, a search revealed no debris, meteoric or otherwise, and no objects.

"Spider Web" Falls On SLC

The October 23, 1962 issue of the Ogden Standard Examiner said that the mystery of "gooey material" which fell on Salt Lake City in the preceding week had been "partly solved." Dr. Grant S. Swynn of the State Health Department said the stuff was fibrous, burns, but is apparently "not hazardous." He said further tests would be made to attempt to determine the material's origin.

The "fiber" drifted down over Salt Lake City on 17 October, coming out of the north. It was described as "white and sticky." Our question: If it were "spider's web" as it was dubbed in the headline on the 23rd, couldn't it have been identified as such after a week's study?

Blue Globe Over Baltimore

At 9 p. m. on 2 July 1962, Mrs. Blanch Rattagin telephoned WFBM, Baltimore to report watching a red flickering flame which seemed appended to a blue-colored balloon-shaped object. The blue object was moving in a northeastern direction against the wind, and below the clouds. WFBM received several calls about it, as did newspapers and Friendship airport, in the area. The object went into a cloud as an aircraft approached from the east and was not seen again.

Shown above is No. 4 in Argentina Photos

Planes Have Unexplained Instrument Failure

"Something unknown caused it to go off course" stated Major Richard Linehan of his C-119 which crashed into a New Orleans private residence on 10 March 1962, killing four of a family of five.

. The Cincinnati (Ohio) Enquirer for 13 March also contained the following: The C-119 had suffered the loss of the right engine at 5,000 feet due to loss of 60 gallons of oil. Linehan said they then turned back to Calendar Field (New Orleans) under radar control. Unable to maintain altitude because the left engine couldn't carry the load, they decided to scuttle the plane. They headed it for sparse country and bailed out. Then the "something unknown" took over and the plane headed toward an inhabited area and crashed into the house.

Five days later, on 15 March, a United Air Lines Boeing 720 jet made an emergency landing at Tinker AFB after all instruments ceased functioning. None of the 48 passengers were hurt. Captain J. L. Jordan, the pilot, said the plane first had radio failure, then smoke in the cockpit. By the time he landed all instruments had ceased functioning.

These are two more examples of planes crashing or nearly crashing from unexplained causes. For another illustration, see headline story, May 1959 APRO Bulletin. Yet another is contained in the "Shadow of the Unknown" series by Dr. Fontes in 1958 Bulletins. In one of these cases a UFO circled the plane, then instruments ceased to function.

Maneuvering Light In Orion

Mary C. Kimball, who is getting extremely curious about how many supposed stars really belong, sighted an extra star in the constellation of Orion on January 20, 1962. It was just to the right and outside the three stars forming Orion's belt making the formation resemble a small cross in the sky. The object began to travel after about five minutes of observation, moving slowly through the two lower stars of the three previously mentioned. Then it faded and went out.

Buffalo Shaken By Mysterious Blast

On April 4, 1961, a rumbling explosion-like sound shook Buffalo, New York causing at least one family to vacate their home. The tower at Greater Buffalo International Airport said that no jets had been reported in the area for two hours.

Object Strikes Irish Field

A mysterious object, about the size of a baseball with four spokes protruding from it, fell from the sky over county Wexford, Ireland and made a crater four feet in diameter on 8 September 1962. Residents in the area reported hearing an explosion within a half-mile radius, at the time the object fell. It was found lying on top of a burned-up patch of yellow clay. Police cordoned off the field while waiting arrival of military experts from Dublin. No further details.

Mystery Lights Aboard Ship

On September 6, 1962, officials at Suva, Fiji Islands released information about strange unidentified lights seen aboard the deserted Japanese fishing vessel Toka Maru No. 8, which went aground on a coral reef near Qelelevu Island on September 1. Qelelevu lies to the west of the big island of Vanua Levu. It was north of Vanua Levu that the mystery ship, "Joyita" was found after disappearing while on passage from Samoa to the Tokalau Islands. The Joyita is now beached at Levuka.

On September 2 an official party approached the Toka Maru without going on board. The party comprised District Officer Peter Westwood, Mr. J. Matheson and a police constable. The official report states that all the Japanese had been taken off by another fishing vessel, but that night (Sunday) they saw a light flashing from the direction of the stranded ship. They replied to the light but got no recognizable signal in return.

The next day the officials went out to the ship and found no one. No light was seen that night.

On Tuesday they stripped all electrical gear from the ship and that night saw a light burning brightly and steadily.

Mr. Westwood commented: "It was most uncanny. It was suggested that Fijian villagers might have gone on board but there is no boat at Qelelevu. The sea was rough and it is a long way to swim. We took bearings on the light and it remained constant. Next morning the same bearing gave us the position of the ship. We could find no explanation for the light."

Monitoring And Scanning UFOs

By C. W. Fitch
(Continued)

There is no doubt in the writer's mind that this fragment was the same segment which had been broken from the edge of the UFO by the bullets from the jet fighter; the only difference being that all of the facts relating to the incident had not been presented to Major Keyhoe at the time.

Yet in its official "News Release" of January 19, 1961, the Department of Defense, Office of Public Relations in its FACT SHEET—AIR FORCE UFO REPORT on page 4, paragraph 8 states: "—and finally, no physical or material evidence, not even a minute fragment of a so-called "flying saucer" or space ship has ever been found."

And the unsuspecting press, having accepted the temperature inversion explanation, dutifully reported the radar blips as such and the episode came to a close. Another classic example, as in the Gorman and Walesville, N. Y. cases, of an occurrence in which only part of the facts were even made known. Again those 'in the know' had succeeded in preventing the portions which might have proved quite disturbing, from reaching the public. Small wonder for Ruppelt's comment that "the complete story has never fully been told."

Oddly enough, while denying the reality of solid objects over Washington, D. C., Air Force intelligence on January 26, 1953, released to the press the account of an incident which took place over northern Japan at 11:20 a.m., March29, 1952. The occurrence involved an American jet fighter-bomber and a small disc. The GRAND RAPIDS (Mich.) PRESS of Jan. 27, 1953 carried the following account of this happening:

"AIR FORCE REPORTS SMALL 'DISC' MAKES PASS AT THUNDER-JET."

United States Airbase, North Japan— AP—The United States Air Force Tuesday night reported a small, metallic, disc-shaped object made a controlled, sweeping pass at an American jet fighter-bomber and was observed at very close range by another pilot.

The report, from Air Force intelligence files, said the sighting was made over northern Japan at 11:20 a.m., March 29, 1952, by Lt. David C. Brighma of Rockford, Ill.

It was a bright, cloudless day, Brigham said he got a very good look at the object from about 30 to 50 feet for about 10 seconds.

"Says It's Small"

The pilot described it as "about eight inches in diameter, very thin, round and as shiny as polished chromium: had no apparent projections and left no exhaust trails or vapor trails."

He said it caught up with an F-84 Thunderjet, hovered a few moments and then shot out of sight. The F-84 pilot, whose name was not repealed, did not see it.

It was the second disclosure in a week by Air Force intelligence of mysterious flying objects over northern Japan near the Russian-Siberia area.

Brigham was flying a prop-driven reconnaissance craft at 6,000 feet when an F-84 drew alongside them, he said, he saw the disc to the right of and just behind the Thunderjet. He said it appeared to be traveling 30 to 40 miles an hour faster than the F-84, which was going 150-160 miles an hour.

"It closed rapidly and just before it would have flown into his fuselage, it decelerated to his air-speed almost instantaneously," Brigham said in his report to intelligence officers. "In doing so it flipped up its edge at approximately a 90-degree bank. Then it fluttered within 20 feet of his fuselage for perhaps two or three seconds, pulled away and around his starboard (right) wing, appearing to flip once as it hit the slipstream behind his wing tip fuel tank.

"Then it passed him, crossed in front of him and pulled up abruptly, appearing to accelerate, and shot out of sight in a steep, almost vertical climb.

An unusual flight characteristic was a slow fluttering motion. It rocked back and forth at approximately 40-degree banks at approximately one second intervals throughout its course."

When it pulled away, "It did so more sharply than a plane could have done. Its maneuvering throughout was always clear and precise." Unquote.

—o—

Diminutive saucers were back in the news again in 1955. On Nov. 9, 1955, Reuters news service of London carried the following dispatch: "Karachi, Pakistan, — Flying Saucers are getting smaller.

Bluish, diminutive saucers, about six inches in diameter, were sighted one night recently over Tejgaon Airport in East Pakistan, the Karachi Morning News reported.

Engineers of the Pakistan International Airlines and airport meteorologists said the tiny saucers were traveling at "roughly 1,000 miles an hour" at a height of about 1,500 feet.

Two saucers were seen for a total of 17 minutes, the newspaper said, and lit up the whole airport area." Unquote.

—o—

Returning again to the year 1952, not only did there take place the aforementioned aerial encounters with small UFOs but this year also ushered in the first of several recorded ground sightings or encounters with strange, eerie lights which appeared to follow the sighters.

THE TITUSVILLE (PA.) HERALD of Monday, August 25, 1952, carried a lengthy article the title of which was: "Editor Sees 'Saucer' Feels Auto Quiver" The sub-title read: "Lights in Sky and On Ground are Watched for Hour by Herald Man." "The following account of an aerial phenomenon was written by a trained newspaperman who is a careful observer and accurate recorder of events. To the best of our knowledge, it is the first to report a reaction on the surafce of the earth—the shaking of a sedan—simultaneously with the display of lights in the sky. The author is careful to draw no conclusion as to what caused the motion. There was no wind. It may have been sound waves on too high a frequency for a human ear to hear, or it may have been an electrical force, such as magnetism, or it might have been a slight earth tremor. But that is for the scientists to say. — The Publishers.

Highlights of Managing Editor Frank S. Holowach's harrowing experience with a moving light are contained in the following paragraphs—excerpts from his article in the HERALD.

"I joined the fraternity early yesterday morning of those who have seen strange lights in the sky. I'm not definitely sure what I saw but I'm not up to joking about the matter yet because at the end of the observation period I was a jittery fellow.

I felt as though I was brushing the supernatural. There may be an explanation for what I saw. There's also probably an explanation for the way I felt, but I know this: I don't want to go through the experience again.

You can laugh if you want to and I'd like to join you, but I felt as though an invisible magnetic force rocked my car and tried to pull me out of it.

That's a pretty tall order for anyone to swallow, but let's just go through this thing once over lightly for the record. I'm not asking anyone to believe anything. I almost don't believe it myself.

To begin with, it happened at half past four yesterday morning.

At that time I was on Route 408 five miles southeast of Cambridge Springs (Pa.) in Rockdale township. I saw a

(See Monitoring next page)

Monitoring

(Continued from Page 5)

light turn on in the sky low over the horizon to my left. It was a bright hard light but not much bigger than a star. In fact, it looked just like a star and twinkled or turned.

Before I was sure I had seen anything, the light went out. Then seconds later it reappeared almost directly ahead at the far east extreme of the horizon.

I stopped my car and turned out the lights. Nothing happened. Probably a shooting star, I thought. So I started up and went around the next curve. The light reappeared riding low in the sky.

"This is what you've been wanting to see, one of those reported lights at night. Let's try to find an explanation for this."

Embarking upon the matter in somewhat the manner of a scientist, which I'm not, I began taking notes of just what was going on and also set down possible explanations. It was a cold night and clear where I was, although foggy in the lowlands. I was enjoying myself and glad I had finally seen "something."

I got out of the car and stood in the roadway while my eyes got adjusted somewhat to the night. The light flickered on and off like a firefly. Could it be a firefly? No, doubt that. It is a whiter light. It covers too much space. It doesn't go away. There is only one light and it seems to cover a regular route.

The light skated around the horizon. I was on rather an elevation, looking to the northeast across a low valley. The light appeared to be just above the next ridge (Brown hill, north of Little Cooley).

The light flickered like a car headlight going past trees. Then it went out. Then it reappeared further north. And then south again. Always just above the horizon, but sometimes going up a little and then coming down a little at a slant.

Now, imagination is a powerful thing. As I look back, I don't think one stray thought entered my head about anything eerie or super-natural. I was just matter-of-factly doing a reporting job, or I thought I was.

I look to see how the eastern sky is getting brighter . .. . and I feel the car vibrate. Ah, shivering because your feet are cold, huh? The car moved again. This time I was watching myself, and I don't think I moved to make the car shift like that.

I look at the valley light. It seems to be increased in intensity and beamed right at me.

For some reason my skin begins to crawl. I told you imagination is a powerful thing.

The car vibrates and I vibrate.

Cut this out .You're thinking things. Nothing's going to hurt you. Watch the car radio aerial against the sky and it'll show you nothing is shaking the car.

But the aerial is shaking. I looked at the light in the valley. It stared at me. It seemed some force was pulling me through the open window. It felt like a giant magnet was drawing my flesh.

Well, I'll be frank with you. My imagination went to work right then. My hair seemed to stand on end. Somehow I felt as if I was going to disintegrate, disappear. Doesn't that light want anyone to watch it?

Right then I switched on the car key, started up and went away as if something was chasing me.

The white light came out and moved ahead of me. The sky in the east was crimson-edged at the horizon. White fog lay in the low places. The countryside was a thing of beauty in that first half morning light, but by that time I was seeing infernal machines behind every bush and the beginning of the day seemed eerie. I havn't had such a crawly feeting since the night a big dog sneaked up on me when I was eight years old and was walking past a neighbor's home." Unquote.

—o—

1956 produced two very unusual small UFO encounters, the first of which took place in Ireland. The CLEVELAND PLAIN DEALER of Sept. 9, 1956 carried an article entitled "EGG-SHAPED SOARING 'SAUCER' SCRAMBLES FREE OF ITS CAPTOR."

"Moneymore, Northern Ireland, Sept. 8, (AP)—A "level-headed, God-fearing" Irish farmer says he was running to the police station with a captured flying saucer in his arms yesterday, but it escaped.

"I had difficulty in holding it down," Thomas Hutchinson explained today.

A Royal Air Force officer said what Hutchinson picked up must have been a weather balloon—but police preferred the farmer's version.

"Thomas Hutchinson is a level-headed, God-fearing chap," said the desk sergeant at Moneymore headquarters. "He's not the sort of man who would imagine he seized a flying saucer if, in fact, he didn't have one."

Hutchinson said he and his wife Maud saw a flying saucer drop from the clouds into a bog 200 yards from his front door.

"It was egg-shaped, about three feet high and 18 inches in diameter," said Hutchinson. "It was bright red with two dark red marks at the end and three

dark red stripes around its smallest diameter." "It had a saucer-shaped base. I kicked it over, but it returned to its original position."

When he got down on his knees for a closer examination, he went on, it began to spin. So he put a hammer lock on it and mused.

"The police station was the only place for such a wicked looking thing as this —and I started to carry it there."

Then Mrs. Hutchinson took up the tale:

"Ah, it was a terrible thing. My husband warned me not to go near it, but you know a woman's inquisitiveness . ."

She said she walked along with her husband and stood there staring at the fearful object when he put it on the ground for a moment to negotiate a hedge.

"Then all of a sudden the monster rose and it nearly pulled my husband off his feet when he tried to hold it."

Asked by police what she did then, she replied:

"I started to panic and then I ran home and prayed." Unquote.

—o—

The second sighting occurred near Butler, Pennsylvania.

The BUTLER EAGLE of October 2, 1956, contained an account of it in an article by John A. Ammon: " 'FLYING SAUCER' SPENDS HOUR CIRCLING YARD IN BUTLER AREA—Object Appeared Lost, Had Small Pegs on Its Top."

"A Butler man revived talk of flying saucers today by relating in detail how he watched one leisurely circling in front of him for an hour.

"I never saw anything like it before or since. It must have been a flying saucer." Charles W. McGrady, 406 Negley Ave., retired car company worker, declared.

The 73-year-old Butler man is not alone, either. He said his brother watched the flying saucer with him.

He described the flying saucer he saw as being shaped like an upside down dishpan with small pegs on top.

It was gray in color and had a light on the front which gave off a grayish light. The contraption was about 2½ feet in diameter and eight inches thick. It ran smoothly without making a sound and gave off a light gray smoke which appeared to have something in it that killed the leaves on a tree.

"I don't think there was anyone in it— it was too small. It must have been controlled by radar or in some similar fashion," McGrady said. But let's let him tell about it. He gave me this account:

(Continued next issue)

The Experience Of Rr. and Mrs. Barney Hill

By C. W. Fitch

On the night of September 19-20, 1961, on U.S. Route 3 in the White Mountains of New Hampshire, a Portsmouth couple had a sensational encounter with a UFO.

The Hills were interviewed on October 21 by Mrs. Walter N. Webb, Chief Lecturer on Astronomy at Hayden Planetarium Boston for a period of six hours and a detailed report of their experience was written up and sent to NICAP. Webb is Chairman of NICAP's Massachusett's Subcommittee, Unit 1, also a member of APRO. A condensation of this report appeared in the "UFO Investigator" of Jan.-Feb. 1962.

Because of my extreme interest in the Hill's most unusual experience, I called them by telephone and talked with Barney Hill at some length in regard to it.

His account at that time was basically the same as at the time of his interview with Mr. Webb and is as follows:

Barney and Betty Hill of 953 State Street, Portsmouth, N. H., were returning home from a vacation in Canada. About midnight in the Groveton area the Hills saw a bright moving object in the southeastern sky. Mrs. Hill described it as being brighter than the planet Jupiter. Mr. Hill said his wife became excited about the object so he stopped the car so they could observe it through their 7x50 binoculars. At first they thought it was an airliner, but when it began curving toward the west and then changed direction and moved eastward toward them as though it had seen them and was coming nearer to investigate, they realized that it was not an airliner. (Reference is made at this point to Case No. 162, CRIFO ORBIT of July 6, 1956, published by Leonard H. Stringfield of Cincinnati, Ohio — "Saucer Descends on Dark Street, Scares Youths" — which related the experience of two girls while waiting at a bus stop in Jacksonville, Florida on the night of May 9, 1956, and their reactions to a somewhat similar situation). (See also APRO Bulletin, March, 1959—article by C. W. Fitch — "Strange Disappearances and Flying Saucers"—The Editor).

At the time of their sighting the Hills were driving through a lonely and nearly uninhabited section.

The UFO seemed to be coming lower and closer. Through the binoculars they could see a lighted band which appeared to be convex as though conforming to the edge of a flattened disc. The strange object came around in front of their car and stopped in mid-air to the right of the highway. They estimated that it was ap-proximately 100 feet above the ground. They could then see that the lighted band was, in reality, a row of windows through which a cold bluish-white glow shone. They could also see a red light on each side of it.

Mr. Hill left the headlights on and the engine running, took the binoculars and got out on the highway to get a better look at the object. He was amazed at the noiseless ease with which it changed position but still felt he was observing a conventional aircraft such as a military helicopter, perhaps of some advanced design.

Fascinated, he watched the object as it began descending slowly in his direction. Through the binoculars he could see from eight to eleven figures which appeared to be watching them from the windows. Suddenly all but one of the figures turned their backs and began to hurry about, seemingly pulling levers on the wall.

One figure remained at a window looking down at them. Just then the two red lights that they had noticed began moving away from the object. Mr. Hill could see that the lights were on the tips of two pointed fin-like structures which were sliding outward from its sides. Mrs. Hill was watching her husband and heard him repeat over and over "I don't believe it, I don't believe it."

Barney Hill said the figures were of human form and were dressed in shiny black uniforms like glossy leather. He was reminded of the cold precision of German officers. The lone figure at the window, who Mr. Hill felt was the leader, both attracted and frightened him. He felt that this figure was concentrating on some plan it had in mind and that they were going to be captured "like bugs in a net."

He said it was then he knew that the craft he was observing was something alien and unearthly and felt that it contained beings of a superior type. Hill estimated that the object at this, its closest point of approach, was from 50 to 80 feet up and between 50 and 100 feet away.

Hill said at this point he panicked and began laughing hysterically. Repeating "they're going to capture us," he jumped into the car and took off down the highway at high speed. Neither of them looked back immediately. When Mrs. Hill did look back she saw no sign of the UFO

They had traveled only a short distance when they heard a series of beeping sounds, like code, on the rear trunk. Each beep caused the car to vibrate. These sounds kept up for approximately 35 miles until they reached Ashland when they ceased as suddenly as they had commenced.

Mr. Hill remarked that they estimated they had observed the UFO for from 30 to 40 minutes for 45 miles, between midnight and 1 a.m.

In a letter to me dated April 23, 1962, Mrs. Hill commented that "The UFO we saw resembled in many ways the one sighted by Frank Edwards (except that the one Edwards saw was spherical) and reported in the January-February, 1962 issue of the UFO Investigator. (See also APRO Bulletin for November, 1961).

"We have been quite upset by our experience," Mrs. Hill said. "It seems to be unbelievable, so puzzling, with so many questions unanswered. We have discussed the situation with a psychiatrist who assured us that it is an impossibility for two people to have the same hallucination at the same time."

(Editor's Note: In the interest of accuracy, we must note that: Opinions pertaining to "collective hallucination" or "mass visions" differ among psychiatrists and psychologists. The late Carl G. Jung, for instance, cites the "Bowman at Mons" as an example of collective hallucination. The Bowman at Mons was a figure of an English Bowman seen in the sky over the British trenches at Mons in the bitter fighting of World War I by a large number of tired and discouraged troops. In that instance it is possible that one soldier "transmitted" the image which was picked up by the rest of the men. At any rate it appears to have been a vision which answered a sub-conscious need of the battle-weary troops. The Hill incident, however, involved an object and entities which were frightening to the observers rather than encouraging or soothing, which leads to the conclusion that it was an objective rather than a subjective experience).

In passing comment on the Hill's sighting, we are definitely inclined to the opinion that there is no doubt as to its reality or that these two people would not be likely to have this particular hallucination at the same time.

(Editor's Note: In this issue, the readers will find a report by Dr. Olavo Fontes concerning the kidnapping of a man in Brazil in August. That kidnappings would be an eventual activity of the occupants of the UAO has been discussed by Dr. Fontes and Mrs. Lorenzen in the past and attempted kidnappings, or at least what appeared to be that, has indicated the possibility).

Check your receipts—please remit dues
$3.50 per year

Boy Scouts Report Sightings —Others See UFO's

An object which changed direction faster than would be possible with a regular aircraft, was sighted by four boy scouts and three staff members of Camp Lakota in Illinois on 12 July 1962. In a letter addressed to Professor Charles Maney, Physics Professor at Defiance College, the J. C. Holley family of Defiance gave this description:

The first object sighted was like a cigar with a pointed tail. The next objects seen were shaped the same, but were smaller and appeared to come from the larger one.

Bob Easley, 11, reported the following information o na sighting which was made on 17 July: The object was sigarshaped, didn't appear to have wings, and changed direction too fast to be a balloon. It blinked on and off, was yellow at first, then changed to light blue and then back to yellow again. It didn't give off a trail.

Ronald B. Baringer, who has 3000 hours flying time and a commercial pilot's rating, gave this account of his sighting on July 30: "It was much larger than a star, was moving at about 1000 mph. It raised straight up to an altitude of about 1,000 feet and lowered again to 200 feet. This raising and lowering was done at speeds much greater than any helicopter was capable of doing. It moved unbelievably faster than the fastest jet I have ever seen operate.

"In the raising and lowering operation there was no flame but just a super bright light and I could observe no definite shape. On every forward motion on a horizontal plane there was a jet of flame about ¾ the size of the object.

"The object itself was a brilliant orange-red glow of light and the jet flame made when traveling was more blue-orange-red and was not present when it hovered. I have seen flares dropped at night, parachutes drop at night, parachute flares dropped at night, airplanes at night, jets at night, and helicopters operate, and this object was certainly none of these."

The names of the scouts who sighted the object at 8:30 p.m. on the 12th were Charles Nelson, Robert Anderson, Ronnie Boweman and LeRoy Hodapp. They were walking along the Power Dam road when they saw the objects.

The sightings were reported to Professor Maney, and the following is additional detail: The boys first thought the object was a jet, when first seen at about 30 degrees elevation, but it proved to be too "globular" in appearance. It

started to move at a slight angle down and to their left and grew in size from a dot to "sigar-shaped." Shortly a very bright speck appeared to the right of the object and stayed stationary while the first object remained in motion. A third object suddenly "fired" from slightly below the second object as if it possibly dropped from object number two. The third object left a bright, clear contrail which hung in the air like a jet trail. It then disappeared behind or into a cloud and never reappeared.

Shortly thereafter, the first (cigarshaped) object changed directions and began to drop over the horizon, and the second object also vansihed from sight.

Strange Lights In S.D.' Neb.

On Thursday, 18 October, residents of Rapid City, S. D., as well as an employee of the FAA in Cheyenne, Wyoming, reported a huge, bright meteor. In western Nebraska several reports were made to authorities concerning a strange bright object in the sky. Highway Patrol officers at Scottsbluff reported a motorist said what he thought was a fragment of a meteor set a grass fire near Kilgore. Fire trucks sent to investigate and extinguish the fire found nothing, however.

Two Ogallala, Nebraska high school boys reported that same night that a glowing object landed north of the town in the hills. A search Thursday night disclosed nothing, and a continuing search Friday yielded the same. One 16-year-old driving on the north edge of Ogallala said he saw a round, green light descending out of the northwest onto a hill just north of the city. He told police he picked up a 17-year-old friend and they drove about 700 yards into the hills where they saw a white, glowing object parked on the ground, and estimated its size as 100 yards by 30 to 40 feet high. Search later yielded nothing naturally.

Maneuvering Star In Calif.

At 10 p. m. and thereafter on the evening of 24 October 1962, Mrs. Harlan Driscoll of El Cajon, Calif. and her daughter, Moyna, observed a bright star-like object in the north-northeast at about a 45 degree elevation. To the naked eye the object appeared about the apparent size of Venus, but through binoculars it appeared as several dots of light arranged in a horizontal row, each of which appeared to give off "rays" of light. The observers trained the binoculars on several stars in the sky, but did not observe the same "ray" phenomena,

as was evident on the unknown object.

The object made several changes of location, each time traveling at speeds higher than those of military planes commonly observed in the area, after which the object hovered motionless for some time before changing location again. According to V. E. Dewey, APRO member who interviewed the observers, there did not seem to be much change in altitude, and only 10 degrees or so net change in location toward the east during the maneuvers. The intensity of the object's light varied somewhat during the maneuvers but did not appear to be correlated with its motions. Observations were terminated by the observers' need to sleep, and the object therefore, was not seen to leave or disappear.

Crises Ahead

During and shortly after the first three (1947, 1952 and 1957) five-year UFO flaps, news coverage and consequently, interest, was at a high point. During the periods of time between these flaps, however, interest, even among "established" UFO enthusiasts, has tended to wane. Lack of interest in the subject means lack of support for participating organizations, and without the support of a considerable number of people it is impossible for a UFO group to survive.

Recently, Norbert Gariety of S.P.A.C.-E., Coral Gables, Florida, announced via the periodical of the same name that the group was discontinuing operations. The same thing has happened to several groups during the past ten years, for one reason or another.

That the time could come when no UFO information would be available outside of skimpy news accounts, is a definite possibility.

APRO has, of course, faced and surmounted the problems indigent to UFO research many times. We can proudly say that we are the oldest UFO research organization. When we are late in our publishing schedules we make up issues instead of simply omitting them. As most of the members are aware, Bulletins have been late consistently since the move from Alamogordo to Tucson. One reason is the fact that Bulletins are arranged for by mail, and there have been other factors. Nonetheless, when this issue is received, the copy for both the May and July issues will be with the printer and we will be current.

We strongly urge members to renew their memberships on time so that some idea of a financial budget will be possible in planning the Bulletin work ahead.

cc 5

THE A.P.R.O. BULLETIN

The A. P. R. O. Bulletin is the official copyrighted publication of the Aerial Phenomena Research Organization (A.P.R.O.), 4145 E. Desert Place, Tucson, Arizona, and is issued every other month to members only. The Aerial Phenomena Research Orgazination is a non-profit group dedicated to the eventual solution of the mystery of the unidentified objects which have been present in the skies for hundreds of years. Inquiries regarding membership may be made to the above address.

TUCSON, ARIZONA — MAY, 1963

UAO LANDS AT BUENOS AIRES AIRPORT

The X-15 And The UFO

On the 10th of May 1962 test pilot Joe Walker reported that film taken during his X-15 flight showed the presence of unidentified objects. So much space in popular periodicals and newspapers was devoted to this revelation that we do not feel it necessary to devote much time or space on it here, except to outline the bare facts and make someobservations.

As it turned out, Col. John Glenn appeared with Walker at a scientific conference in Seattle on the 10th of May. He had also seen "strange objects" during his historic orbiting of the globe. In the case of Walker, the objects were disc-shaped and white in color and showed on the film taken when Walker was at the high point of his flight—246,700 feet. Walker admitted he hadn't seen the objects himself, but that had viewed them on the film after the flight. He also stated he didn't care to comment on them.

Authorities had speculated, shortly after Glenn's flight, that the objects he saw had been "snowflakes" (condensed crystals of water vapor from his capsule) or paint peeling off his capsule. "I don't feel they were snowflakes or paint peeling off the capsule. I don't feel they originated from the capsule at all—because some of them were coming toward me," Glen commenteed during the conference.

Of the objects he saw, Walker said: "We just haven't had time to analyze the characteristics of these objects. From what we can tell, they shaped or erha s even c lin l It's impossible to estimate their size or their distance from the camera." Walker also said that considerable more study of the objects would be carried out.

Flotsam and jetsam (garbage) of space (possibly originating from other space shots) could be considered as a possible answer to these mysterious objects. Also considering the size of the object which paced the jet over Korea in 1953, the objects seen by Walker and Glenn could possibly be remote-controlled monitoring devices.

Saucer Dunks In Reservoir

The area in and around Oradell, New Jersey was the setting for some spectacular happenings in the middle of September 1962. It started this way: At 7:55 p. m. on the evening of Saturday, 15 September, 3 boys, Robert Decker, Steve Nagy and David Finley were at the Oradell reservoir when they saw a strange, saucer-shaped object land in the water just south of the dam near Oradell Avenue. According to the trio, the object landed, with a splash (which they heard) then took off at high speed. It was disc-shaped with a band around the middle, "spots" on the upper half, protruding from the lower

The next morning, they went back to investigate, and found what they thought was a bear tracks, and tion w ich appeared to be banana-shaped. The boys then reported their experience and findings to police, who checked with Teterboro Airport and found that no airplanes were scheduled for that area at that time. Police then called in Air Force authorities from McGuire AFB. The Operations Officer, Major Vance, asked for drawings of the object and asked that he be kept informed.

Haworth police located a man who was working near the Haworth side of the servoir at about 8 p. m. The man informed the police that he had heard a splash at that time.

On Sunday night, the Finley boy, with two more witnesses, Paul Bitetti and Ed Lombi, returned to the site of the incident at about 8 p. m. A half hour later they were at police headquarters, all talking at once, and re ating w at they had seen only minutes before. The Bitetti boy and Lombi said they hadn't believed Finley before they went to the spot Sunday night, but were convinced by what they observed. Police said the boys seemed frightened, and said they had pointed out the object to a fisherman who ran away as soon as he saw it. The boys described the object seen

(See "Saucer" on Page 3)

At 12 p.m. on 23 December 1962, a glowing football-shaped object sat down on the runway at the Ezeiza International Airport at Buenos Aires, Argentina. Mr. Horacio Alora, a technician, and ose Besutti, tower operator observed the landing of the unconventional aerial object from the control tower. The object parked near section 40-28, about 2,000 meters little over a and 1/5) from control tower. Alora an esutti described the object as flowing and football shaped.

At the time of the sighting, Besutti and Alora were controlling the landing of a Panamerican DC8, and paid special attention to the object during the landing of the plane. There was excellent visibility at the airport, and all facilities were functioning well, according to newspaper reports. When the object left, it ascended vertically at high speed, to an altitude of about 500 or 600 meters (about 1500 feet), then disappeared over the horizon in level flight.

The above is the sum total of information we have to date, however, if further information is forthcoming, it will be printed in this Bulletin or a subsequent issue.

Strange Light "Goes Out"

The mother of member Kathryn Liehl forwarded the following information about an unusual sky object which, through Miss Diehl, reached APRO: Gene Hunter (apparently of Cleveland) was traveling on Center Ridge Road near Dover Center on September 1 at between 9:30 and 10 p.m. She observed a round object which had a fan-shaped white light about it. It traveled from north to southwest at about the speed of a plane. No motor or other noise was heard. She stopped her car to watch, and suddenly the light either was extinguished or the object carrying it turned in such a way that it was no longer visible. This brief sighting, with few details, correlates with the sighting of November 23, 1960, in Indiana and Ohio.

The A. P. R. O. BULLETIN

Published by
THE AERIAL PHENOMENA RESEARCH
ORGANIZATION
4145 E. Desert Place
Tucson, Arizona
Copyright 1963, Coral E. Lorenzen
Editor and Director

Information appearing in this bulletin may be used by other UAO research periodicals providing names and address credit is properly given to this organization and periodical.

Coral E. Lorenzen ..... International Director and Editor
A. E. Brown, B.S.E.E. .... Director of Research
L. J. Lorenzen .... Director of Public Relations
John T. Hopf .... Photographic Consultant
Oliver Dean .... Photographic Consultant

SPECIAL REPRESENTATIVES
(The following listed individuals participate in planning and policy-making as Staff Members, in addition to coordinating investigative efforts in the areas indicated following their names.)

Dr. Olavo T. Fontes, M.D. ...... Brazil
K. Gosta Rehn .... Sweden
Graham Conway .... Eastern Canada
Aime Michel .... France
Horacio Gonzales Gauteaume
.... Venezuela
Peter E. Norris, L.L.D. .... Australia
Jun' Ichi Takanashi .... Japan
Juan C. Remonda .... Argentina
Sergio Robba .... Italy
Arist. Mitropoulos .... Greece
Rev. N. C. G. Cruttwell, New Guinea
Eduardo Buelte .... Spain
Norman Alford .... New Zealand
Austin Byrne .... Ireland

SPECIAL CONSULTANT
Prof. Charles Maney,—Physics

ALAMOGORDO PRINTING CO., INC.

Object Seen Again Near Quarry

On Friday, September 21, four policemen as well as William Stock observed a brightly-lit object above Hawthorne, N. J. Stock had seen the same type of thing early on Thursday morning, saw it again at 3:45 a.m. on Friday and called the police to corroborate his sighting. Patrolman Joseph Snyder, dispatched Patrolmen George Gordon and George Jediny to the quarry where they confirmed Stocks' report. A second patrol car with Patrolmen Frank Saal and Edward Welch was dispatched to the scene. Saal, who served five years as an AF pilot in WW II, as well as the Korean War, said he estimated the brightly lit object at between 20,000 and 25,000 feet high when first seen by him. The sky was clear with a three-quarter moon overhead. The object came from a southerly direction and then hovered for about 25 minutes. "I could clearly make out two lights on it, but could not make out the outline. The object then moved off rapidly in the direction from which it had come," Saal said.

Submarine Saucers

From time to time through the years before saucers became newsworthy in 1947, various naval vessels reported the presence of huge "wheels of light" in the sea. Some of these have been documented by FATE magazine. Since 1947, several mystery submarines have been spotted which have not been successfully tracked or identified.

On October 25, 1962, the Los Angeles Times writer, Marvin Miles (Aerospace Editor) wrote a feature on "Soviet Subs." According to the article, on July 28 the skipper of a chartered fishing boat spotted lights in the darkness just before dawn about six miles southeast of Avalon, (on Catalina). He noted the lights were low in the water and apparently stationary as he swung his 46-foot craft through a change of course toward the tip of San Clemente. The lights were almost dead ahead by then and he trained his binoculars for a good look.

The fisherman was startled to see a squat, lighted structure in which several men were working, although the enclosure seemed empty of any objects. The skipper and another member of the crew viewed the strange sight. They described it thusly:

"It appeared to be the stern of a submarine. We could see five men, two in all-white garb, two in dark trousers and white shirts and one in a sky-blue jumpsuit. We passed abeam at about a quarter-mile and I was certain it was a submarine low in the water, steel gray, no markings, decks almost awash, with only its tail and odd aftstructure showing."

The strange aspects of this encounter which qualified it for printing in this Bulletin were these: "Then it started toward us and I turned hard to keep clear," the skipper reported. "It swept past us at surprising speed and headed toward the open sea, still on the surface. There was no noise that I could discern, no trailing white wake, just a good-sized swell."

The skipper thought for a while it was just an American sub on the surface for a small repair, but the odd superstructure puzzled him, so he reported to Naval Intelligence. The Navy reacted fast, taking detailed statements, having the skipper study alien submarine silhouettes and carefully checked his log for course changes, times and distances involved.

The Los Angeles Times, after hearing about the incident, checked with the Navy, got a cryptic answer: "There's nothing to it." Washington, D. C. public information reacted the same.

Mr. Miles' feature went on to say that no identification was made, and described various types of known submarines. One bit of data was completely missing: What kind of U.S. or other submarine, could travel at high surface speed, leaving no wake, with a huge, mysterious swell. We have an idea.

1831 Sighting Of 80-Minute Meteor

The Corvallis Gazette-Times of Corvallis, Oregon contained a very interesting record of a sighting of a strange meteor sighted by the crew of a ship off Puget Sound. The article, by Kenneth Holmes, takes from "Lights and Shadows of Sailor Life," published in Boston in 1848: "At ten minutes past 8 o'clock on the 31st, (May) a meteor of immense magnitude and brilliancy shot across the heavens in a northwest direction, illuminating the heavens to such an extent that there was a resemblance of a sheet of fire until it nearly reached the horizon, when it exploded, sending off myriads of corruscations in every direction. When it first commenced its flight, it was exceedingly slow in its descent, but as it increased its distance towards the horizon it increased its velocity considerably, until it burst. Many old seamen on board never witnessed a meteor half so large, nor one whose light remained so long visible. From the time it was first seen until it disappeared, was one hour and twenty-five minuites." Unquote. (This apparently encompasses time of sighting plus duration of observation of trail. —The Ed.).

Another "meteoric display" of the 1800s is also recorded in the same article. It involves a display observed by a huge wagon train during the "Great Migration of 1843." William T. Newby, a founder of McMinnville, Oregon, recorded the event in his diary for August 4, 1843. According to him, there was a curious explosion at noon; first there was "something" which passed over the train which looked like a ball of fire which was followed by a long streak of blue smoke in zig-zag form "about 200 yards long." Then the report or explosion was heard. Another member of the wagon train, James W. Nesmith, noted in his diary for the same day that about 2 p. m., he heard a loud, sharp report which sounded like a piece of heavy artillery, after which there came a loud rumbling sound overhead.

Don't forget dues!
$3.50 per year.

Saucer . . .

(Continued from Page 1)

Sunday night approximately the same as the object of the Saturday evening sighting.

Also, on Sunday night, William Cooper and Alfred Tauss, both 16, were coaxed by Cooper's mother to tell police and the newspaper "The Record" about the object they had seen. The two boys were in the vicinity of the new junior-senior high school near the reservoir on Saturday evening, about 8, they said, when they saw a brilliant light (many times brighter than a star, they said) which moved quickly back and forth over the pines: "Like it was looking for something," Cooper said. They said they watched it dip behind the forest of pines rimming the reservoir. "Then we heard a loud bang, like a car door slamming, only louder," Cooper related.

After verification of the initial sighting on Saturday night, hopeful sighters began to collect at the reservoir. The newspaper reported in its Wednesday, 19 September issue, that Patrolmen Emil Rudloff and Eugene Troy said they were on Kinerkamack Road about 4 a. m. Tuesday (18th) morning when they saw a huge, object, round at the top and tapering into a cone. They said it was to the east of them, traveling very fast and only visible for 7 or 8 seconds. They described the object as bright yellowish-white. Oradell Patrolmen Martin Hanlon and Peter McHale said they saw a bright light in the sky at about 4:45 a. m. on Tuesday.

James Rafferty and Ernest Kuver, maintenance employees at the Record, reported seeing two brilliant white lights in the sky at about 5 a. m. Tuesday. The lights did not move, but suddenly disappeared in the east in a puff of smoke, they said. They told newsmen that two maintenance men at the City Incerator plant also saw the lights.

At 5 a. m. on Tuesday two milkmen reported a strange sight at Kohring Circle in Harrington Park. Robert Pega said he and a friend saw a tremendous beam of light high in the air at that time. Mrs. Robert Mischa of Westwood reported sighting a round, red object Saturday afternoon (the 15th).

Oradell Chief of Police George Brugnoli theorized that the boys only saw a bird on its way south, on Saturday night. He said birds with four-foot wing spans stop off at the reservoir every year on their way south.

The Newark Evening News for 24 September 1962, printed some additional facts: It seems that at 4:08 a. m. on the 24th, five Hawthorne policemen, one Passaic County Park policeman, a nightwatchman and a photographer, after keeping a lonely, cold and damp vigil all night, saw "the object come into view above the quarry," as it had several times previously.

The paper gave no description beyond that, except to go into the subject of an unsigned letter which read: "Our flying saucer was made of a balsa wood frame, filled with helium balloons for neutral buoyancy. Power was supplied by a radio controlled 1/8 horsepower model airplane motor with a variable pitch propeller. Please do not think that the boys that reported this were involved, because to them it was a flying saucer." The letter was signed, "The of Gergenfield."

A few observations: No sounds wer heard during any of the sightings. The descriptions of the objects purportedly seen do not fit that of the purported hoax.

Further, Sam Braen quarry was visited on the 20th, and again on the 21st (see articles, "Discs Illuminates Area" and "Object Seen Again Near Quarry," this issue.

About the letter: It appears too grammatical and pseudo-technical to be the work of youngsters. Also, for people who deliberately perpetrate a cruel hoax, it seems somewhat unfitting that they should be concerned about the people who were the victims. The type of individual who perpetrates such a hoax is quite likely to want to take name credit for all his efforts—these "pranksters" didn't.

"The Record" for 25 September notes that the boys "thank one and all for participating in the September 15 Flying Hoax Day." If these boys were responsible only for the 15th, who takes credit for the 16th (Sunday), the 18th (Tuesday) and the rest of the sightings, including the sighting at the Sam Braen Quarry? There is more to this than meets the eye, especially when we consider the other sightings of objects in the vicinity of water deposits during 1962. Those Bergenfield pranksters really get around, don't they? Was it real important for someone to disprove the sighting of the 15th in particular? Why?

Another Strange "Satellite"

Harvey B. Courtney, of Stratford, Conn., observed a steady but dim light which proceeded from south to north, and took about 10 to 15 seconds to travel 45 to 50 degrees of arc. No noise—atmosphere clear, bright moon.

On the morning of 20 July, 1962, at about 8:45 p.m., Miss Lita Ward of Cleveland, Ohio, was traveling east on Pleasant Valley Road (Independence, Ohio) when she sighted an elliptical-shaped object of a brilliant white color, in the northeast. It appeared to be a long way away and at a high altitude (Miss Ward compares it to a half dollar at arm's length which would make its size tremendous). She estimated the object was in her range of vision for about 3 minutes, during which time it was moving in a straight line at quite a rapid speed. Then it suddenly changed course and ascended vertically until it disappeared from view. When she first saw the object, she shut off the car radio and opened her windows to see if she could hear the object, but there was no emanating from it, to her knowledge.

Another Wandering "Star"

APRO Member Dorothy Lefler, of Cincinnati, Ohio, noticed what seemed to be a variable star that appeared to be really wandering around, at 8:50 p.m. on 24 April 1962. She stared hard at it, and it seemed to be moving. She used guide lines of telephone wires, trees and telephone pole. She called to her mother and was just explaining how such an illusion is caused by atmospheric refraction when she realized that it really had moved because it had crossed telephone wires. When it was first sighted, it was in the WNW and it traveled straight across the northern sky, heading NNE. She and her mother observed it for approximately 5 minutes. It appeared to bob only slightly but no doubt this was due to atmospheric refraction, she decided. She estimated it traveled approximately 160 degrees of arc during this time at 60 degrees elevation. She felt it was quite high, perhaps outside the atmosphere, but there was no way to estimate either size or distance. No sound, no trail, object was same apparent size as average star. Binoculars did not resolve the object.

Fireball Over Israel

A ball of fire described as a "blaze of colors" leaving a trail of smoke, passed over Israel in a north to south trajectory on the evening of 26 September 1962. Police sources in Jerusalem said the object was a small rocket from Jordan, another theory identified it as an American satellite launched in 1960. The satellite, however, was due over Israel in the late afternoon, about 4 p.m. The fireball showed up at between 5:30 and 5:45.

Yellow Light At Amboy, California

At 9:15 p. m., on August 16, 1962, Mr. and Mrs. L. J. Lorenzen of Tucson were driving west on Route 66 approaching Amboy, California, when Mrs. Lorenzen spotted a large, yellow light at about 15 degrees elevation in the west—apparently over Amboy. She called it to Mr. Lorenzen's attention and they proceeded to watch the object as they approached the small desert town. The object was occasionally obscured by buildings, etc. as they came into Amboy, but after they had passed through the town the yellow light was still very obvious in apparently the same position, but appearing to be larger, leading them to believe that they were nearing it or it was coming toward them slowly. After they had passed the last buildings of the town, they were startled to see the object blink out. It had been about four times the size of Venus at peak brilliance. Shortly, at about the same spot, the object suddenly appeared again. Until this time the Lorenzens had decided against stopping, not sure that the object wasn't a beacon of some sort, although no mountains were visible on the horizon. Then, after the first blink-out they noticed that there were cars stopped at intervals along the highway, the occupants on the shoulder of the road looking in the direction of the light. Once more within the space of just a few minutes, the light blinked out and on again. The final "blink-out" took place fifteen minutes after the Larenzens emerged from the western city limits of Amboy, at about 10:15 p. m. They continued to watch but the object did not appear. Several miles on they stopped at a small roadside lunch stand and queried the proprietor who verified their suspicion that there was no beacon in that vincity of that size or color.

Strange Light—N. Zealand

On the 22nd of July, 1962, J. Baker, transport operator and his wife and family were traveling to Greymouth (Westland Prov.) from Hokitika when they observed a bright green light, much larger than brightest star, which changed color at varying intervals. It appeared to emit sparks also. Baker called a reported at the Grey River Argus who accompanied him to Mawhera Quay and the object, now a brilliant green, was still visible low on the horizon. Nothing was being emitted though the object appeared to change color to yellow and then pale pink.

A press report from Auckland stated that Aucklanders, at 8:50 p.m., on the 22nd, saw a bright object over the city which came from the northeast. Mr. E. S. D. Luckens, of Hobsonville, said he saw pieces of red material or sparks flying off the object, which he said had the appearance of a meteor.

Colored Ball Over Dunedin, Hovers

On the 11th of July 1962 at 11:10 p. m., many residents of Dunedin, New Zealand, watched a vari-colored light flash over the city and appear to hover over the sea to the south. Although no time estimates were made by witnesses, it is apparent by the report that the object was evident in the sky for several seconds. The object apparently changed color, as there were different descriptions of color. Mr. B. A. A. Seesink of Waldronville said it was a blue ball preceded by a brilliant flash; Mr. Russell Clark of Canongate, sitting in his car at St. Clair beach, was startled when the water and were lit a strange light. light changed red and then to blue at regular intervals, he said, and persisted for several minutes. A Canongate woman saw it from her front gate and said it was a round yellowish ball with a blue tail traveling north to south and disappearing out to sea.

Clark observed the object as it hovered above the seashore before proceding out over the sea.

Twin Dumbells Seen In Wisconsin

At 8 p.m. on the evening of 18 July 1962, Mrs. Florence Cummins of Stanley, Wisconsin, observed two unusual objects with the aid of 7x35 binoculars. The objects were first seen with the naked eye and Mrs. Cummins thought it was a refueling operation. Through the glasses, however, the objects resembled dumbells with rather thick appearing heavy bars with bulging ends. Both objects were bright silver, clear and s o tline the rear object g owing red They were spotted in the south, disappeared in the southwest at about 20-30 degrees elevation. The flight was fast and level with no wavering or hesitating, no sound, trail or exhaust.

"Wronk-Way" Satellites

On the evenings of July 26, 27 and 28, Mr. and Mrs. E. Vaughan of Phoenix, Arizona, after watching earth satellites, also observed an unidentified object which appeared to be about the size of earth satellies, which proceeded from due south to due north, traversing the sky in about 5 minutes. The object, in each instance, on all three nights, were observed with th id of 7x50 Navy binoculars. On 28th, u an hour a ter thei observation of this unidentified object, they observed another similar object which came out of the north, (the direction into which the others had disappeared) and disappeared into the south. This observation supports others to us by ADC personnel in Colorado, concerning unusual satellites, as well as other data indicating that the UFO occupants are orbiti sa e ites.

Objects Over Washington State

The following is an excerpt from a letter from member Gene Thrune relating an experience occurring on the morning of March 19, 1962:

"I entered Ellensburg, Washington at 11:55 a.m. and was just tuning my car radio to receive the noon news broadcasts. I observed two objects which I assumed to be jet fighter planes. One was slightly behind the other and traveled at an extremely fast climb—leaving two distinct contrails—beginning from what I assumed to be Geiger Air Force Base (or Fairchild) at Spokane, Washington.

"The start of the contrails formed a "loose s" shape at the horizon and climbed at almost a 45 degree angle up into the sky. I couldn't make out the exact shape of the "planes" for I couldn't see any wings—but I could make out the two "objects." I pulled off to the side of the road and watched the contrails and objects for two full minutes—noting the time on my wrist watch. Suddenly, when the objects were directly overhead, THEY VANISHED MOVING TRAIGHT UP — and (this is the difficult part to believe)—the entire length of the two white contrails—all the way down to, but not including the "S" — VANISHED ALSO."

Thrune asked a service station operator nearby if he had seen them, but the fellow replied no, that he had just previously glanced up and noted the two contrails and when glancing up seconds later, "wondered where they went." Mr. Thrune watched the "S" part of the contrail for a distance of 38 miles to Yakima, Washington and it was still there when he arrived at Yakima.

Monitoring And Scanning UFOs

By C. W. Fitch
(Continued)

"It happened about a month ago when McGrady was visiting his brother at the McGrady homestead about nine miles out the Kittanning Road and off to the left a mile on a slag road.

At about 9 p.m., McGrady's brother called to McGrady from the front porch that "something funny" had gone past the porch. Asked what it looked like, the brother told McGrady it was "white."

"I just presumed it was an owl," Mc-Grady recalled today.

McGrady joined his brother on the porch and suddenly his brother pointed and exclaimed "there it is again." They both had plenty of time to get a good look because "it" made 25 or 30 trips in front of them during the next hour.

"I looked and saw it coming under a telephone wire. It was about fifteen feet from the ground and came within 20 or 25 feet of me," McGrady related. He continued: "It looked like a dishpan turned over and was not quite as big as a tub. It was kind of light gray and round. It had a light—a gray light in the front. The light wasn't bright like an electric or gas light.

"We could see it plainly. It passed under the telephone wire and under a tree by the porch. It made 25 or 30 trips in an area of about 200 feet and we watched it for over an hour.

"It kept the same elevation and went under the same wire each time, to a foot above the ground. It didn't make a bit of noise.

"There were pegs on top like on a battery in a car, six or eight little pegs. It was about 2½ feet in diameter and about eight inches thick.

McGrady said he went to a shanty near the house where he thought he would get something to throw at the flying saucer. He found a heavy bolt.

"I was waiting for it to come through again. Then something told me not to throw, and I didn't throw anything at it. I was afraid it might have gas in it or might explode."

He said he had read digests about flying saucers and "would say this is one." Asked how his vision is, McGrady said he only needs glasses for reading.

Finally "it seemed to disappear the last time it passed in mid-air."

McGrady said it was traveling so slowly "if you walked fast you could have kept up with it." Each circling trip took about 1½ minutes.

The brothers checked the tree near

where the machine passed the next day and found the leaves were dying, "like there had been a frost, but there was no frost."

"I'm pretty sure the smoke made the leaves die," McGrady explained. He said the smoke "rolled out" but not like it came from an exhaust. The smoke had no noticeable odor.

"It had no motor, or, if it did, it ran silently. I had never seen anything like it before and it kind of fit into what I've read. I don't know what else it could be. But I kept wondering why it would go around and around out there. It seemed to be lost." Unquote.

—o—

The writer drove to East Butler, Pa., and visited Charles McGrady in his home there. His verbatim account of his experience was a repetition of the news version of it, but it served to convince us of his sincerity as did viewing the dead catalpa tree in the grass-grown yard of the then abandoned farmhouse lend conviction as to the reality of his sighting.

Cases in which actual contact was made between the observer and small UFOs are indeed rare. In this category fall the Washington, D. C. incident, the David Lightfoot and Thomas Hutchinson experiences and the following occurrence which took place in October, 1959.

THE DAILY PRESS of Newport News Hampton, Virginia on Wednesday morning, October 21, 1959 printed the account of such a happening: "TENTH GRADER SEES SAUCER IN THE SKY."

POQUOSON—"It appeared in the sky amidst a loud, rushing wind noise and hovered about 100 feet over my head."

That's the way 15-year-old Mark George Muza, Jr., of 176 Ridge Road described his encounter with an unidentified flying object "just about dusk Monday."

"It was about four feet in diameter and had a black body encircled by a silver rim about six inches wide," the Poquoson tenth grader added.

"I stood petrified for several seconds and then raised my 12-gauge shotgun and poured two blasts into it. I knew I hit it both times but nothing happened so I loaded my gun with a shell which had a little more lead in it and shot at it again as it disappeared.

(Larry Bryant, investigating for the Air Research Group of Newport News, Va., interviewed Mark Muza at the boy's home on the evening of Oct. 21st. During the interview Muza related that he at first thought the sound he heard was coming from a flock of wild birds, but then he glanced up to see the thing

gently coming down—right toward his head. This frightened him and he fired a load of No. 4 shot at it, and heard the ring of metal striking metal. At the 55 foot level the object stopped in time to receive his second blast of "Maximum 4's; for his third and final shot, Muza used a steel bearing. After hearing the clear hit of the slug, Muza wiped his brow in relief. When he looked up again the object was gone.)

The episode took place just after sunset Monday while Muza and Harold Moore, Jr., 14, of 220 Ridge Road were hunting in the marsh near their homes.

Harold stated that his attention was called to the "queer looking thing with a silver rim around it" when Mark began shooting at it. He said he saw it for only a few seconds before it disappeared.

Mrs. Muza pointed out that her son came home very upset and told her he had shot at a flying saucer. "He's a pretty steady boy and I was surprised to find him so upset. He drew a picture to describe what he saw and the thing preyed on his mind all night long. He was still a very nervous boy when he went to school, Tuesday," she declared.

"I don't know what I saw and I don't claim it was a flying saucer. I would like for someone to tell me what it was as it was the most frightening experience of my life and something I won't get over for a long time," he said. Unquote.

—o—

Note: The above is the third one in which a UFO has been fired at and hit, the other two being the Washington, D. C. 1952 incident previously related and the Lloyd C. Booth sighting on the night of January 29, 1953 near Conway, South Carolina. THE STATE of Columbia, S. C. under the date of Sat., Feb. 7, 1953 printed a full account of this happening under the heading: "SC MAN TELLS OF STUDYING HOVERING FLYING SAUCER — SHOOTING INTO IT." In this instance Booth shot at the low flying saucer with his .22 caliber rifle and heard his bullet hit the object with a metallic sound, after which it took off at a high rate of speed. (See APRO Bulletin, March, 1953).

—o—

In a tape-recorded talk entitled "What We Are Doing in Ottawa" Mr. Wilbert B. Smith of that city relates an experience which he and two other members of his group had with a small disc. "We saw one of these little monitors doing exactly that trick." (This occurrence was cited as an illustration of his explanation of how flying saucers by in—

(See Monitoring, next page)

Monitoring

(Continued from Page 5)

creasing the tempic field in the vicinity of the saucer can cause _____ rays to bend around it thereby creating an optical illusi_____ o its actua size caus_____ smaller than it actually i) "We had very good reason to believe that a certain conversation we were having with a friend of mine was being monitored by one of these little fellows. So when we came out of the house we made a definite effort to locate it. We did. It was down in the ditch just in front of the house and as soon as we spotted it apparently the people who were controlling it became aware of the fact—as soon as we spotted it, we saw what appeared to be just like a heat wave— something about a foot in diameter and there popped out of the center of this what appeared to be a little disc about so big (approximately 4 to 6 inches) and it just took off like that and disappeared in the great blue yonder. I think the whole operation probably occurred in less than maybe two seconds, but we were looking right at it and there were three of us and we all saw the same thing, and knowing this trick about the fields we figured that was how it was done."

—o—

As an introduction to another phase of this phenomena we quote at some length from another talk by Mr. Wilbur B. Smith entitled "Why I Believe in the Reality of Spacecraft":

"There have been several close brushes with these objects and in one case at least the aircraft pilot lost his life as a consequence. (Captain Mantell was reported killed as a result of chasing a flying saucer on January 7, 1947. The incident is described in detail in THE REPORT ON UNIDENTIFIED FLYING OBJECTS by Edward J. Ruppelt, pages 51 to 60).

People who have been near these objects have described physical sensations which are unusual to say the least, but which are quite consistent with what is known of the technology under which they operate.

While the foregoing may seem rather incredible, nevertheless there exists quite good records in support of these occurrences. Furthermore, the technology of which we have been able to get a glimpse, namely that of the manipulation of the three basic fields, electric, magnetic and tem_ic, indica es qui e straight-forward answer to these phenomena. In Mantell's case the altered field configuration in the vicinity of the craft reduced the binding forces within the structural members of the aircraft to a value below that of the load which they were expected to carry, so they just came apart.

These altered binding forces have been measured by simple instruments by people in my group and have been found to be quite significant. Furthermore, there was probably a substantial reduction in tempic field intensity in the vicinity of the craft which Mantell approached, which would result in an effective rise in temperature of the aircraft and contents. I understand that Mantell's body gave every indication of having been subjected to considerable heat and not from the outside in.

A rise in temperature in the vicinity of these craft from elsewhere has been reported on many occasions, * as has also an apparent alteration in the direction of gravity. Both of these phenomena are tempic field functions and would be expected if the craft were making use of combinations of fields which involved substantial modifications of the tempic field function."

*Five such instances come to mind and will be mentioned at this point by way of confirmation and for readers' reference:

The Walesville, New York case of July 2, 1954. In this instance an F-94-C Starfire jet fighter was scrambled to investigate an unknown over Utica, New York. According to accounts of the occurrence contained in THE FLYING SAUCER CONSPIRACY by Major Donald E. Keyhoe, pages 174-175 and the C.R.I.F.O. NEWSLETTER of Oct. 1, 1954, page 5, published by Leonard H. Stringfiedl—as the jet approached the UFO, a wave of heat suddenly filled the cockpit and in a matter of seconds became so intense that the pilot and radar observer were forced to bail out. The jet crashed in the tiny village of Walesville killing four persons. According to Stringfield "The press handed the unsuspecting reader a front page story without the facts." That is, 'all' the facts, since the portion relating to the stifling heat being due to the jet getting too close to the UFO was omitted from the news version of the disaster.

Also related in THE FLYING SAUCER CONSPIRACY on Page 272 is another similar instance in which a French Air Force pilot was pursuing a flying saucer when "Suddenly a mysterious heat filled the cockpit." Though he was half-dazed the pilot was able to turn away from the object and escape the heat. He was sure that the heat was coming from the UFO but was unable to account for it.

The SULLIVAN (Indiana) DAILY TIMES of Monday, November 11, 1957 carried a headline "Ironworker Burned By 'Shiny Object',"—Condition Similar to Burns by Arc Welder." Rene Gilham of R. R. 1, Merom, Ind., a 33-year-old iron wor er suffered _____ ns which he said were inflicted by a "bright light in the sky." Gilham stood in the back yard of his farm home on Highway 63 and watched an extremely bright light that he estimated as being about 40 feet in diameter and 1000 feet overhead and which remained motionless for about 10 _____ be ore going straight up and hea ing west. Gilham said "It bathe his farm with an _____ ht _____ was so bri _____ loo a it or brief intervals at a time. Treated _____ of Friday morning, Nov. 8th, Gilham the physician that the facial burns began to bother him on Thursday following the lighted object's appearance the nigh before. Gilham's condition worsened Sa urday and he was admitted to the Sullivan County Hospital on Saturday where he remained until Tuesday when his condition had improved sufficiently to permit his release.

or of thi

casions and can ers all attest to the veracity of his ex erience.

A fourth instance of burns received from a low-hovering UFO is that of the two sentries in the Brazilian Fortress Itaipu attack case, first disclosed and related in detail in the APRO BULLETIN of September, 1959, in the article entitled TOP SECRET REPORT UNVEILED. See also Coral Lorenzen's book, "The Great Flying Saucer Hoax).

The APRO BULLETIN of November 1958 featured an article: MAN CLAIMS FACE BURNS FROM UAO. This was the Loch Raven bridge incident which took place at 11:30 p.m. on the evening of October 26, 1958. Philip Small and Al vin Cohen of Baltimore, Maryland, de scribed how they watched a "large, glowing, egg-shaped 'thing' floating over the dam" for a period of about a minute. Suddenly the object began to glow "intensely" and threw off a lot of heat. It then shot straight up into the air and a loud clap of thunder or sound was heard just before it went out of sight. Small said that he felt the heat of the object and that his face felt as though it was burned. When interviewed later, Mrs. Small said her husband's face was bright red and hot to the touch when he arrived home.

In the October, 1954, issue of the English publication URANUS on page 27 appeared the following account from an article by Jimmy Guieu.

(Continued next issue)

THE A.P.R.O. BULLETIN

The A. P. R. O. Bulletin is the official copyrighted publication of the Aerial Phenomena Research Organization (A.P.R.O.), 4145 E. Desert Place, Tucson, Arizona, and is issued every other month to members only. The Aerial Phenomena Research Orgazination is a non-profit group dedicated to the eventual solution of the mystery of the unidentified objects which have been present in the skies for hundreds of years. Inquiries regarding membership may be made to the above address.

TUCSON, ARIZONA — JULY, 1963

SAUCER PANICS CATTLE

"Meteor" Panics Baseball Crowd

Another one of those huge, phenom-enal, several-second meteors scared the daylights out of players and spectators alike at a baseball game at Vancouver, B. C., Canada, on May 28, 1962. Descrip-tions indicated that this beauty had an angular displacement of at least 10 de-grees, traversed a 30 degree area of the sky in 5 seconds. Fans in the third base bleachers at Capilano Stadium were the first to spot the object during the 12th inning. They cried out in panic, players looked up from the diamond, then ran for the dugout along with the umpires. The object was huge, and glowed with a brilliance like a magnesium flare. A control tower employee at Vancouver International Airport said it was "as big as an aircraft hangar."

Reports to police switchboards describ-ed an off-course rocket, a comet or a flaming airplane. The object was seen in Vancouver, Victoria, Calgary, Fort Assiniboine, (Alta.), Spokane and Lew-iston, Idaho.

Research scientist Frank Hughes of nearby North Surry said he had observ-ed 200 meteors, and this was the largest he had ever seen. Dr. R. M. Petrie, head of the Dominion Astrophysical Observa-tory at Victoria said the descriptions "applied to meteors" (quotes ours), that it must have been a big one. "A meteor is usually seen for just a second or two. This one would have to be huge to have been visible for so long or it would have burned itself out more quickly," he said.

Some observations: There has been an increase in the observation of these unusually large, brilliant meteors in 1962, coincidental with the appearance of larger number of saucer and cigar-shaped aerial phenomena. Some curious things about the giant fireballs: Very brilliant, large, low, sometimes emitting flashes of blinding light (see recent bulletins) they are seen over very large areas, they make no noise except an oc-casional thunderous crash, and are never observed to crash.

Barometers React To "Meteor"

A mysterious bright object flashed across the western sky in Western Wash-ington state at 10:45 p. m. on 31 July 1962. The Weather Bureau said the ob-ject apparently caused pressure changes similar to those noted after large nuc-clear explosions. Observers said the ob-ject "looked like a jet," but didn't sound like one—it made no sound at all, and was going much too fast. Needles re-cording barometric pressure "jumped" in Seattle, Olympia and Toledo. It was not immediately determined whether or not the change was a rise or a fall in pressure.

The object, first seen in the southwest sky, disappeared in the northeast. It moved horizontally about 35 degrees above the western horizon, and appeared to be disintegrating, with pieces drop-ping off. Then it flared up even brighter and seemed to die out.

A Tacoma woman who saw the object said it was quite large, had no tail, was the color of the sun and about "half the size of a soccer ball."

At McChord AFB, tower observers said they didn't see the object. Robert Grib-ble, of National Investigations Commis-sion on Aerial Phenomena feels the ob-ject was not a meteor due to its hori-zontal flight path, and duration of his observation, which was 20 seconds. His conclusion seems to be reasonable.

Saucer Lands In Italy

In the early hours of the 18th of De-cember, 1962, a watchman on duty in the courtyard of a suburban factory in Milan, Italy, reported to police that he had seen a "3-foot, 4-inch man climb out of a "flying saucer" after it landed in the courtyard. The little creature beck-oned to the watchman, then another small man gestured the first one back into the ship which took off. Police frowned upon the report, but launched an official investigation. More will be printed on this incident when more de-tails are received.

From Peter Norris comes the follow-ing information gleaned from "The Sun": Dairy farmer Mr. Charlie Brew of Ole Sale Road, Willow Grove, northwest of Moe, Australia, has reported that a "thick disc" frightened a horse and his cow herd on 16 February 1963. The disc, "battleship grey" in color, appeared to have a band of glass or plastic around the circumference and number of pro-trusions which looked like scoops, ac-cording to Brew.

Mr. Brew and his son Trevor were milking the cows at shortly after 7 a. m. on the morning of the 16th. It was rain-ing heavily at the time. Brew looked out of the cow shed, saw the object coming down in a fairly steep but slow descent. Brew said he thought it was going to land when it reached an approximate altitude of 75 to 100 feet. Suddenly, how-ever, it shot off in a westerly direction at what seemed to be about two or three times the speed of a jet, then it dis-appeared into a cloud.

Trevor did not see the object, Brew reported, but he did hear the "pulsat-ing, whooshing" sound it made as it re-volved overhead. "The cows turned som-ersaults and the horse reared up in panic," Mr. Brew said. "The whole visit last only a matter of seconds."

Brew admitted that he had often scoff-ed at reports of UFO, but swears the thing he saw was real. If more informa-tion comes in as a result of Mr. Norris' investigation, it will be printed in this or a forthcoming issue.

Saucer At Sheffield Reservoirs

Until August 19, cutlery worker Wal-ter Revill of Sheffield, England, had be-lieved flying saucers were "rubbish," and didn't mind saying so. On that date, however, he changed his mind. He and a friend, Mrs. Teresa Spotswood had been out, and when they returned to Mrs. Spotswood's home, Mrs. S. opened the back door because it was warm inside. She started outside in amazement, then called Revill. Together, for about 15 minutes they watched a bright orange

(See Sheffield, Page 3)

The A. P. R. O. BULLETIN

Published by
THE AERIAL PHENOMENA RESEARCH
ORGANIZATION
4145 E. Desert Place
Tucson, Arizona

Copyright 1963, Coral E. Lorenzen

Editor and Director

Information appearing in this bulletin may be used by other UAO research periodicals providing names and address credit is properly given to this organization and periodical.

Coral E. Lorenzen ..... International Director and Editor
A. E. Brown, B.S.E.E. .... Director of Research
L. J. Lorenzen .... Director of Public Relations
John T. Hopf .... Photographic Consultant
Oliver Dean .... Photographic Consultant

SPECIAL REPRESENTATIVES

(The following listed individuals participate in planning and policy-making as Staff Members, in addition to coordinating investigative efforts in the areas indicated following their names.)

Dr. Olavo T. Fontes, M.D. .... Brazil
K. Gosta Rehn .... Sweden
Graham Conway ...... Eastern Canada
Aime Michel .... France
Horacio Gonzales Gauteaume
                                Venezuela
Peter E. Norris, L.L.D. ...... Australia
Jun' Ichi Takanashi .... Japan
Juan C. Remonda .... Argentina
Sergio Robba .... Italy
Arist. Mitropoulos .... Greece
Rev. N. C. G. Cruttwell, New Guinea
Eduardo Buelte .... Spain
Norman Alford .... New Zealand
Austin Byrne .... Ireland

SPECIAL CONSULTANT
Prof. Charles Maney,—Physics

ALAMOGORDO PRINTING CO., INC.

In Argentina

The 1962 "flap" seemed to have officially opened with the January sighting of a UFO at such close quarters that details were easily observed. (See recent issue of the Bulletin). However, the interesting Argentinian series of sighting seemed to get under way with a vengeance in May. The following reports came to APRO via our Argentinian representative Juan Remonda as well as our ex-representative in that country, Bernard Passion, who now resides in Los Angeles, U.S.A.

On the 12th of May 1962, at between 4 and 4:40 a. m., residents of Cordoba, Argentina saw a strange object plowing through the atmosphere. It traveled at high speed. News reports were skimpy, but Mr. Remonda forwarded the following: Two young ladies, Yolanda and Miriam Curas, of Cordoba, driving from Rosario to Cordoba, in the area of Oncativo, saw a great thick fog which covered the road. They were forced to travel with the car in low gear to prevent a collision. Before encountering the fog, however, they had observed an elongat-

ed, brilliant object with streaks of green, red and yellow, cross the road at high speed ahead of them. Then they encountered the fog. When they observed, later on, the strange object sitting beside the road and partially hidden by bushes, they notitced that the fog was considerably decreased. The object was described as a "reddish hut-shaped thing." Windows or portholes were evident.

Both of the young ladies said nothing until they read in the newspapers that others in the area had observed unexplainable objects in the samemorning.

The next report came from Chumbica, Catamarca, where, approximately 30 minutes after the Cordoba sighting, a number of people waiting for a bus from the Cadol Line which provides passenger service between Cordoba and Catamarca, saw a luminous body which followed a horizontal line of light at a very low altitude. It appeared to throw out bright white and blue streaks behind, and was so bright it illuminated the ground beneath it. Observers said the object "turned the night into day with its brilliance." The object disappeared over the horizon and later, when the bus and other passengers arrfived, they told of the strange object they had seen at about 4:40 in the vicinity of Carranza. This corresponds with the direction of disappearance of the object seen by the observers at Catmarca.

Early in the morning of the next day (Sunday 13 May), in the region of Mayor Buratovich, Senor Rene Ottavianelli, his wife and a relative observed two shining "dots" flying parallel close paths and emitting a bright orange light. The objects traveled at very high speed toward the southwest. The observation was corroborated by many others in nearby areas.

A resident of La Barrera, about 15 kilometers from La Rioja informed correspondents for "La Nacion" that he saw an object surrounded by a brilliant halo of yellow and red light which moved speedily into the west at a constant altitude. The claims of the observer, Senor Raul Diaz were corroborated by hunters in the same area.

In Ameghnio, Dr. Jorge M. Vallina and companions reported seeing a shiny, phosphorescent green object with a tail the "color of fire." Upon nearing the object, the witnesses observed that there were four or five slightly elongated balls which, when seen together, gave the appearance of a cigar-shaped object. The object was low and traveled from Northwest to Southeast.

The Villa Harding Green airport was the setting of another sighting 5 days

later, on the 18th of May. Personnel at the airport saw a small, reddish object of high luminosity moving in a horizontal path over the landing field during the early morning hours. The object resembled a saucer, and moved with great speed. Its altitude was so low that tongues of flame could easily be seen coming from the object. After flying over the field for a brief time, the object disappeared over the bay.

After the above described sightings aroused public and press interest, a special commission to study the information was set up and on the 24th of May the arrival of said commission was expected at the naval base of Puerto Belgrano.

With a group of newsmen and witnesses of former sightings, Captain Luis Sanchez Moreno of Naval Intelligence went to Kilometer marker No. 72 on route 35, the road to La Pampa, to examine the site of an incident involving several truck drivers. Drivers Valentin Tomasini, Guaro Tomasini and Humberto Zenobi told their story:

At about 4:10 a. m. on the morning of the 12th of May they saw what appeared to be a brightly lighted railroad car about 100 meters away from the highway. As they came closer to the object it moved and flew at low altitude across the highway about 70 meters ahead of the lead truck. The lights on the object, which they estimated to be 20 or 30, flickered, and shortly after it crossed the road the lights went out.

Then a red flash about 1.29 m by 50 cm shot out and the vehicle rose from the ground. After it took off, they noted that it was actually two objects which separated and flew off in different directions until they disappeared into the distance.

The duration of the landing was approximately one minute, and the lights seemed to come from about 20 little windows in the vehicle. A hum was heard which the witnesses compared to the dial tone of a telephone.

The drivers continued on their route and when they came back they stopped to inspect the spot. They were surprised to find a number of damp, greyish stains. Samples of the earth were taken later in May for analysis at Puerto Belgrano. Captain Sanchez Moreno, Chief of Intelligence at the Puerto Belgrano Naval Base, stated that the Navy had been concerned with the UFO phenomena since 1952, also he had had occasion, with two others, to observe unidentified objects. He said, "Logically it (his sighting) was not a matter of stars or planets but of mobile bodies with incred-

(See "Argentina", Page 4)

Sheffield . . .

(Continued from Page 1)

object "shaped like two soup plates, one upside down over the other." The main part of it was somehow translucent and the rim glowed even more brightly. After watching a while, Revill went inside for his camera. The object had begun to move away rapidly and by the time he could photograph it, it was just a fast-vanishing point of light. But it showed up on his film.

Mrs. Spotswood, meanwhile, called two neighbors, Mr. and Mrs. Tony Pellegrina, who both saw the object and confirmed Reevill's description.

The Sheffield area is the site of many reservoirs.

On the 28th of August, John Needham, a butcher who lives in Upper Whiston, a few miles from Sheffield, stepped into his garden to look at the weather. Directly above him he saw an object "like two soup bowls with their rims together" which was glowing with a bright blue light. Round its rim, a series of what looked like tennis balls, were evident. "It was bigger than the moon," said Mr. Needham. As he watched, it soared away and became quite small. He went inside and called the Sheffield Telegraph, and shortly two reporters and a photographer arrived. They were Sheila MacGregor, Christine Cartwright and Keith Graves, all of whom saw something . . . a bright light, high in the sky. According to Miss Cartwright, the light was much too large to be a star, and appeared much larger than visible astronomical bodies. "It seemed to move like a yacht tacking," she said. They looked at the light through a naval telescope and binoculars, and had the firm impression that its outer rim was brilliant and consisted of a series of straight edges like a threepenny piece.

Rancher Sees Hovering Object

A. T. Gray, dairy rancher in the Capay district near Orland, California, reported to the Sheriff's department that he had seen a strange saucer-shaped object hovering over an alfalfa field in September of 1962. The article containing the information was written by Chal Green in the Enterprise-Record, but the exact date of the paper and the name of same was not included by the sender. We would appreciate this information.

Gray reported that he went to the field to shut off pump irrigation as a favor to a friend, John Gilmore, the owner. As he arrived, between 9:45 and 10 p. m., he saw the lights, thought it was a car parked there. As he drove into the field he discovered the object was not a car, but an object about 20 feet in the air. It had two lights, one on each side which seemed to be shining on the ground. It made no noise.

Gray had difficulty seeing the object's shape, but said it was oblong in shape, "it's edges blunt-shaped." The lights seemed to protrude from the main body. Gray moved toward the object, got within 50 yards of it when it moved toward him, skimming the ground, then it zipped off into the southwest. In three or four seconds it was out of sight. Then it came back again, finally veering off east toward Chico.

The object, while hovering, was occasionally silhouetted by lightning behind it, and Gray said it was an eerie sight. He said it was extremely fast, and didn't resemble anything he had ever seen. He further commented that the only noise was a "swishing sound." Note that the object was in the vicinity of a pumping apparatus and irrigation ditches.

Another "Mother" Ship?

On the 26th of August 1962 at 12:30 a.m., APRO member Walter T. Jones, Jr., of Philadelphia, Pa., observed a light in the west traveling on a north-south course. He first thought the glowing object was Echo, but noticed a dip in its course at regular intervals. The following is the remainder of his report, word-for-word:

"It increased in size as it came directly ahead of us, until it was several times the size of the planet Venus. As it became larger it was increasingly brighter, and when it remained motionless in the sky, I knew Echo had nothing to do with it. Fortunately, I had my binoculars with me. It hovered at such a distance I couldn't give you a more detailed description than already mentioned, except several smaller, bright round objects appeared beside the large one. This was noticed by my mother, Mrs. Jones, without the use of binoculars.

"The large object disappeared, and from the same area came a row of six of the smaller orbs, with one bright green light following in what I would call an imaginary triangle. This group came directly our way, and passed over our house as low as perhaps several hundred feet. I had the impression they were no higher than a plane would fly when we consider it to be flying very low. The formation headed east, and I saw all of the objects clearly—the six in front, followed by one bright, glowing green light, and nothing in between, or connecting them. It was a completely silent operation, and the entire incident took no more than three or four minutes."

Green Flash Over Cincinnati

On May 3, 1962, at 8 p.m. a bright greenish-white flash spread across the southern Cincinnati sky. Reports generally agreed its light was visible for three to 10 seconds, that the object or light had a luminous tail and traveled horizontally toward the southwest. The object, described by witnesses as "rocket-shaped," "a soft blue puff," huge in front, skinny at the end" and "a huge ball of fire with a tail, sort of greenish," or "no particular shape," was at an elevation of 30 degrees in the south, traveling from southeast to southwest. Although the object was explained as a possible "meteor," the Cincinnati Enquirer noted that no one had a ready explanation at the time of the sighting. Reports also came from Wheeling, W. Va., and Columbus and Dayton, Ohio airports also received reports.

Antarctica Sightings Corroborated

Thirteen-year-old newspaper boy, Mark Channing of Dalrymple Street, Invarcargill, N. Z., reported seeing a cluster of three lights at 7:05 p.m. on 7 July 1962. (See APRO Bulletin for May 1962, Page 3, and correct sighting date to 7 July instead of 9 as stated). The boy reported that he and a friend were standing outside on a street when the object traversed the northern sector of the sky, from west to east. It traveled fast, being in sight no more than 3 minutes and appeared to be losing altitude as it traveled eastward. Mark said the object appeared to be three separate white lights that flashed on and off, the center light being brighter than the others.

A South Hillend farmer who declines to be identified, reported seeing a strange sky object at 4:55 p.m. on the same day. The object he reported was traveling into the southeast, was egg-shaped and bright green in color. It appeared to be at low altitude and released a shower of sparks, of orange and green as it passed over the Wyndam district. The observer did not believe he saw the same object as seen at Antarctica but did forward his information to Mr. Taylor of Hallett Station.

Argentina

(Continued from Page 2)

ible speed and irregularity of movement."

Captain Moreno went on to further elucidate concerning a sighting in his official files which documents the experiences of four people who were traveling in a car on May 12th at 4:30 a. m. when they saw three luminous objects at very close range and very clearly. The witnesses, Captain Moreno said, claimed that the objects followed close to the car for a distance and gave off such a bright light that the passengers could see each other in the car as well as they could have in full sunlight. One of them had to have treatment for an injured retina, thought to be a result of the intense light from the object. The men watched one of the objects fly over the horizon and back, slanting as it cleared a grove of trees, indicating that it was very low in altitude.

At the same time as Captain Moreno's interview with the press, Rear Admiral Eladio M. Vasquez, and Captain Aldo Molinari, second in command of the naval district, revealed that they were at the U. S. Military Mission in Espora on the 11th at 1940 hours (7:40 p. m.) when they saw a "flying saucer"—probably the one photographed by the "La Neuva Provincia" photographer. The photo was published in "La Razon," and APRO has a copy, but it shows only a somewhat flattened globe of light with no details.

The May 1962 issue of the APRO Bulletin carried a short article on page 5 concerning the sighting of a UFO and robot-like occupant. At this date we have the following additional information: The wife of a well-known and respected rancher in the Speluzzi, Vertiz area, saw a landed unconventional aerial object from which came a robot-like creature. It carefully explored the area around the craft, then suddenly apparently became aware of the woman watching, re-entered the object after which the craft ascended into the sky and disappeared toward the north. The woman, in shock, ran crying to her husband. She eventually had to be hospitalized for shock. However, her husband arrived in time to see the object take off. He and others approached the place where the object had rested and found a round area of burned grass. No date was given, nor time of day of the appearance, but "authorities" and neighbors confirmed the fact that the UFO was there, and that the grass had been burned. The object appeared during the "rest" hours, which is probably between 12 and 3 p. m.

Scores of witnesses were cross-examined concerning what they had seen during the night of May 14, 1962, in the near vicinity of the Puerta Belgrano Naval Base. Little or nothing is known about this specific case, but the Navy seemed to be somewhat agitated about the incidents. It is interesting to speculate whether the upset might have been caused by incidents similar to the Texas Army camp affair and the Itaipu Fortress incident (Brazil) in 1957.

A third-hand case forwarded by Bernard Passion from his friend Mr. Echinique, involves the May or possibly June sighting (no exact date) of a saucer landing by four people. The people (4) were traveling in a pickup truck bound for a town in Juyjuy, and ran out of gas. They pulled up alongside the road and waited for a car to come along so they could go for help. It was 4 a. m. and drizzling rain. Suddenly they saw a bright light coming up the road in their direction. At first they thought it was another car but then realized it was not when it was about 200 yards away. It veered off the road, shot up into the air, "lighting the area as if it were daylight." Then it landed. The object was round in shape, very luminous, and blinked its lights on and off several times. It remained on the ground for about an hour. After that, it took off and disappeared into the distance at high speed.

In "La Opinion," a Spanish language paper published in Los Angeles, a sighting appeared in the August 4 issue. From Entre Rios Province, Argentina, came a report that a flying saucer landed on a road near Parana. Out of it came human-like beings over 6 feet tall, fair-haired with very large eyes. The sighting was reported by Dr. Gazua, of Parana, who was traveling in his car with his wife on their they way to Goya City.

Dr. Gazua said that he was driving when he spotted the luminous object about 10 yards from his car. The beings then came out of it and signaled him to stop. When he overcame his surprise, he sped off. His wife was shocked at the incident but was soon well.

The same article stated that a truck driver who was also driving along the road, claimed he saw three beings whose shape he could not tell.

Another report, this time possibly in June, was reported in the June 4 issue of La Voz Del Interior: Dr. Felix Di Pinto and his companions, Pablo Chiavassa, Doctor Raul Oliva Otero, Angel Slinsky and Castaneda and Engineer Carlos Alberto Carena, were out on Dike of the River, Los Molinos, Cordoba, along with approximately 40 others when two brilliant blue objects flew overhead. They

were first attracted by the reflection and upon looking up they saw two shiny blue spheres which left a blue "wake" or "trail." They came out of the west at a relatively slow speed, about 500 KM per hour. They were observed to change color as they passed over and disappeared.

Although La Voz Del Interior gave no date, La Razon of Cordoba, in its 15 May issue, stated that several residents of Cordoba observed a strange object "plowing through the air" at about 4 to 4:30 a. m. "It traveled at high speed in the direction of the dike of Los Molinos and then disappeared," it said. There is only one object in this instance, but the coincidence of the early morning hour and the Los Molinas dike indicate that it may have been the same sighting of at least one of the objects.

—o—

The above concludes the somewhat skimpy information gleaned from South American reports. Besides difficulties with translations, we have the problem of obtaining information. Richard Hall of NICAP was kind enough to furnish the copies of clippings they had obtained, but unfortunately the information was almost a complete duplication of what APRO had gathered. If further information is obtained on these sightings, we will feature it in a future issue.

Seattle—Another Fire Ball

On May 19, 1962 at 9:15 hundreds of Seattle, Washington residents were startled by the swift passage of a huge yellow ball of fire which appeared to burn out in the atmosphere. Reports of observations came from various points in Oregon, California and Washington. It was generally believed to have crashed near seattle, but reports that it was seen west of glamath Falls, Oregon and northwest of Red Bluff, Calif., placed the object over the Pacific Ocean when it either burned out, continued through the atmosphere, or crashed into the sea. Two hours after the spectacular sight, many people in Seattle reported another strange object, a bright light, moving from west to east. The Seattle Post Intelligencer, in the May 29 issue, said that there was speculation that the second mysterious object which "appeared about the size of the U.S. Balloon satellite Echo I, may have been the same one first spotted yesterday at Jupiter, Fla." According to UPI, the article continued, the Smithsonian Astrophysical Observatory in Cambridge, Mass., later sent out a request that satellite tracking stations around the world help follow a "suspected (and) unpredicted bright satellite."

Monitoring and Scanning UFOs

By C. W. Fitch
(Continued)

"On Saturday, July 17, on the road to Istres, a textile merchant and his wife were cruising along in their little van at some 100 k.m. an hour. All at once the driver noticed at a slight distance from the windshield, a strange bluish light. Theen everything happened in a flash!

Did the bluish light reach the windshield, or did it emanate from it, immediately preceding the invident proper? Impossible to say. The fact is, that after the appearance of this mysterious light the windshield flew into splinters. The driver braked hard and stopped. At the same time as the windshield spintered, a strange whitish mist, an impalable but sharply defined cloud, formed in the van. The driver's wife felt an inexplicable heat envelope her bust. A kind of uniform pressure pressed her nylon blouse to her skin; we must emphasize that neither the wind nor the surrounding warm air had any part in this phenomenon.

Imagine this business lady's astonishment on discovering, immediately after experiencing this strange sensation, that her white nylon blouse had become straw yellow." (For another example of color change, see March 1962 APRO Bulleting story, "Saucer Blocked Road in Norway).

The CHICAGO SUN-TIMES of August 19, 1960 carried an item "Blue Lights in the Night Add to Meteorite Mystery."

"Consider the hair-raising experience of four occupants of an auto southbound on Illinois 49 during the early-morning hours of July 2.

Dave Darnell, 58, of 1745 N. Drake, a punch-press operator, was driving. Next to him was his wife Alean, 49. In the back seat, sleeping, were the Darnells' daughter, Mrs. Nell Braddy, 20, and son-in-law, Jerry Braddy, 22, both of the Drake address.

The family was Tennessee-bound. Nothing out of the ordinary occurred until they were about two hours' journey south of Kankakee.

And then, as Mrs. Darnell tells it:

"The sky lit up with a beautiful blue light. It began in the south and got brighter and brighter until the whole earth was bathed in a light that was bright as the moon, and then bright as the sun. It was so bright you could see to pick a pin off the highway.

An object like a ball of fire came out of the south and passed right over our car with a tail like a streak of blue lightning behind it. We speeded up because we were afraid and the car got so hot we could hardly breathe. It woke up my daughter and her husband in the back seat. They actually woke up 'fighting for air.' Then gradually the light faded and the thing in the sky went away in the north." Unquote.

Another strange and frightening experience appeared in THE EAGLE BEND NEWS of Thursday, May 25, 1961, under the heading: "What Was It? A Phenomenon?"

A strange, frightening phenomenon was witnessed a week ago Wednesday evening, May 10th, by Richard Vogt, who resides south of Eagle Bend. The incident, which as yet has University of Minnesota scientists baffled, occurred on the aforementioned evening at about 11:30 p. m. about one and one-half miles south of Osakis, Minnesota.

In an interview with the individual involved, the News learned that Richard Vogt was enroute home from a business trip which had taken him several miles south of Osakis. When enroute to his home Vogt noted what he described as a ball of fog approximately three feet ni diameter, and somewhat elongated, descending toward him from a perfectly clear sky at about a forty-five degree angle. It approached with such rapidity that Vogt was unable to take any evasive action and the mysterious object struck the automobile on the upper section of the hood and windshield. The sound of the impact of the strange matter with the vehicle Vogt describes as he imagines it would sound if driving at a high rate of speed into a thrown shovel full of fine gravel.

A tremendous amount of heat was generated and the interior of the vehicle was heated almost instantaneously to a near unbearable heat, and the windshield which received the full impact of the "fog mass" was extremely hot to the touch. It was so hot, in fact, that to have held the hand in contact with the glass for more than a very brief moment would have resulted in a burn.

Mr. Vogt was so startled by the unusual happening that at first he envisioned an atomic blast, a disintegating rocket or nose cone, or perhaps even some other newer and more deadly weapon as the result of scientific research. He admitted having felt very uncomfortable as a result of his experience.

As proof of his harrowing experience, Mr. Vogt has his Chevrolet automobile. The pit marks which were burned into the windshield, the circular cracks in the glass which resulted from the intense heat, and the burned specks in the finish of the hood, are all there to corroborate his story.

This strange phenomena has been reported to the University of Minnesota scientists and one, W. J. Luyten, after discussing it with several colleagues, seems to have no definite answer as yet. His personal feeling is that it might have been either a collection of small meteorites, surrounded by some gas produced when they came through the atmosphere or that it was what is sometimes called "ball lightning." This latter is, however, usually a very dangerous affair, and if it hits anything such as the windshield of a car, the object that is struck usually disintegrates.

The matter has been referred to other colleagues of the University scientist who are more informed on matters such as this, and will be evaluated to a greater degree."

—o—

Consideration of the foregoing cases which offer evidence of the validity of Mr. Wilbur Smith's statement that "A rise in temperature in the vicinity of these craft from elsewhere has been reported on many occasions," serves to prepare one for the possibility that a UFO could conceivably have been the unknown factor involved in the following tragedy.

THE PIKE COUNTY NEWS of Pikeville, Ky., on November 23, 1960, carried the headline "Foul Play Theory Out in Deaths of 5 in Burned Vehicle."

"Foul play has been ruled out in the deaths of five Greasy Creek residents whose bodies, charred beyond recognition, were found about 8 a. m. Sunday in a burned automobile on the right fork of Grassy Creek.

County Attorney John Paul Runyon said autopsies performed on two of the bodies have ruled out the possibility of foul play.

The five bodies were identified as those of four men and a youth.

The bodies were seated in an upright position and they had not been pinned in. The right front door of the vehicle was open and blood was found near the car. Only fire damage to the vehicle was reported. The car appeared to have been driven off the side of the road into a shallow creek.

The autopsy report on the two bodies were returned yesterday and indicated that the two were definitely alive when fire began consuming the automobile. "Quite a bit" of carbon monoxide was present in the bodies, and the exact percentage will be reported later.

Dr. Frank Cleveland of Cincinnati's Kettering Laboratory examined two of

(See Monitoring, Page 6)

Monitoring

(Continued from Page 5)

the bodies yesterday and said death was caused by fire fracture or internal heat.

Runyon said the presence of blood near the car remains to be explained, and added "The investigation will continue in order to explain what is evidently an accidental death." Unquote.

(Additional factors included in the coroner's report, and recorded at APRO headquarters indicate the presence of a heat source from above the car. See APRO Bulletin, July, 1963. The Editor).

Individual experiences with night-flying balls of light have found their way into the news on a number of occasions.

The LONDON FREE PRESS of Dec. 2, 1957 reported the following incident:

"Mrs. Gerald Alderman has had a weird, almost eerie encounter with an UFO. The incident took place Friday, the night of November 29, 1957. She described the object in detail.

It was within 75 feet of her car. "It was a little thing, a round ball about six to eight inches in diameter and aglow with a fiercely bright white light. It had a 'tail' of light two or three feet long, and it was spinning as it moved in an orbit twenty or thirty feet across."

Mrs. Alderman was driving the family car on No. 80 highway, about two miles north of Glencoe shortly after 5 p. m., when she saw the object first, "quite high in the sky." It dropped fast she said, cleared the highway and fences and hovered about a foot above the road just ahead of her car. It was within range of the car headlights set on dim. It paused a few minutes, then shot away at extreme speed, angling upward. "It looked like a star, but much bigger and brighter," she said. Unquote. Credit: THE VISITOR, Vol. II, No. 1, Nov. Dec., 1957.

Comparison is made to a somewhat similar sighting which appeared in the August, 1962 issue of SPACE, published by Norbert F. Gariety of Coral Gables, Florida. The incident is described under the heading "UFO THROWS TELEVISION SET OUT OF KILTER IN JERSEY.

"The TV set was acting up all night. Then about 11 p. m., it got very bad," Mrs. Jessie Bilancio of Homestead Ave., Bordentown, Township, explained.

Investigating the cause of the disturbance, the woman walked out into the rear yard and there "off to my right—about the size of my fist—was a very bright object." It was last Friday (June 1, 1962) evening when the UFO apparently touched off the electrical disturbance in Mrs. Bilancio's TV set.

"It didn't reflect light," the woman explained the strange sighting. "It—the light—hovered in the top of a tree in my yard less than 30 feet above me. Then it moved to the lower limbs, something like a firefly. "I first thought it was a spotlight," she continued, "but then when it moved from branch to branch and finally flashed away into the sky, I realized it was something that was giving off its own light." Mrs. Bilancio said it all happened so fast she did not have time to become frightened.

"When I told my husband about it inside the house, he started kidding me," she added." Unquote.

—o—

Incidents in which small UFOs or lights have followed or 'pursued' cars are also on record. (If APRO readers know of other such cases we would like to hear from you about them.)

The following experiences are typical: THE LAMPASAS (Texas) RECORD, Thursday, Jan. 29, 1959.

"Lampasas Couple 'Victims' of Mysterious, Fast-Flying Lights."

"Unidentified Flying Objects!"

Ghost Lights!

"You may not believe in them but you would have a hard time convincing Mr. and Mrs. Franklin Richardson that they don't exist.

The Richardsons say they have been 'victims' of fast-flying lights for about the past six weeks, always in the same general area and the same general time (12:30 to 2:30 a. m. on Sunday mornings).

Latest episode with the lights ended with a wrecked automobile and cuts and bruises suffered by Mrs. Richardson Saturday night after the lights "chased" them a short distance.

It all began the Saturday before Christmas when the youthful couple were headlight-hunting rabbits about 10 miles north of Lampasas on the Spivey-Tapp Road, close to School Creek, the couple related.

That night they spotted six, blue-white lights, approximately four times the size of a headlight on a car, hanging about 75 feet in the air. The lights were about a quarter of a mile from the road, Richardson said, and in brushy country.

"We didn't pay much attention to them," Franklin said, "but after noticing them for a while, they began moving around so that sometimes they looked like a string up and down, sometimes they would blend into one light and sometimes they would dance crazily without pattern."

"The lights would jump and race and blink off and on," said Mrs. Richardson. "We watched them for a while and suddently two of them broke loose from the rest and approached us very rapidly," she stated.

"They came within about 150 feet of our car and then stopped and sank slowly into the ground. Shortly afterwards, two lights came up through a pasture, skimming the tree tops and although they were out of range of a .22 rifle, they lit up the interior of the car," Mrs. Richardson state.

Each of the nights several boys and girls from the high school have gone to the hills east of the city to watch them. Tuesday night there were between 30 and 40 boys and girls watching them. Jim Tichenor who has been watching them each night said they looked to be about 18 inches in diameter. They swooped down over the city, from the hills in the east and from the hills in the west from Iowa. Sometimes they just miss each other. They show a white light."

On subsequent trips, the couple said, they saw lights coming out of the ground and sinking back into the earth.

"Peculiarly enough, we would only see the lights on Saturday night and between 12:30 and 2:30 in the morning—always on clear nights."

Saturday night, January 24, the Richardsons pulled up and parked on the roadway purposely to see if they could spot the lights again.

"We hadn't been there but just a few minutes when we soptted a huge light about 20 miles north and to the east of us. The light hopscotched across the mountain and in nothing flat it was directly east of us. Without slackening speed the light made a right angle turn and headed directly for us," Franklin said.

"I was driving," said Mrs. Richardson, "and I started the car and was trying to get out of there."

"I looked over my shoulder and saw the light to the right and in back of us, real close," she said. "I was trying to get away from it and trying to watch the road and the light at the same time when we approached a curve and I hit the brakes.

"The loose gravel made the braking car swerve to the right and it bounced off a tree and crossed to the left side of the road and hit another tree," she said.

The car was severely damaged and Mrs. Richardson suffered cuts and bruises and has been in bed much of this week.

"I brought my wife into the hospital early Sunday morning for treatment and when she was okay, I hunted up the highway patrolman and we went back to the wreck," Franklin said.

"When we got back there I saw two of the lights but neither one was close

(See Monitoring, next page)

Monitoring

(Continued from Page 6)

enough to get a good look at it," he said.

The Richardsons described the lights as "blue-white, very similar to the mercury vapor lights used in some street lighting. There were no direct rays and there was nothing solid around the lights —just the brightness without reflection or rays."

The young couple would be hard to convince that the lights are hallucinations, vapors, St. Elmo's fire or other figments of imagination, because to them—THEY'RE REAL!" Unquote.

The SUPERIOR (Nebraska) EXPRESS of July 16, 1959 carried the following account of an equally strange experience:

"Anyone Else See the Flying Saucer or Whatever It Was? Three Saw It."

They didn't get a close-up view of it, and they do not claim to have seen a flying saucer. There must be some logical explanation of it they agree, but they haven't figured out what it is. There certainly was something flying around Nuckolls county one night recently, and at least three persons saw it.

First to sight the strange object was Jim Chapman of Nelson. Jim had been at a ball game in Oak and saw it first at about 10:30 p. m., on his way home, just before turning west at the corner three miles southwest of Oak. It was ahead of him then, he said, and when he turned west, it turned too, then went north in front of him, and again followed him west along the road.

Jim said that he was just "plain scared," and that the first thing he thought of was to turn around and head back where there were some people. On his way back toward Oak, he met Mr. and Mrs. Gerald Kubicek, who were on their way home to Nelson. Jim turned around and the three headed for Nelson. The object followed them about the same as it had been following Jim. It changed directions several times, seemed to stop and start again, and finally flew off in another direction and faded from view.

The object was not bright, appeared to be round and several inches in diameter, and was at about a 30-degree angle in the sky and about a quarter of a mile distant. Anyone else see it?" Unquote.

(An attempt was made by the writer to contact Chapman relative to his experience but he would not correspond. Since he did not have a phone the effort did not meet with success. However, the Kubiceks were reached by phone and Mrs. Kubicek confirmed their sighting. She was unable to add any additional details to the printed newspaper version of their experience related above, but did remark that they felt the strange light must have been a reflection but didn't know what from and were badly frightened by the weirdness of the experience.

In THE CAPITAL TIMES of Madison, Wisconsin, on Thursday, Nov. 24, 1960, appeared an item. "Flying Discs Are Seen at Prairie." "Prairie du Chien — Getting quite a thrill watching flying discs here. They were first noticed by Darwin Tichenor Saturday morning while waiting for the deer season to open in Grant county. Since that time, on Saturday, Sunday, Monday and Tuesday evenings they have been seen over the city.

Two letters received from Mr. Darwin Tichenor give such an excellent, firsthand description of his experience with these small discs or lights that they have been included for the reader's enlightenment.

Prairie du Chien, Wis.
June 5, 1961

Dear Mr. Fitch:

I received your letter of May 24, and was very much interested in it.

I first sighted these objects about 5:00 a.m. one November morning while I was going deer hunting. I was crossing an open field on a hill when I noticed a strange light just about the horizon. I paid no special attention to it until it began moving back and forth at a tremendous speed. I continued watching it until it suddenly zoomed high into the sky and became stationary. I continued watching it until I saw three smaller, perfectly round discs appear as if from nowhere. These discs gave off a cool, fluorescent light. The three discs flew in the same plane and were equal distances from each other. They moved slowly like this in perfect formation until they were very close to the first light. Then when they reached a certain point just a little way from the first disc, they completely vanished, as if they had been taken in by the larger one. As I continued to watch I saw several more of the smaller discs move across the sky and disappear in exactly the same manner. The sky was overcast that morning so the objects were definitely under the cloud cover, but I was unable to judge just how far away they were.

I do not know what these objects were but I do know that no balloons, airplanes, meteorites or other known objects could act like the ones I sighted did. The light from them was very steady. They made absolutely no noise and left no vapor trail. I told several friends about my sighting but they showed the typical reaction of disbelief.

As I was driving along that night I noticed a light on the horizon which I had never seen before. I stopped the car to get a better look. I noticed then that this light was moving back and forth while remaining in the same general location. I watched it for a while and then decided to drive to a nearby hill where I could see much better. When I got to the hill I could not see the original light any more. Instead I saw two lights which were not moving. As I watched them they would suddenly go out and then slowly light up again and gain intensity until they wiuld suddenly disappear again. These lights repeated this cycle without moving even slightly.

After watching them a while longer I went to get some of my friends to show them the objects. When I returned with several friends the large lights were still in the sky and we noticed several other moving ones. They would seem to come up over the nearby hills and then move along down through the valleys and suddenly disappear.

Sometimes the objects would move steadily along and again they would make sudden dashes, slow down and zoom off again. We were sitting in the car watching the objects because of the cold outside. I was becoming somewhat disappointed because the lights did not come any closer. Then one of them that we were watching appeared to 'creep' slowly over the hills and came toward the car.

It did not disappear but came closer and closer. Then it came directly toward the car. It appeared that it was surely going to hit the car and everyone, including myself, ducked down. When we looked up, the object was gone. It was probably about 50 feet from the car when I ducked. The object was probably two or three feet in diameter. Because of the very brilliant light, I could make out no definite outline or shape of the object itself. This was the closest that any of the objects came.

For several nights these objects were seen. Many people would go up on the hill and watch them. Even the local authorities saw them but did not report them. Then one night they were gone and I have not seen them since.

Since then I have become very interested in trying to learn more about these objects.

Sincerely,

Darwin Tichenor."

In a second letter dated June 27, 1961, Darwin Tichenor replied to questions asked him by the writer:

"My younger brother and two friends

(See Monitoring, next page)

Monitoring

(Continued from Page 7)

were out one night looking for the objects when one of them started coming in very close. He told me that when he shone the beam from his flashlight in the direction of the light, it suddenly disappeared. This bears a close resemblance to the behavior of the four lighted objects above the freight train described in the pamphlet which you sent me." (Tichenor's reference here is to the Monon Railroad sighting which is described in detail by Frank Edwards in the February, 1959 issue of FATE magazine).

"You also asked why I described the light as "creeping" toward us. This was because the light seemed only a few feet off the ground and moved somewhat like a cat creeping toward an intended victim. By this I mean that the light would move very slowly and then suddenly speed up and again slow down. It usually moved slowly but occasionally would make these little bursts of speed.

When it came directly at the car, it appeared to keep at the same level and come directly toward us. I do not think that it continued to go on over the car with the light on. Rather it seemed that the object stopped giving off light. We did not see it after we ducked our heads."

—o—

An even more weird and frightening experience is related in the LEWISTON-AUBURN, (Maine) JOURNAL of Nov. 9, 1961: "Former Lewiston Couple Has Weird Experience as Car Is Chased By Lights."

"Mr. and Mrs. Richard DuBois of 13481 Shirley St., Westminster, California, formerly of Lewiston, (Me.) returning home from a brief visit to Maine, were the disturbed victims of a somewhat macabre game of tag played on the moonlit reaches of America's famous route 66, it was learned today.

"For more than 30 miles between the towns of Datil and Pie Town in New Mexico, the DuBois car was accompanied by a brilliant ball of white light which climaxed its frightfully persistent visit with the travelers by breaking up into four individual smaller lights.

It was about 2 a. m., when Mrs. DuBois' attention was attracted to the light as it flashed across the front of their car, slowed down, and then turned back, and seemingly followed the automobile as it proceeded along the highway.

Her first thought, as she pointed it out to her husband, was that it was from a plane seeking an emergency landing area.

Its strange behavior shortly put the idea to route, however, when it began its game of tag. Flashing ahead of the car with great speed it slowed and then waited until the car caught up with it. Again it flashed ahead and returned.

DuBois attempted to quiet his wife's alarm with an explanation that it was a reflection, a trick of the moonlight, but this idea, too, was soon refuted when the car entered a dark canyon, not reached by the moonlight. The light when traveling in front of the car suddenly broke up into four smaller lights which followed along side the machine for some distance until the car reached a small roadside motel and service station.

When DuBois brought his car to a stop the lights flashed up into the sky and flitted out of sight.

Mrs. DuBois said they stopped at the next town and asked if there had been any reports of flying objects, but people only laughed at them.

"They may have thuoght it was funny, but we were plenty scared," she said.

An account of the Dubois' experience appeared in the Jan. 1962 issue of the APRO Bulletin. In a letter to the writer under date of Nov. 4, 1962, Mrs. DuBois made the following enlightening statements:

"The object or ball of light was just about 30 yards from us and was about as big as the car and it was more like a ball of white fire. I also feel that it was under intelligent control for it would be right by the car and when we stopped the car, it would stop also. The object followed us for about one hour. We were driving at about 90 miles an hour.

"At one point my husband stopped the car and ran out into a field to see if he could get a better look at it but he did not, for at that time it went up into the sky, but as soon as he got back in the car it came right back down. It would come close to the car and then it would go up on top of the mountain. At one point it went up into the sky and broke up into four small round discs which looked about as big as golf balls." Unquote.

—o—

THE REGISTER, Storm Lake, Iowa, of August 21, 1962, reports the following experience of a motorist with a small disc.

"While returning irom Cherokee, Gus Goettsch reported that his car was struck by what appeared to be a flying saucer.

According to the report, Mr. Goettsch was on a gravel road south of Aurelia when he noticed this object about the size of a paper plate spinning along outside his car. He said it had what appeared to be sparks dropping from it.

Goettsch reported that the object struck the rear fender fo his car and disappeared. It left no mark on the car and he was traveling about 30 miles per hour when the incident took place." Unquote. (Credit: Wash. State NICAP Sub-Committe, Seattle, Washington).

Clues On
Mysterious Cremation

On 20 November 1960, the badly charred bodies of five people, later identified as four men and a youth, were found in a burned car at Grassy Creek, Kentucky. One door was open—there was blood outside near the car, and the upright position of the bodies showed no indication of a struggle.

The autopsies showed the deaths were caused by fire fracture or "internal heat". The skulls of the corpses, explained by Cincinnati's Kettering Laboratory, indicated that they had fractured as a result of extreme internal heat. One puzzle was tiny bits of metal found in the bodies, which were first thought to be shotgun pellets. Careful examination, however, showed that the fragments were bits of molten metal from the top of the car which had dripped down into the bodies.

Authorities told the Pike County News that they had no idea what had happened. Some points to be pondered:

The car appeared to have been driven off the road and into a shallow creek. The only part of the car which was melted was the top, the rest had just burned, indicating an intense heat source from above.

On the basis of what we know the car and bodies and their position, we can hypothesize that after feeling the sudden, intense heat, the driver may have panicked and started to drive the car into the water to combat the heat while the passengers on the right front flung the door open in preparation for getting out. Apparently, however, no further action was possible.

If we consider the evidence in this case along with repeated reports of glowing objects following cars, causing intense and sudden rises in temperature in the interiors of the vehicles being pursued, we begin to see the correlation of data which has led researchers to conclude that at least some UFOs are dangerous, and that the occupants are, at best, not concerned with the welfare of humans.

For references on above reports, see C. W. Fitch's article this issue, also APRO Bulletin issues containing sightings of UFOs pursuing cars in Brazil, Venezuela, etc.

THE A.P.R.O. BULLETIN

The A. P. R. O. Bulletin is the official copyrighted publication of the Aerial Phenomena Research Organization (A.P.R.O.), 4145 E. Desert Place, Tucson, Arizona, and is issued every other month to members only. The Aerial Phenomena Research Orgazination is a non-profit group dedicated to the eventual solution of the mystery of the unidentified objects which have been present in the skies for hundreds of years. Inquiries regarding membership may be made to the above address.

TUCSON, ARIZONA — SEPTEMBER, 1963

THE CASE OF THE FRIGHTENED COWS

Solar Transit Made By UFO

On February 15, 1963 at 10:16 a. m., EST, Mr. Cyrus Fernald of Tangerine, Florida, witnessed the transit across the sun of an unknown object. The equipment used was a Questar telescope using a 40x eyepiece. Seeing conditions were good.

The object was perfectly round and well defined and appeared to be black in color. No sunlight showed through it. The apparent size was between 1/30 and 1/20 the sun's apparent diameter, something over one second of arc. The passage was almost a central transit and total time in transit was about 20 seconds. As the object left the sun's disc, its edge remained perfectly sharp. Mr. Fernald's wife observed the transit also. There were no other people involved.

An explanation has ben offered by Mr. Clinton D. Ford which was published in the April Abstracts of the AAVSO. He feels that it is possible that Mr. Fernald saw a Saturn C-5 rocket end on or nearly so for the 20 second duration of the transit. Any other man-made device could possibly account for the conditions if it were located within a few miles of the earth's surface. Mr. Ford feels that the Saturn C-5 rocket is the only apparent explanation for the observed round shape. though he views this with some skepticism.

Blue Light Seen In Ark.

Mr. Frank Hudson, APRO member, observed a rapidly-moving unidentified object on the night of 2 July 1963, at 9:15 p. m. He was located 1½ miles southwest of Huntsville, Arkansas, when the light was first seen about 70 degrees above the northern horizon. The light emitted a steady blue-tinged glow and passed directly over the observer. No noise was heard nor were there any other visual phenomena other than those mentioned. Mr. Hudson said the object's speed was faster than a jet plane. He used 6x30 binoculars during the observation. The UFO was lost from sight as it passed behind clouds while traveling toward the south.

Disc Buzzes House

In the early morning hour of June 26, 1963, Mr. and Mrs. Enrico Gilberti of Weymouth, Mass., experienced a most unusual and interesting encounter with an unconventional flying machine.

At 1 a.m. (Eastern Zone, Daylight Saving Time) they were awakened by what sounded like a low-flying, slow-moving jet aircraft. Looking out a window, they saw a low-flying object that resembled two saucers which were inverted, edge on edge and placed together. Around the outer periphery was a "lip" where the two "saucers" joined. On the top and bottom of the vehicle were two lights, the shape of which resembled Turkish fez hats.

These two lights were described as being as bright as lamp post lights and enabled the observers to distinguish the outline of the machine. The UFO hovered momentarily and then moved slowly on. It was at an altitude of about 100 feet and was estimated as being "about the size of a 10-wheel trailer truck," or approximately 30 feet at its largest dimension.

Mr. and Mrs. Thomas Merrill, neighbors of the Gilbertis, heard the vehicle although they did not see it. On the morning of the 26th the Gilberts called the local Naval Air Station and found that no jet aircraft were active in the area at the time of the sighting.

It may have been this vehicle which was photographed accidentally when Mr. Richard Pothier, a newspaperman was photographing star trails. (See this story elsewhere in this issue). Other individuals also apparently saw the same object but in different localities.

Ice Fall In Russia

Russian scientists are studying fragments of ice—11 pounds of it, which fell from the sky in an orchard at Domodedovo near Moscow. The Soviet News Agency Tass said tests were being run on the ice and that the scientists assuming it was part of an ice meteorite which came from space although science does not know of any precedent.

At about 7 a. m., on the morning of 15 February 1963, Farmer Charlie Brew and his son Trevor were milking the cows when a disc-shaped object descended out of the rain at an estimated height of about 70 to 100 feet. At the appearance of the object, the cows became very agitated and the horses reared in panic, Brew told investigators later. His farm is located near Moe, about 80 miles southeast of Melbourne, Australia.

Brew described the object as about 25 feet in diameter, battleship gray in color, with what appeared to be a band of perspex (plastic) or glass around the circumference and a number of scoop-like protrusions.

The disc appeared about to land, but it suddenly shot off in a westerly direction at "2 or 3 times the speed of a jet" and disappeared into a cloud. Brew's son Trevor did not see the object but did hear the "pulsating, whooshing sound" as it traveled overhead. They both said the whole episode only lasted a few seconds.

The above are the basic facts about the sighting forwarded by Sylvia Sutton, Secretary of the Victorian Flying Saucer Research Society. A transcript of a tape recording interview of Mr. Brew by APRO Representative Mr. Peter Norris, which is most revealing, follows:

(Tape recorded interview with Mr. Charles Brew by Mr. Peter Norris, President, Victorian Flying Saucer Research Society).

Question: What time did you make the sighting, Mr. Brew?

Answer: It would be about 10 past 7, it was. Yes, 10 past 7, definitely.

Q. What were you doing at the time?

A. We were milking and half way — approximately halfway — through, I'd say.

Q. Yes. How did you first notice the object come down?

A. Well I was lookin' out over the cows as I referred to you a while ago and it came down very steeply out of the east. Oh, I'd say at about 45 degrees.

Q. And what did the object look like when you first saw it? What were your reactions?

(See Cows—Page 3)

The A. P. R. O. BULLETIN

Published by
THE AERIAL PHENOMENA RESEARCH
ORGANIZATION
4145 E. Desert Place
Tucson, Arizona
Copyright 1964, Coral E. Lorenzen
Editor and Director

Information appearing in this bulletin may be used by other UAO research periodicals providing names and address credit is properly given to this organization and periodical.

Coral E. Lorenzen .... International Director and Editor
A. E. Brown, B.S.E.E. .... Director of Research
L. J. Lorenzen .... Director of Public Relations
John T. Hopf .... Photographic Consultant
Oliver Dean .... Photographic Consultant

SPECIAL REPRESENTATIVES

(The following listed individuals participate in planning and policy-making as Staff Members, in addition to coordinating investigative efforts in the areas indicated following their names.)

Dr. Olavo T. Fontes, M.D.........Brazil
K.Gosta Rehn .... Sweden
Graham Conway ...... Eastern Canada
Aime Michel .... France
Horacio Gonzales Gauteaume
                                        Venezuela
Peter E. Norris, L.L.D. ....Australia
Jun' Ichi Takanashi .... Japan
Juan C. Remonda .... Argentina
Sergio Robba .... Italy
Arist. Mitropoulos .... Greece
Rev. N. C. G. Cruttwell, New Guinea
Eduardo Buelte .... Spain
Norman Alford .... New Zealand
Austin Byrne .... Ireland

SPECIAL CONSULTANT
Prof. Charles Maney,—Physics

ALAMOGORDO PRINTING CO., INC.

Menzel's Book—A Further Extension on An Old Theme

In 1954 Dr. Donald Menzel, astronomer and science fiction writer, published a book called, simply, "Flying Saucers" in which he generally parroted the current authoritarian line that UFOs or flying saucers do not exist and attempted to back up his contention with gobbledygook about temperature inversion reflections. At the time it was generally felt by many who had studied the subject, and especially by people in countries other than the U.SS., that there was insufficient data to warrant any conclusion, whether it favored the reality or nonexistence of UFOs as space ships. However, Menzel jumped into the UFO publishing field head first and came out smelling like a rose because he had a reputation as an astronomer and because his book concluded what the public in general and the authorities and, therefore, the press, wanted to believe. The discs did not exist.

In 1963, 9 years and some 30 or 40 thousand sightings later which have yielded some damning evidence on the side of the reality of the discs, Menzel has found it necessary, in partnership with another science-fiction writer, Mrs. Lyle Boyd, to reiterate his predisposed conviction that UFOs are nothing but psychological abberations, tempature inversion reflections (naturally), misconceptions of conventional aircraft, etc.

Before going into any great detail, and we won't do that to any extent because the importance of the book does not warrant much space, we would like to emphasize the fact that Menzel's method, touted as scientific, leaves much to be desired and his motives are not above suspicion. Some observations:

Menzel and Boyd claim that although APRO challenged the AF to a joint test of the magnesium samples, we never did publish the results. This is not so. The entire report was published, in the book, "The Great Flying Saucer Hoax," and Menzel can hardly deny having read it, as he admits to being a reader of the magazine, "Flying Saucers" edited by Ray Palmer, which has carried a full-page ad concerning the book for the past year. We herewith invite Dr. Menzel to study the entire report, including spectrographic film, and a report by a metal historian at one of the U.S.'s top atomic laboratories. We also invite Dr. Menzel to reiterate his statement concerning the amount of magnesium found in meteorites. It is evident that Menzel was writing for a group of people, namely UFO researchers, whom he appears to be convinced are absolutely without scientific training.

As we said before, we cannot devote too much space to Menzel's diatribe, but the following is quite important: On page 181, paragraph 3, Menzel insinuates that James Stokes was a personal friend. Mrs. Lorenzen met with Mr. Stokes a total of four times, the first of which was a social introduction long before the Stokes incident took place. Two meetings took place after the Orogrande incident, in order to gather the information needed for a report. Of course, Menzel and Boy's definition of friendship may be considerably different than Mrs. Lorenzen's. If Menzel took someone else's word as fact in the above issue, he was being anything but careful or scientific. The fourth meeting was accidental and had nothing to do with Stokes' experience.

On page 278, Menzel says that Mrs. Lorenzen has published her conviction that nobody in the Air Force, the Navy or the Marines 'has the brains' to contrive so successful a scheme and that the alleged plot "could only be . . .", etc. The reference given for this quotation by Mrs. Lorenzen is the October 1958 issue of Flying Saucers magazine, an article entitled "The Psychology of UFO Secrecy." It should be pointed out that nowhere in that article do the words 'has the brains' appear.

Menzel and Boy's account of the IGY photographs and incident is very incomplete. The thing that is puzzling is that so much evidence is left out and in view of the fact that Dr. Menzel was in Rio de Janeiro in February 1963 (and states so in a footnote) it is difficult to understand why so much fact is missing from Menzel's account. In the case of the official Navy release, Menzel leaves out a most important paragraph which reads: "This Ministry sees no reason to forbid the publication of pictures of said object, taken by Mr. Almiro Barauna—who was at the Island of Trindade as a Navy guest—in the presence of a number of elements from the NE 'Almirante Saldanha' garrison, aboard that ship from whic hthe photos were taken." This paragraph completely nullifies Menzel's claim that there were no witnesses to the actual photographing of the object.

The last paragraph, however, poses an even greater mystery, for this supposed scientist, Dr. Donald Menzel, or perhaps his co-author, Mrs. Boyd, either mistakenly or deliberately inserted a word which completely changes the meaning of the statement. The correct sentence reads thusly: "Evidently, this Ministry cannot make any statement about the object sighted over the Island of Trindade, for the photos do not constitute enough evidence for such a purpose." Menzel's version reads: "Clearly, this Ministry cannot make any statement about the reality of the object, for the photos do not, etc." In leaving out the words, "sighted over the Island of Trindade" and inserting the words "reality of the," Menzel effectively changes an official Navy release to suit his own purposes. Perhaps this is only a mistake, but that kind of mistake is not what is expected by a man who is ranked among the world's first-run astronomers

The hanky-panky with the Official Brazilian Navy Release of February 22, 1958, becomes somewhat illuminated when we read Menzel's chapter which includes the IGY incident. He mentions, but only in a footnote, that he visited with astronomers in Rio who said the photos were a hoax. In a recent conversation with Dr. Fontes, the Dr. pointed out the fact that Menzel apparently did not visit the Navy Ministry in his quest for information, or he would have mentioned it. Also Menzel and Boyd insinuate that Bacellar, commandante of the Island of Trindade, had more or less disassociated himself from the incident. They also stated that there were no witnesses to the sighting and photography except Barauna and a friend. Without seeming to be pedantic, we will

(See Menzel—Page 5)

Cows . . .

(Continued from Page 1)

A. Well I thought it was a helicopter, at first.

Q. What made you think that?

A. On account of it being round and I've naturally never, ever seen one of these turnouts before. That would be asking too much!

Q. Yes, and what did you see when the object came fairly close to you?

A. Oh well, I noticed first of all the coloring and after that, the top 2/3 when it came down and hovered, was stationary and the lower section was turning in an anti-clockwise direction—noticed that—and also as I pointed out, those scoop-like protrusions around the side which I think was making the noise—the swishing noise, that is.

Q. And at this stage, how far was the object from you?

A. Oh I'd say 5 feet away—perhaps a little further—and about the same distance up in the air.

Q. How did you calculate the height of the object?

A. Well I calculated the height by those trees. I'd say they were approximately 75 feet hight. It might have been a shade higher than those, of course.

Q. Yes, that would be quite right I would say. Now once again, getting back to the general appearance of the object, can you describe the top part of the object?

A. Well, the top, the very top section, the dome section, that is, was sort of what we would call Perspex or glass material or whatever that was, I couldn't say. The middle section between the Perspex and the part that was rotating, was sort of battleship grey and looked to me like some bit of metallic material. I couldn't say for sure, of course, and the bottom as I said, was rotating on an anti-clockwise direction. Well I couldn't say what sort of material it was definitely made of but the Air Force chaps asked me that too. As near as I could say, it seemed something the same material as motorcars. Just by lookin' at it, you know.

Q. What was the size of the object?

A. Well I'd say as near as I could judge, about 25 feet across—perhaps a little more—if anything a little more.

Q. Well what about the height?

A. Oh I'd say overall, about 9 feet as near as I could judge. Might have been a bit more but of course it's hard to judge when you only see a thing for a few seconds, but I'd say 9 or 10 feet.

Q. You didn't actually see anybody in it through what appeared to be the glass portion on the top, on the dome?

A. No, on a clear day you may have

but as I said, it was raining heavy and no, I can't honestly say I did see anybody although I was lookin' hard enough.

Q. Looking at the object from the underneath part, what could you see there?

A. Well, when it was hovering, I could see those scoop-like protrusions, or whatever they were, which seemed to be making the swishing noise. After that, when it took off, it was the bluish or sort of pale bluish color underneath. That's as near as I can tell you, as much as I can tell you really, about the lower section.

Q. And when it took off, what did you notice? Well first of all, of course it did hover, didn't it, for some little time?

A. Well I'd say for a space of 4 or 5 seconds, which is not long, I know.

Q. Yes, and then after that it took off, did it, and if so, at what speed would you calculate?

A. Oh well, we reckon, Trevor and I reckon, a jet would probably have to add up speed to match the speed.

Q. And it took off instantly?

A. Yes, flying from a flying start—you know, not a flying start but a standing start—and very fast and very steep.

Q. It went straight up, did it?

A. I'll say it came in and went out at about the same angle of 45 degrees, as near as I could judge.

Q. Getting back to the appearance of the object, I think you said you noticed something on top of the dome?

A. Yes, it seemed to be an aerial sort of a thing—I'd say about 5 or 6 feet long and it did seem to be either chrome or some lightish metal thing. Whether it was the aerial or not, I couldn't say. I was speaking to the other chap and he said it was.

Q. I know there were some cows and other stock in the yard at the time of the sighting, Mr. Brew?

A. Yes, we had half done. We were half way, half of them were milked out and the other half still had to go through.

Q. What was their reaction to the sighting?

A. Well, as I said to your other chap who was here, they done everything but turn somesaults. They put in the paper that they did turn somesaults but that's carrying it a bit far! They certainly played up. I've never seen cows play up like that before and they never take any notice (quite happy before) of an ordinary jet. A jet can go over and they just take no notice at all, but they really played up this day.

Q. Did you have anybody helping you milk the cows?

A. Yes, we had Trevor there and as I said, unfortunately he never seen it, but he did hear it and he said: 'What was

that?' and I said: 'A flying saucer,' and he said: 'Don't be so and so silly, you know those things don't exist' or something to that effect and I said: 'Well this was a flying saucer, definitely.' He said: 'Well it certainly moved off the mark, it travelled twice as fast as a jet.' I said: 'Well it certainly went away fast, just like somebody had it on a blooming Yo-yo or something. Really went off with a bang.'

Q. So he didn't hear it until it actually moved away and then of course, it was too late?

A. No, he didn't see it, unfortunately, but he certainly heard it go.

Q. Have you been interviewed by any representatives of the Government?

A. Yes, as I said, the C.S.I.R.O. were here and number one question as far as they were concerned—he asked me did I get a headache. I said: 'Well it's strange that you should ask me that because I thought it was too ridiculous, I would never have mentioned it. But I did get an awful headache just behind the eyes. I never suffer with headaches normally and I took a Bex and I went in but it didn't seem to have any effect. It just wore off itself toward night—took all day long to wear off.

Q. When did you first get the headache?

A. Oh when I was sort of gazing at the Perspex canopy business I noticed it.

Q. It came on immediately, did it?

A. Yes, more or less. Yes. Yes.

Q. What did the C.S.I.R.O. man say? Incidentally, do you know his name? What's his name?

A. Er, Mr. Berson. Yes, Mr. Berson was his name.

Q. And what did he say about the headache?

A. 'Well,' he said, 'that ties in with our theory, we always had the impression that it was . . . ' (what would you say?) he gave the impression it was electro magnetic or something to that effect — that's beyond me—but he said that would more than likely cause a headache and it certainly took all day to get rid of it anyhow. I know that.

Q. What else did the C.S.I.R.O. do?

A. Well as I said, he took away samples of rock—they were very interested in that—because he said being a sort of an iron-stone, it may have some attraction for it. And there is the reef as I said and winds right through here and it came over that reef, more or less parallel with it.

Q. How long after the sighting occurred, did the C.S.I.R.O. come down here?

A. They were here about 4 days after and the Air Force about a week, or near

(See Cows—Page 4)

Cows

(Continued from Page 3)

the best part of a week after that.

Q. Oh, the Air Force came down as well, did they? Who came down from the Air Force?

A. Well Mr. Murdoch was one of them, the only name I can recall.

Q. Was he in uniform?

A. Yes, they were all in uniform.

Q. They were officers, were they?

A. Yes, I would say high officers, high-ranking officers, anyhow.

Q. What did they do?

A. Well they photographed the surrounding country, that was the Baw Baws, Mt. Macdonald. Long distance cameras and took light, cloud and cloud plus, you know, how much blue was showing in the sky—all that sort of thing. It's a bit beyond me, some of the things they done but, all those things.

Q. Did they have instruments?

A. Yes, they had the cameras and they lay tapping the rocks and took particular notice of the rock formation also. Don't know for what reason but they did. Yes, they said that after I drew them the sketch, that it was similar to other sighting to what had been seen in other countries. It tallied almost exactly with what's been seen over there, but they didn't think it was quite so big as that. Yes, they said it was, approximately, to the best of their knowledge, the lowest it had been and the best sightings.

Q. That was in Australia, was it?

A. Yes, from what I could gather, here.

Q. Did anyone else come down from the Government?

A. Yes, I had the Aeronautical expert from, I think liaison officer, I think that was the Sale Air Base. He asked similar questions and he wanted to know if there was any engine noise but we never heard any engine noise, not as we know engines today.

Q. To get back to the object itself, did you notice any light coming from the object itself at any time?

A. No. There was no light, no light in the dome busines sand no lights underneath.

Commonwealth of Australia

Department of Air
Canberra, A.C.T.
1 April 1963

In reply quote 580/1/1(11)
Mrs. S. Sutton
Hon. Sec.
Victorian Flying Saucer Research Society
P. O. Box 32
TOORAK, VICTORIA
Dear Madam:

1. I refer to your letter dated 8th March, 1963, regarding the investigation of a sighting of an unidentified object by Mr. Charles Brew.

2. Our investigation and enquiries reveal that there are scientific records of certain tornado-like meteorological manifestations which have a similar appearance in many ways to whatever was seen by Mr. Brew.

3. The information available is such however, that while we accept this as a possibility, we are unable to come to any firm conclusion as to the nature of the object or manifestation reported.

Yours faithfully,

A. B. McFARLANE,
Secretary.

Division of Meteorological Physics

Station Street,
Aspendale, S.13
Vicotria
8th April, 1963

Mrs. S. Sutton,
Hon. Sec.,
Victorian Flying Saucer Research Society
P. O. Box 32,
TOORAK.
Dear Madam:

I apologize for the delay in answering your letter of the 19th March last.

I visited Mr. Brew in company of a friend of mine, but we did not take any rock sample. But I know that somebody else did.

To obtain more information about the mentioned sighting, please contact the R.A.A.F., Dept. of Air, Canberra, who were investigating this case.

Yours faithfully,

F. A. BERSON.

Inquirer Says Mars Moons Artificial

The July 28, 1963 issue of the tabloid, "National Inquirer" headlined a U. S. plan to investigate the possibility that the Martian satellites are artificial. It quotes astronomers Shklovsky, Slipher, Sinton and Singer as endorsing the possibility—and Clyde W. Tombaugh as objecting on the basis that "such a satellite would severely strain the capabilities of a world rich in resources." The extreme poverty of mineral resources on Mars would have deprived them of the necessary materials, Tombaugh asserted.

The APRO Bulletin endorses both view points, pointing out that when all the evidence is considered it appears likely that the Mars satellites are artificial but originate somewhere other than Mars — probably some other solar system and that they are implements through which aliens established a base on Mars during the 1870s.

Do Scientists Stifle New Knowledge?

The September 23 issue of the National Observer contains an article entitled "Do Scientists Snuff Out the Lights of Learning?" by Dr. Robert M. Hutchins, former president of the University of Chicago, and which includes the following nugget: ". . . that professors are somewhat worse than other people, and that scientists are somewhat worse than other professors. The foundation of morality in our society is a desire to protect one's reputation. A professor's reputation depends entirely upon his books and his articles in learned journals. The narrower the field in which a man must tell the truth, the wider the area in which he is free to lie. This is one of the 'advantages' of specialization."

Our hats are off to this brave professor. The art of lying seems to be more important these days than such silly pastimes as research. The latter entails work, the former merely a reputation, a whale of an ego and a glib tongue.

High Altitude Satellite Type Object Seen

On the night of August 16, 1963, at approximately 9:41 p. m., Kevin Fitzgerald of East Hartford, Conn., observed a satellite-type object which he described as being like a large bright star in appearance.

Its speed was approximately three times that of the American Echo Communications satellite as it moved from South to North through the sky. The object was at high altitude and seeing conditions were good. Pulsing at four second intervals, the white object moved in a straight line from the upper part of the contellation of Delphinus to about five degrees under and at a slight angle to the star Eta Cassiopeia.

Fiery Object Over Fijis

New Zealand Naval and Air Force personnel as well as civilians and police witnessed the passage of a huge, glowing green and white object with a long orange tail on April 3, 1963 at 3:20 a. m. The New Zealand Navy survey ship HMS Cook was also within range and personnel aboard saw it.

The direction of travel across the Fiji Island was from northwest to southeast. At 3:25 a. m. the object was visible from the Royal New Zealand Air Force Station at Lauthala Bay. This and other reports correlated in time and description.

Menzel . . .

(Continued from Page 2)

refer Dr. Menzel to the May 3, 1958 issue of O Cruzeiro, in which Bacellar's full statement is printed, and to the 25 February 1958 issue of Folha Da Tarde and O Estado De Sao Paulo, both of which are Sao Paulo newspapers and which list names of witnesses and include their statements concerning the incidents. In the event Menzel and Boyd should attempt to claim the Air Force files furnished them with the official Navy release, we would like to point out that in paragraph 5 of a letter from Lt. Col. Tacker, on page 188 of Mrs. Lorenzen's book, the word "reality" does not appear in the third paragraph as claimed by Menzel and Boyd.

Inasmuch as the original text in Portuguese is on file here at headquarters, along with a Portuguese-English dictionary, we also invite Dr. Menbel and/or Mrs. Boyd to study the IGY file and to do their own translation if so desired.

At the time the book was sent out for review, this office contacted Dick Hall of NICAP concerning Menzel's statement that Donald E. Keyhoe had refused to allow the authors of the book, "The World of Flying Saucers" to quote from his writings. In a statement which will be presented elsewhere, NICAP and Keyhoe expressed their opinion that Menzel tended to misquote and quote out of context and therefore permission was not given. It appears that this was a very wise move.

Although the authors of "The World of Flying Saucers" mentioned Aime Michel, and his book "Flying Saucers and the Straight Line Mystery," they failed to comment on the straight lines or orthoteny, mentioning only "the little men" it documented. Another example of omission is the authors' failure to mention either Mrs. Lorenzen's book or "Flying Saucers—a Modern Myth of Things Seen in the Sky" by Dr. Carl Jung, although considerable space was given to various cult leaders and their writings. This omission may be due to the fact that both of the above-named books were not too generous in dealing with Menzel's theory and convictions.

Last, but not least, we feel the membership will be interested in the following incident: In March of 1963, Mr. Lorenzen was asked to come to the office of a superior at Kitt Peak Observatory Laboratory to discuss an article published in Flying Saucers magazine, and bearing his name and a mention of his employment. When first considering changing positions from Holloman to Kitt Peak in 1960, Mr. Lorenzen discussed quite thoroughly his activity in the flying saucer field with the man who interviewed him. It was agreed that what he did in his spare time was his business. It appeared, however, during the discussion in March, that "someone" on the Board of Directors had read the article and objected to Mr. Lorenzen using his connection with Kitt Peak Laboratory in a forward to the article. Actually, as Mr. Lorenzen pointed out, he had not written the forward, only the article. The article in question was an answer to a criticism of Mrs. Lorenzen's book written by a Frank Patton who is suspected to be a woman and a member of APRO who is favorably inclined toward the "contactee" cult .

Mr. Lorenzen has stated that he resents being sniped at "from an Ivory Tower." Although he said he felt he should know the name of the sniper, this information was not given him. It is interesting to note, however, that Dr. Donald Menzel, admitted reader of Flying Saucers magazine, science fiction writer, astronomer, chief of the Harvard Observatory, is also on the Board of Directors of Kitt Peak National Observatory.

Keyhoe On Menzel's Book

In a footnote on page 10 of "The World of Flying Saucers," Dr. Menzel alleges that one recalcitrant UFO author, Major Donald E. Keyhoe, prevented a "scientific" presentation of the beliefs of UFO-logists by refusing permission to quote from his (Keyhoe's) books. The truth of the matter is that Holt, Rinehart and Winston, Inc., publishers of "Flying Saucers from Outer Space" and "Flying Saucer Conspiracy" had misgivings about apparent misquotes and misrepresentations by Dr. Menzel of books they had published, and on their own initiative had sent the galleys to Major KeKyhoe so he could judge the matter for himself.

The galleys (available for inspection at NICAP) show that Dr. Menzel at numerous points combined partial quotations with incorrect paraphrasing, creating a seriously misleading effect; lumped Major Keyhoe's name in with several other authors in a statement enclosed in quotation marks—a statement including comments Major KeKyhoe had never made, which were not and had never been his beliefs.

Dr. Menzel also attributed certain details of sightings and witnesses' statements to Major Keyhoe's imagination, when in fact these details and statements were taken verbatim from Air Force Intelligence records specifically declassified and released to Major Keyhoe in 1952 and 1953, with a signed clearance letter and signed clearance sheet. Under such circumstances, Major Keyhoe told

APRO, no author would allow his views to be so completely misrepresented. (He can say that again and again!—The Ed.)

RNZAF Pilot Spots UFO

At 7:30 p. m. (NZ time) on March 26, 1963, Flying Officer Hosie of the RNZAF, while piloting a Canberra light bomber, sighted an unidentified object. He was the only witness as his navigator was busy performing his duties.

The altitude of the plane was close to 20,000 feet and sky conditions were clear. The ship's speed was between 380 and 400 knots ground speed. There was no radio interference during the observation and the object was apparently beyond radar range of ground installations at Wellington, NZ. At the time of observation the plane was 40 miles northeast of the Ahakea RNZAF Base.

Flying officer Hosie saw a rapidly flashing light ahead of him at 10 o'clock, a position somewhat above his ship, and moving at about the same speed. The light was moving on nearly an easterly heading and the Canberra was moving on 60 degrees true by the compass.

The flashing light was clear white in color and very bright. Two flashes per second were observed for the full minute of the observation, and the brilliancy of the light did not change at any time.

Careful checking showed that there were no known aircraft in the area except Hosie's plane, and no chase was given as the Canberra was required to carry out its flight exercise.

Strange Substances Falls On Ranch In Washington

Larry Robinson of Sequim, Washington, found an unkown object on May 2, 1963 which apparently fell from the sky. He made the discovery on his ranch which is located on Sherbourne Road near Sequim, Washington.

Several pieces of the "thing" were found in a corral. The largest piece measured about 12 inches long, 6 inches wide and 3 inches thick. It appeared to be lava-like and porous. Its color is described as grey, but the pieces were covered on the outside by a white powder. Tiny bits of crystal appeared underneath the powder. When tasted, the stuff had a salty taste.

A local science teacher, Mrs. James Scott, felt that after microscopic examination the object was not a meteorite, primarily because of the deterioration of the white powder. A piece of the stuff was sent to the University of Washington Geology department for analysis and no results have been announced concerning their findings.

Strange Lights Over Long Island

The Long Island press reported on Tuesday, 26 March 1963, that mysterious lights were seen in the skies over Long Island, the preceding night. Witnesses included police officers, residents and officials at MacArthur Airport in Islip Town. The witnesses gave various descriptions of what they saw, such as "lights in the sky" and "streaks of light."

The most detailed account was given by Mr. Victor Agne of Garden City, N. Y. At 10:08 p. m., he saw an object which he described as traveling at a speed "five times that of a jet." He said it was similar in shape to a jet and was fluorescent green in color, and gave off white fire streaks from the rear.

Added Data On Long Island Sighting

The following information which adds to the Long Island sighting of 25 March reached this office in time to include in this issue: At 10:00 p. m., two interesting observations of unidentified lights over Long Island were made. A Dr. Lang of Mount Crane Road, Port Jefferson and Mr. Victor Agne of 38 Kilborn Road, Garden City, were the witnesses.

Dr. Lang reported seeing a streak of light plummet into Long Island Sound off Crane Neck. Mr. Agne while driving along the Long Island Expressway in East Hills at 10:08 p. m., saw an object which he described as being circular and giving off a fluorescent greenish light. It trailed white sparks. Its speed was estimated to be about five times that of a jet plane. It moved in a southerly direction and was abo e the level of clouds in the area at that time. At Islip Town, MacArthur Airport officials also saw lights in the sky. No aircraft were considered as a possible explanation.

Blue "Satellite" Over Ark.

At 8:35 p. m., CST, on June 29, 1963, Frank Hudson of Huntsville, Arkansas as well as other members of his family, observed the passage of a fast-moving UFO. Seeing conditions were good and there was moonlight. 6x30 binoculars were used during the observation. The UFO, described as being a light larger in size than the Echo I Communications satellite, had a bluish tinge and was moving faster than a jet plane. It maintained a steady sped and did not pulsate. It noiselessly moved from south to north, traveling a distance of 135 degrees in a minute or slightly less. No vapor trail was seen and all witnesses agreed that it was not a conventional aircraft or a meteor.

Strange Object Over Canada

On August 1, 1963 at 8:30 p. m., two Canadians, Lyle and Kim Crosbie of S. W. Calgary Alberta, saw an orange-red colored object described as being shaped like a piece of pipe. The coloration was as metal would appear if heated until it became red hot. The observers described its length as being approximately that of the sun's diameter.

The UFO came from a high cloud and moving at a speed described as about 8 times that of a jet plane, traveled horizontally toward the southwest. As the vehicle's speed decreased, its color changed to a grey such as that associated with the moon. The observers noted that when the orange color changed, the vehicle seemed to "shrink" in size.

From the rear of the object came other strange objects, apparently some type of contrail, shaped like written "i's." As one disappeared another would appear. The main object then assumed a vertical attitude. At this point an object described as being dome-shaped appeared on the side of the UFO. From the "dome" came flashes of "white lightning." Five flashes or strokes were observed. The "dome" then disintegrated "like plant cells dividing under a miscroscope." The UFO, still in its vertical attitude sank slowly until it disappeared from view behind obstructions on the horizon.

Phoenix Lights Seen On Three Nights

Mr. and Mrs. Earl Vaughan of Phoenix, Ariz., observed the passage of some UFOs on the nights of July 6, 7, and 8, 1963. All objects were at a very high altitude and of a bright white color. The instrument used for the observations was 7x50 field glasses mounted on a tripod.

The first object was seen on July 6, 1963 at 8 p. m. as it traveled from north to south. At 9:35 p. m. that same night another UFO type object made its appearance, traveling roughly in the same direction. Both lights traveled in straight lines.

The night of July 7 brought the appearance of object number three. At 8:30 p. m. it traveled from the northwest to the southeast. This object made an alteration in its course in an easterly direction before proceeding on. The maneuver occurred while at the zenith.

On July 8 at 8:45 p. m., the fourth object made a passage from the southwest to the east. Its path was a straight line but was confined to the southern half of the sky. Mr. Vaughan expressed his doubts that all the objects involved were man-made satellites. He felt their origin was somewhere other than this planet.

Cloud and Light Phenomena Observed by Ship Crew

At 0500 GMT on April 4, 1963, the Captain and Junior Second Officer of the Swedish Motor vessel Kungsholm observed a strange, white cloud bearing 315 degrees by the compass and at an elevation of 45 degrees. The Kungsholm was running between Honolulu, Hawaii and Los Angeles, Calif.

This particular cloud appeared more noticeable than others in the same area. Seconds after spotting the strange cloud broke up into several concentric rings. These then began to spread out and in the middle of the inner ring 6 or 7 bright star-like dots appeared. Cloud and all were moving westward swiftly. After a period of about 3 minutes the dots broke up into two groups. One group remained inside the inner ring but the other turned away and vanished.

The total time of the observation was approximately 7 minutes and visibility was good.

Greek Ship Sights Strange Fireball

At 1630 GMT on March 18, 1963, the second officer and Captain of the Greek M.V. Hellenic Laurel observed a bright fire-ball type object. The ship was proceeding from Bombay to Port Sudan. Her position at the time of observation being latitude 16 degrees, 49 minutes N., longitude 63 degrees, 41 minutes east in the Arabian Sea.

The UFO traveled from 290 degrees by the compass to 45 degrees. In appearance it was white and about the apparent size of the moon. A bright white, thick contrail was left behind as it moved across the sky. The time of visibility was one minute, and seeing conditions were very good.

Whining Object Seen At Invercargill, NZ

Witnesses have reported a strange encounter with an oval-shaped object which was also described as silver in color with a blue hue. The object made a whining or whirring sound.

The incident took place on February 24, 1963 at 1 a.m. The object was both heard and seen by residents and one man chased it in his car. Some alarm was expressed by those involved. The same clipping which reported this incident also cited the observation of a slowly moving cigar-shaped light blue object over Half Moon Bay in June 1962.

THE A.P.R.O. BULLETIN

The A. P. R. O. Bulletin is the official copyrighted publication of the Aerial Phenomena Research Organization (A.P.R.O.), 4145 E. Desert Place, Tucson, Arizona, and is issued every other month to members only. The Aerial Phenomena Research Orgazination is a non-profit group dedicated to the eventual solution of the mystery of the unidentified objects which have been present in the skies for hundreds of years. Inquiries regarding membership may be made to the above address.

TUCSON, ARIZONA, NOVEMBER, 1963

FAMILY BESEIGED BY DISCS

What Did Cooper See?

In may 1963 while American Astronaut Gordon Cooper was in his 15th orbit over Australia, he reportedly saw an unidentified object going in the opposite direction. The following is a direct quote from the KFI Los Angeles radio broadcast which was piped in direct from Cape Canaveral: "However, during his 15th orbit NBC has reports from West Australia which indicate that an unidentified and somewhat mysterious light was visible from the capsule. These reports all said that the unknown space phenomenon was of a green color with a red tail. Spokesmen at Muchea (spelling may be wrong — the transcript is blurred here) the station in Australia, tracking this, said that the light, of course, had nothing to do with the capsule or its journey through space but the spokesman did not discount its presence up there."

The second report direct from Cape Canaveral May 16, 1963 8:00-8:05 a.m. (PDT). This portion began with Ellis Abel, NBC New York, who switched immediately to John Chancellor NBC Space Control, Cape Canaveral. Portion of his report pertaining to the UFO follows: "And after that he will be in the dark again over Australia as he was in the 15th orbit. At that time NBC News reports he saw unidentified light in the sky preceding in the opposite direction. Reportedly the light was green with a red tail. A spokesman at the Australia tracking station at Muchea said the light, of course, did not have anything to do with the capsule's flight but did not discount reports of its existence."

Rumors dribbling back to APRO via Cape Canaveral indicate that both Cooper and the Australian trackers observed the object. It is suspicious, to say the least, that after that one small report, no further information was available concerning the mystery object.

This brings to mind, however, the "snowflakes" or tiny lighted particles seen by Glenn and subsequent orbiting

(See Cooper—Page 5)

News Photog Snaps UFO

APRO HAS in its possession a colored slide of an object photographed on time exposure by news photographer Dick Pothier of Wollaston, Mass. In a by-lined story in the Quincy Patroit-Ledger, Mr. Pothier described his experience which took place on either the 25th or 26th of June 1963.

Pothier was taking time photos of stars in order to record the tracks of same, from his back yard at Wollaston, Mass. His equipment consisted of a Japanese 35 mm. camera on a tripod. He was using Kodachrome X film. Other than checking the distance he did not touch the equipment until 30 minutes after he opened the shutter, when he returned to close it.

Two weeks later Potheir had the film developed. On the slide he immediately spotted something which shouldn't have been there—a clear pattern of lights which moved into the camera's view, hovered in at least 10 spots, maneuvered, then left the camera's view again.

In Pothier's own words: "The time exposure was able to capture all this, and the intensity of the lights on the color slide clearly show just where the lights stopped and moved, leaving either an image of the lights or a colored track. In back of the orange, white and silver lights and tracks were the star trails which was originally the purpose of one of the shots."

Pothier eventually showed the photo slide to Stephen Putnam, a mechanical engineer, APRO member and President of the Two-State UFO Group, of Egypt, Mass. Putnam, in a statement to the Patriot-Ledger said after a three-hour study of the slide, that the lights seemed to be arranged on a single object which never changed its attitude relative to the ground, and appeared to make 90 degree turns without turning itself. Because the lights ranged in color from orange to white to silver, never changed their relative position, they were apparently mounted on the same frame-

(See Photog—Page 4)

At 9:30 p. m. on the 21st of October Senor Antonio de Moreno was awakened at his ranch near Tranca, Argentina by a 15-year-old employee who told him there had apparently been an accident at the railroad tracks about a half mile distant as there was a lot of light and people moving around at that location.

De Moreno, 72, wakened Senora Teresa Kairus de Moreno, 63, and they both looked out the window. Over the railroad track just a few feet in the air there hovered an oval-shaped object which was projecting light to the ground where the de Morenon saw "people" walking to and fro, apparently always in single file. Senora de Moreno then spotted another similar object very close to the house. She could see a dome-shaped structure, about 25 feet in diameter, as well as windows or ports around the circumference of the object. This object also was just a few feet off the ground. The Senora got a flashlight and shone it toward the disc, whereupon it shot a bright white tubular beam of light at the house. Although she stayed fairly calm throughout the whole episode, Senora de Moreno, not knowing the meaning of the incident, rounded up the children in the ranch house, with the help of her sister, and hid them. Then the de Morenos began a systematic check of all the windows and shortly discovered that there were five discs near the house—three stayed about 210-225 feet distant, and two, including the nearest one which she saw first, were within only a few feet. One shone the white tubular light at the house, the other a reddish-violet tubular light.

House Heated Up Like Oven

Shortly after the lights struck the house, the inside of the house began to heat up until it was "like an oven" and there was a strong smell of sulphur in the air. Although the heat became so intense that the occupants didn't think

(See Beseiged—Page 5)

The A. P. R. O. BULLETIN

Published by
THE AERIAL PHENOMENA RESEARCH
ORGANIZATION
4145 E. Desert Place
Tucson, Arizona
Copyright 1964, Carol E. Lorenzen
Editor and Director

Information appearing in this bulletin may be used by other UAO research periodicals providing names and address credit is properly given to this organization and periodical.

Coral E. Lorenzen ..... International Director and Editor
A. E. Brown, B.S.E.E. .... Director of Research
L. J. Lorenzen .... Director of Public Relations
John T. Hopf .... Photographic Consultant
Oliver Dean .... Photographic Consultant

SPECIAL REPRESENTATIVES

(The following listed individuals participate in planning and policy-making as Staff Members, in addition to coordinating investigative efforts in the areas indicated following their names.)

Dr. Olavo T. Fontes, M.D. ....Brazil
K. Gosta Rehn .... Sweden
Graham Conway ...... Eastern Canada
Aime Michel .... France
Horacio Gonzales Gauteaume
　　　　　　　　　　　Venezuela
Peter E. Norris, L.L.D. ....Australia
Jun' Ichi Takanashi .... Japan
Juan C. Remonda .... Argentina
Sergio Robba .... Italy
Arist. Mitropoulos .... Greece
Rev. N. C. G. Cruttwell, New Guinea
Eduardo Buelte .... Spain
Norman Alford .... New Zealand
Austin Byrne .... Ireland

SPECIAL CONSULTANT
Prof. Charles Maney,—Physics

ALAMOGORDO PRINTING CO., INC.

The Reason?

From time to time in the past 12 years, a concerted effort has been launched by a segment of UFO researchers to force a Congressional Investigation of the handling of the UFO mystery by the USAF. Various reasons have been professed for supporting this effort, the main one of which has been that the people should have access to such information—it is their right as individuals and citizens.

Most of us have tried to divine the "big reason" for the alleged censorship and mishandling of the UFO mystery, and the most popular theory has been that the military authorities fear a panic, economic as well as emotional, among the masses. UFO researchers cite the Orson Wells "War of the Worlds" scare of 1938. In view of the extensive propaganda and speculation dealing with space travel and the possibility of life on other worlds, it is not longer a valid argument. The resistance to the idea of interplanetary or interstellar travel by extraterrestrials has weakened considerably, and most people would not have any great difficulty accepting the presence of such visitors were they to become a reality through official announcement. However, despite the publicity during the early years which took form not only through the press, but via books by authorities on the subject of flying saucers, most people hesitate to accept the reality of space visitors without the sanction of official cognizance. This has not come, and it is not likely to come unless a definite move on the part of the visitors has been made.

These are many UFO "believers" who are caught up in a pseudo-religious movement, who pay little attention to sightings or landing incidents, etc., for they are more concerned with perpetuating a doctrine than dealing with and digesting facts. Another segment concerns itself mainly with trying to find a "big answer"—some think differently in the line of origin of the visitors, purpose, etc.

The third group of UFO enthusiasts is definitely a minority and are those engaged in serious scrutiny of the facts available. Among all three of these groups there is a small sub-group with a common factor, and that is egotism. They do not seem to be satisfied to learn by observing and studying the information available, and seem more inclined to find someone to blame so that they can justify their position.

Before going further it should be pointed out that as a result of this article many fingers will be pointed and many rumors will be started, the gist of which will be that APRO's Director has been "talked to" and "hushed up." It must be estabalished before continuing that this has not happened and is not likely to happen and if it did every effort wouldd be made to relate such an incident to APRO members.

APRO has been, to our knowledge, the first organization to accept the existence of the "little men" or humanoid occupants of the discs, and since then to consider the possibility of hostile occupants. Both theories met with no little resistance at the time they were first discussed. Except for a small number of researchers, most of us accept the humanoid occupants as realities, but the hostile theory has yet to be seriously considered and FACED.

Upon this latter premise could hinge the REASON for authoritarian censorship when feasible, and official reluctance to even admit the substance of 12 years of UFO sightings. Let's take a look at some basic facts:

The mystery supposedly began in 1947, but sightings were logged by the military without civilian knowledge in 1944 and 1945, during World War II, and over military and civilian areas in 1946. In 1948 a pilot was killed (Mantell) while chasing a UFO. By 1952, it was quite evident to any intelligent individual with access to the facts available that something odd was afoot and that if these things were interplanetary they were not bent on contact and were certainly interested in the defensive and offensive installations in the United States.

This was known to some civilians in 1952, and must have been more than evident to military people in those early years inasmuch as they had access to all military sightings.

Since then, serious discussion and press notices of UFO sightings have been discouraged by an attitude of ridicule. This attitude seems to be authored by official sources which apparently cannot be dissuaded or indeed even reached. Attempts to bring about Congressional investigations and hearings have been costly and futile. All through this, some disturbing threads have been woven, and if they indicate what they seem to, any real effort to bring about public enlightenment, at least through one media of news, might amount to eventual disaster.

Many incidents have taken place which indicate that the UFO are capable of monitoring radio broadcasts and if that is possible, TV monitoring would be simple. Also it should be noted that although it is almost impossible to get radio or television time via interview programs and the like, to seriously discuss UFO research and the conclusions reached by serious researchers, no one has made any effort to stop the publication of the many periodicals dealing with the subject, or books.

It is impossible to get a big publisher to accept a manuscript dealing with UFOs on the positive, interplanetary theory side of the question, and therefore widespread circulation of UFO books is no longer possible. The only books dealing with UFO which have been published in the last five years (since the 1957-58 flap) have been serious books dealing with interplanetary space ships which were published by the "vanity" or "subsidy" press, or books heavily laden with crackpotism and religious understones, or anti-saucer books such as Menzel's. Menzel's and Boyd's book, incidentally, was published by a large publisher and was given the stamp of approval of the press and TV and radio media via many reviews of same and interviews with the authors. Not so with Keyhoe, Hall or Maney, after Hall and Maney's book, "The Challenge of the UFOs." Not so either, with Mrs. Lorenzen's book, "The Great Flying Saucer Hoax." Both of these books had to be privately published and neither received the notice they should have. It seems ironic that Mrs. Lorenzen received so many enthusiastic comments about her book from scientists who subsequently have joined APRO and are working diligently to solve some of the enigmas of the UFOs, yet has not been able to promote adequate press notice on the book.

Publications do not seem to be affected by this insidious effort to keep UFO news from public notice. Whoever or whatever is behind the stifling of information about UFO seems to be more concerned with information which is electronically disseminated, and therefore quite easily monitored by ships or satellites which could be circling our globe. It has been at least fairly well substantiated that UFOs can monitor radio and therefore TV, and this brings us to the crux of the whole situation.

The Air Force of the United States is charged with the protection of this country; their specific responsibility is the air space over this land. The same is true of all the other Air contingents in other countries. The American Navy is investigating UFOs—they have their own program, for although UFOs are generally and for the most part seen in the air, they have been known to fly over the sea and enter the oceans, and this of course is the Navy's domain. The Army is in the act, too, for UFOs have hovered over and landed at or near Army installations.

Although publicly the Air Force has the responsibility for the UFOs, it is obvious that it cannot be everywhere at once, so the AF public relations department is responsible only for public pronouncements about UFO. However, it is quite probable that all military groups in the United States have a central reporting place which is possibly the CIA or a similar outfit set up exclusively for this purpose.

It all boils down to this: If as is suspected, certain authoritarian groups deduced by 1952 (when discs were seen over prohibited areas of the nation's capital and news of saucers became scarce) that they were faced with a formidable problem. With little or no knowledge of these visitors they would have to set up a system by which to learn as much as they could about the visitors but they would have to ultimately PREVENT THE VISITORS FROM LEARNING HOW MUCH THEY KNEW ABOUT THEM.

Counter-intelligence is most import-

ant in a military campaign. It would be impossible to keep the visitors from observing a lot, but if we could prevent them from knowing just how much we were aware of their existence and capabilities, we could at least effectively "stall for time." Meanwhile, a concerted attempt to devise defenses against the possibility of attack, etc., could be made, but the whole success would hinge upon the stall for time which would hinge upon keeping the visitors in ignorance concerning our knowledge of them.

If we can picture the occupants of the UFOs monitoring TV and radio broadcasts and being lulled into a sense of security by official announcements that one of their soirees in the vicinity of a military installation was evaluated as only mistaken observation of a planet, ordinary earth-made vehicle, etc., the visitors would not be concerned with any immediate action. It seems so far that they are only bent on observation and preventing us from any real successes in space exploration. We have experienced considerable difficulty in probing the mysteries of the moon, the only successful probe being that of the Russians in 1959. Since then we (the U.S.) have lost a total of 14 moon probes. The phony baloney coming out of NASA, Washington, D.C., indicates that either there is considerable ignorance in that quarter concerning the capabilities of the UFO, or that they also realize there is an outside effort to keep man off the moon.

If this analysis of the UFO situation and the reason for the alleged censorship is correct, some might postulate that APRO and similar groups no longer have a function, if they cannot disseminate information about UFOs.

This is not true. If for no other reason, APRO would continue to function out of intellectual curiosity. Also, the policy of denial which authorities have instituted as a means of misleading the UFO occupants has worked against them in some ways—many people will not report a UFO incident for they feel that it is useless to report such if the general opinion is already formed. But these people DO report to civilian groups whom they trust. And there is little doube that the groups of authorities who control UFO information and carry out correlation and evaluation of sightings keep close tabs on the information contained in private UFO periodicals. Therefore, in publishing the results of our investigations we are helping to some extent.

If this theory is true, some groups will have outlived their usefulness if their whole justification for existing depends on a "cause," this cause being the cause of truth for the masses and public con-

demnation of the agencies responsible for the censorship.

Some researchers depend on an emotional need for attention and power, and might find it difficult to continue if they had no "goat" to blame things on. Of course, egotism is also prevalent among the anti-saucer people, also. They too, would have difficulty in accepting this thesis concerning UFO motivation and governmental censorship.

An excellent example of censorship for a good cause is the way in which the investigation of President Kennedy's assassination has been handled. At least 14 points of information, if presented in trial court, would have won an acquittal for Lee Oswald. These 14 points indicate at least ONE co-conspirator and Kennedy was shot from the front. For a study in censorship motives for the common good, take your time and think this one over!

The big weak spot in all of our contentions concerning authoritarian censorship has been the motive for same. Just a possibility of hysteria when that possibility is so small, is not an intelligent reason for censoring news of such portent. Even the possibility of economic disaster is not sufficient in itself or even if coupled with the hysteria angle. But if authoritarian powers are faced with the idea of defense against apparently superior powers, it would do their defense measures no good to tell the people and inadvertently admit to the suspected enemy that they have not gone undetected. All things considered, if the motivation for the alleged censorship is a stall for time in the face of almost impossible odds, the choice has been a wise one. It would be senseless to expose ourselves to a potential enemy without first assuring ourselves of having every advantage.

Slow Moving Discs

Sometime between 6:30 and 7:00 p. m., on July 7, 1963, the Le Blanc family near Bantam, Connecticut, observed a total of eight disc-shaped UFOs. They were seen first by two of Mrs. Angela Le Blanc's children as the objects floated slowly and silently over hills southwest of Bantam. The entire family was called to watch as the discs moved from the northeast to the southwest. The estimated altitude of the discs was from 2000 to 3000 feet and the objects appeared to be metallic.

The length of the observation was longer than one minute but the exact figure was undisclosed in published reports. Police were unable to provide an explanation

Photog

(Continued from Page 1)

work, he said.

"Except for a brilliant orange nucleus, which remained in a central position, no matter which way the object stopped, turned or paused, the lights defy interpretation," Putnam said.

Putnam pointed out that the structure of the object would be invisible on the slide, as it was, just as a night picture of a car would show only headlights.

Obviously the lights were not caused by a balloon or airplane and the color of the lights precludes the helicopter explanation. The focus of the camera was set at infinity, thus ruling out close-in objects such as fireflies, etc.

For camera enthusiasts, Pothier elucidates the details about his: It was a Heiland Pentax 35 mm. with an FL-55 mm. lens. The film was Kodachrome X,—ASA 64—lens wide open and set for infinity.

Exit and entrance trails of the object which made the image are very dim indicating that whatever it was is was either accelerating rapidly or descending into camera range during its exit and entrance upon the scene. In a letter dated August 5, John T. Hopf, APRO's photo analyst, had this to say: "There is no question but that this is a real image of some light source, we have positively ruled out processing or film defects. I don't agree with the Harvard astronomer who said that if there was a solid body behind the light it would obscure the star trails. I know from my own experience that an object passing in front of the stars for a short time will not show an effect on the trails in an exposure as long as 30 minutes as this one was. I think this photo is worth running in the Bulletin although we will probably never know just what caused it. I have talked to the fellow (Pothier) at great length, and believe him when he says that no accidental double exposure occurred. I happen to own one of the same cameras (Pentax) and will will make some tests myself when I get a chance, but don't expect to duplicate the photo."

After Pothier's story the Patriot-Ledger carried an account in its July 30 edition which was headlined: "UFO Photo Baffles Astronomer at B.U." and quotes Dr. Gerald S. Hawkins, Director of the Boston University Observatory: "I would hesitate to say the photograph does show a flying saucer although I admit it is very difficult to explain the photograph." He also said: "If there were a solid object in the sky it would obscure some of the star trails. None of

the trails in the picture were obscured. There were several areas on the film where no light has fallen. This is probably obscuration of some sort and it is very unlikely that the glow from a flying saucer would be shining through some sort of grid. And, the complicated pattern, similar to those found in multiple reflections, does not agree at all with the eyewitness descriptions of flying saucers."

It is obvious from Dr. Hawkins' comments that he has had little experience with the study and research of flying saucers. Mr. Hopf has deftly and correctly disputed Hawkins' theory about the obscuration of star trails, and most UFO experts, upon seeing the slide, remark about the similarity between the color and apparent placement of lights and the many sightings which describe almost those exact characteristics.

It would seem the UFOs suddenly attained some sort of legitimacy after being commented upon by Dr. Hawkins, for shortly, Pothier and others received accounts of various UFO sightings in the area.

On June 26, Mr. and Mrs. Enrico Gilbert of East Weymouth spotted a UFO at 1 a.m. Next morning they reported the sighting to the Naval Air Station at South Weymouth and Mrs. Gilberti said the authority who took the report "didn't seem too surprised." The description of the sighting: Both Mr. and Mrs. Gilbert described the craft as 'very large,' bigger than a truck, with brilliant orange light on its bottom and a white light of equal intensity on its top. They said the object flew "with a deafening roar" about 100 feet over the ground, apparently following the path of some high-tension wires near the Gilbert home. Its shape, Gilberti said, was best described by using the traditional "flying saucers" concept, or more exactly, two saucers inverted toward each other. Around its middle, he said, was a protruding lip. The two lights were shaped like a Turkish fez hat, or a cone with the top cut off, he said. It flew smoothly, very low, almost right above the treetops, Gilberti said. The roar was deafening. "Up to now I've always thought of those people who believe in flying saucers as nuts," he said, "but my wife and I both saw it and it was some sort of machine, not a balloon or some other explanation."

Another June 26 sighting was made by Mr. and Mrs. Richard Tonsberg of Rockland, Mass. They were sitting outside their home along with Mrs. Tonsberg's brother-in-law William Henderson. They saw a lighted obect with the same exact colors and light relationship but flying much higher. They heard no

sound. All three reported the obect traced a zig-zag path, making a series of sharp 90-degree turns without pausing in its flight. The glow the object emitted was orange and white. Mr. Henderson reported the object's flight path was sharp and irregular as in the photograph taken in Wollaston about 1:30 on the 25th or 26th. He said it appeared to be heading northwest, but repeatedly doubled back and forth over its path. "All three of use watched it for about five minutes," Henderson said, "and the main reason we did so was the lare number of almost-perfect right angles taken by whatever it was." The trio first saw it when a commercial airliner bound for Logan Airport passed over their house. When the plane had passed, all three saw the orange-white light source "much higher than the airplane, tracing this zig-zag pattern."

On July 4, at 8:30 a.m. Mr. and Mrs. Robert Carr of Weymouth reported seeing "a dark object" emmitting an orange glow and moving in an irregular path fairly high above the ground near Archbishop Williams High School. "We couldn't see how big it was but it was not small. It appeared dark at the top but there was a strong orange glow at the bottom. It was fully light, about 8:30, and we could see only a very rough outline of the object. The most pronounced detail was the orange hue at the bottom and a dark surface or area at its top," she said.

Several weeks earlier on June 13 a North Scituate woman who declines to be identified, spotted the same or a similar object, which she reported on July 7. The yellow-white light, she said, seemed to be plunging into the ocean off Scituate, but suddenly reversed its direction and doubled back on its original path. A friend with her saw it also. "It denly stopped and moved erratically for a few seconds, reversed its direction, and went back from east to west," the woman reported. She also said she watched the maneuvering light source for at least 10 or 15 minutes and when it stopped moving and hovered for a while she stopped watching it.

The foregoing are only a few of the more detailed sightings seen at or about the time of the Pothier incident, and the Patriot-Ledger announced in a subseuent issue that a total of 21 sightings hads been reported to them. All seemed to be of the same or a similar object sighted within days or at most, 3 weeks of the Pothier sighting.

Please Renew Now
$3.50 per Year

Beseiged . . .

(Continued from Page One)

they could stay there, they were afraid to leave because of the machines hovering outside, so Senora de Moreno instructed all to be as quiet as possible.

After forty minutes of this discomfort and fear, the witnesses, who had watched the proceedings outside all the time, saw the object at the railroad tracks elevate and move away, followed by the discs which surrounded the house. Just before taking off, the light on the two closest discs went out and they followed the others off in the direction of the neighboring farms. Where the two closest discs had hovered there remained a misty smoke-like deposit for several minutes.

Several hours later a reporter for "Clarim," a newspaper at Cordoba Province, also providing information for France Press Service, visited the de Morenos. He later reported that the strong sulphur smell was still apparent both around and inside the de Moreno house and the inside of the house was still suffocatingly hot when he arrived there.

Corroboration

Corroboration of the presence of the discs in the area between 9:30 and 10:20 was furnished by Francisco Tropuano, who, not knowing of the de Moreno incident, had reported seeing a formation or "squadron" of lighted disc-like shapes moving through the sky at about 10:15 p. m. when the de Morenos said the discs were leaving their area.

The presence of the heat and odor when the reporter arrived, plus Tropuano's testimony concerning the discs leaving at about the time the de Morenos claimed they left, seem to indicate that this incident is true, especially in view of the good reputation for integrity and honesty of the de Moreno family.

Cooper . . .

astronauts. Although Russian astronauts had supposedly preceded American astronauts into orbit around the earth they did not mention such bits of information until they were publicly mentioned by Glenn. However, at last inspection of reports concerning the mystery lights encontered by Glenn and others as they orbited into the sunrise, NASA had no explanation. Some researchers and UFO fans have noted this chain of occurrences with the implied notion that they could be spacecraft of a sort—monitoring objects, so to speak. The fact that these objects laid along the orbit of the astronauts at least strongly suggests that they may have had something to do with past orbits, of which there have been

many. It is a known fact that all American space launches have been along a prescribed orbital route. Whether or not these tiny and not identical particles are pieces of spacecraft long since disintegrated, or bits of matter from a spacecraft refuse system whether it be earth originated or not, is not likely to be determined for quite some time until, at least, samples can be obtained. That they are some kind of inert matter which are orbiting around earth or suspended at a specific altitude is quite obvious. If they were some type of tiny monitoring objects, it is difficult to understand why their sponsor would be intent on making them all apparently of a different size and shape. Their light, according to the viewers, was reflected, for they were only seen at sunrise.

Widely Seen UFO In Calif.

Shortly after 4:00 a. m., on the morning of 25 September 1963, a fast-moving UFO was reported over Santa Clara and San Mateo counties. Reports came in from the town of Woodside and San Jose also. Sheriff's offices in the above-mentioned counties received twenty reports. Some descriptions given by witnesses were as follows: "A half moon pulsating object," a "circular object lighted from the interior." The light, which appeared to turn off and on was visible intermittently The Federal Aviation Agency, when queried, was unable to account for the UFO.

Scout Leader Observes Strange Light

On the afternoon of March 22, 1963, between 3:30 and 4:00 p. m., Mrs. Barbara Warren, an assistant den mother at Richardson, Texas, witnessed the passage overhead of unusual aerial objects. The four UFOs were described as being white in color and oval in shape, more rounded than oblique. The outlines were not sharp and were fuzzy around the edges. They moved at great speed and didn't reflect sunlight although it was a sunny day with good seeing conditions.

The first two which traveled toward the east passed one after the other and were not in formation. A few minutes later another one appeared, going west. This was immediately followed by a second object which was going west also, and which changed course suddenly and moved toward the north. No more were seen.

Triangle In The Sky

On the night of 17 August 1963 at 7:30 p. m. EDT, Mrs. Bradberry, a resident of Baltimore, Maryland, observed a most unusual UFO in the sky overhead.

Viewed through binoculars from her location the object appeared to be triangular in shape with a red light emanating from one corner. By 10:00 p. m., the triangle was still in approximately the same location but clouds obscured it. At 1:15 a. m., the triangle was visible again but it was smaller in size and the red light had dimmed. The position had changed somewhat in regards to a reference point she was using. Investigation by Robert D. Briele, associated with radio station WFBR in Baltimore, failed to turn up an explanation.

Pear-Shaped Object Over Balto.

On the same night as the Bradberry sighting Mrs. George Spec of Baltimore observed a pear-shaped object high in the sky over the northeast portion of the city. She reported the object to WFBR immediately and viewed the object from 9:10 to 10:00 p. m. No sound or motion were detected and Mrs. Spec said the object pointed earthward and the whole object was red in color. No optics used in sighting, and investigation showed no weather balloons over Baltimore for three days.

Sky Object Strikes Building, Causes Fire

On Friday, May 10, 1963, shortly after 10 a. m., an object described by witnesses as round, about 15 inches long and blue or green in color, struck a warehouse in Belfast, Maine and exploded.

The building belonging to the Maple Upholstery Company suffered minor damage from a fire which broke out as a result of the collision. It was reported that the first flames visible following the explosion were of a greenish hue. People in the area reported hearing a blast and Mr. Rene Gagine, a foreman, witnessed the occurrence. No traces of the mysterious object were found.

Mr. Floyd G. Drinkwater, Waldo County Civil Defense Director, investigated the site with a geiger counter and a slightly high radiation reading registered on the instrument. It was reported, however, that this was not enough to indicate contamination from an object from space like, for instance, a meteor. The general consensus among people interested in and investigating this incident was that the object was not an ordinary space object.

Falling Spheres Found

In early April 1963, newspapers were printing the news of a mysterious metal sphere found by Mr. J. McLure on station property near Broken Hill, New South Wales in Australia on 8 April. It was shipped to Broken Hill for examination by scientists there. It could not be cut or broken into by the use of a file or hack saw. Metallurgists at the Zinc Corporation said it had been subjected to great heat, was 14 inches in diameter, weighed 12 pounds and was spherical and hollow. McLure, who found the object said that no one had been in the area of the sheep station where the object was found, for about 50 years.

After the initial news release from Broken Hill which contained the foregoing information, the obect was shipped to the Weapons Research Establishment in Salisbury for examination. Mr. R. Pitman-Hooper, the Zinc Corporation's manager, refused to make any real comment on reports that the Corporation's metallurgists at Broken Hill had determined via X-ray spectographic examination that the object contained beryllium, titanium, and magnesium and had only this to say: "All I can say at this stage is that our scientists have had a look at the object, that any tests they may have made so far are inconclusive and that the sphere has been placed in the charge of a senior Army officer." The Director of the Broken Hill division of the U. of New South Wales, Mr. T. K. Hogan, said that university scientists had made a visual inspection of the object and that what they saw would not be "inconsistent with the report that it contained beryllium, titanium and magnesium." He said further that the metals were certainly of modern origin and were also non-magnetic. He also commented on an unusual "submerged arc weld" around the surface of the sphere which was a "most beautifully executed job." He disputed the idea that the object was some sort of tank or cistern float, and said it had the remains of two lugs still attached to it. Hogan also said that the object was definitely hollow and that they would have "dearly liked to ope nit." He theorized that the object probably had originally been protected by some sort of heat shield which protected it from the intense heat which melted the lugs.

On the 30th of April, a dispatch out of Canberra said that the sphere had "definitely been identified as part of a space vehicle." It went on to explain that Mr. Allen Fairhall, Australian Supply Minister, told the House of Representatives that the sphere was identified as part of a space vehicle, and that Australia was "communicating with the overseas Governments from whose spacecraft it might have come." The dispatch also said that the sphere carried the faint outline of a hammer and sickle, the Soviet emblem. Fairhall said the sphere had not been opened as it might contain "something of scientific interest." "It's a million-to-one chance that a piece of orbiting hardware should survive the temperature of re-entry and be recovered in one piece," he said. Various other newspapers carried the news that scientists (unnamed) had determined that the object was a pressure vessel from a space vehicle, designed to withstand great pressure.

Apparently no more information was released concerning the mystery sphere, but a small article in the Omaha World-Herald (Nebraska, U.S.A.) for 2 October 1963, carried the information that the first sphere had not been identified when the second one was found in October about 35 miles from the location of the first one.

The press release divulged the fact that despite inquiries abroad, the Australian government had not located the origin of the first sphere. The second sphere was described as 16 inches in diameter and weighing 18 pounds. It was also said to be a "stainless steel ball" on which a valve had been turned into a fused mass, apparently as a result of intense heat.

It is interesting to note that to this date no definite news concerning the metallic makeup of that first sphere has been released, nor has there been any further description or clarification of the physical properties of the second. This brings to mind another mysterious object which was found in South Africa in early 1962. This object was identified as a spherical titanium pressure tank from the fuel tank of an Atlas rocket. There was no doubt that this object, at least according to press reports, belonged to a U.S. space vehicle. The question now arises concerning the reason that the Australian spheres have not been identified. The most recent releases state unequivocally that the sphere has been disowned by Russia and the U.S. Then whence?

Youth Chased By Fiery Object

On the night of 20 May 1963, a 17-year-old saw an object which he at first thought was a truck or a bulldozer at the side of the road between Glencoe and Mt. Gambier, near the Victorian border, in Australia. He refused to let his name be used as he feared he would be called "crackers" (crazy). As he drew to within about 20 yards of the object, a bright light came on which was dazzling and the young man stopped his car. The object then moved across the road, and the boy started driving again, speeding up. Then the light shot straight up into the air and the car went underneath it. "Although I was going 50 or 60 miles per hour, the light followed the car. It was as bright as an arc welder's light," the youth said. The boy's father, who reported the incident, said that the boy arrived home "white, upset and frightened."

The same press report said that a similar object was seen by a carload of people on the night of the 15th of May and was reported to Mt. Gambier police. The people claimed the light, which turned from red to white, followed the car for several miles.

Fiji Has A Fireball

On the 3rd of April 1963 Mrs. A. E. Kennard, a Tamavna housewife, woke about 3:30 a.m. and gazed through her window at what appeared to be a ball of fire in the sky over Beqa. It appeared to be moving toward Laucala Bay. She said it was "horrifying."

Ten minutes earlier three Fijian policemen at Ba had reported seeing a similar object and at 3:30 a.m., members of the Royal New Zealand Air Force also saw the object. Men on HMS ship Cook had reported seeing strange objects "falling into the Fiji Islands group" at about 3:20 a.m. the same morning. They said they watched a huge fireball fall into the sea while they were anchored in the northern Yarawa group. An officer reported that at the time the area was bathed in a light as bright as moonlight which seemed to be coming from a falling object. Another officer said the falling object looked to him "like the classic example of a Hollywood spaceship." It was glowing with a bright greenish-white light and had an enormous, long fiery orange tail.

The same or a similar object was reported by several people at Lakota.

As this issue goes to the press, APRO is winding up the investigation of the UFO incidents in New Mexico. This investigation has been expensive and has nearly depleted the treasury. We are not asking for donations, but ask merely that you renew your membership if you are due.

Please check your cards and send in your dues, if you are due or renew early. Thank you.

Made in the USA
Middletown, DE
21 July 2021